SILVER PHOENIX

SILVER PHOENIX

BEYOND THE KINGDOM OF XIA

CINDY PON

WITH CHAPTER DECORATIONS BY THE AUTHOR

GREENWILLOW BOOKS
An Imprint of HarperCollins Publishers

Silver Phoenix

Beyond the Kingdom of Xia

Copyright © 2009 by Cindy Pon

The text of this book is set in 12-Point Weiss.

Book design by Paul Zakris

Library of Congress Cataloging-in-Publication Data

Pon, Cindy, (date).

Silver phoenix: beyond the kingdom of Xia / by Cindy Pon.

p. cm.

"Greenwillow Books."

Summary: With her father long overdue from his journey and a lecherous merchant blackmailing her into marriage, seventeen-year-old Ai Ling becomes aware of a strange power within her as she goes in search of her parent.

ISBN 978-0-06-173021-4 (trade bdg.) — ISBN 978-0-06-178033-2 (lib. bdg.)

[1. Supernatural—Fiction. 2. Voyages and travels—Fiction. 3. Fathers and daughters—Fiction. 4. China—History—Xi Xia dynasty, 1038-1227—Fiction.] I. Title.

PZ7.P77215Si 2009   [Fic]—dc22   2008029149

09 10 11 12 13 LP/RRDH First Edition 10 9 8 7 6 5 4 3 2 1

 GREENWILLOW BOOKS

For my *wai gong*, who taught me the importance of journal keeping
and told me fantastic tales.
For my *wai po*, whom I never met,
but whose slender fingers I inherited.
I miss you both.

PROLOGUE

In the Kingdom of Xia, within the Palace of Fragrant Dreams,

nineteen years past

The eunuchs said the windows were ceiling height to allow the concubines their privacy, but Jin Lian knew it was also a way to keep them trapped. These quarters had walls taller than any courtyard tree. No one could survive the drop to the other side. Not that any concubine in possession of her wits would ever attempt to escape the Palace—or her duties to the Emperor.

Jin Lian pushed the tray of rice porridge and pickled cucumbers away. The ache in her swollen belly robbed her of any appetite. Her devoted handmaid, Hong Yu, eased her onto the platform bed, one firm hand beneath her elbow. The girl rearranged the silk drapes to encourage air flow. But the night was hot and still.

Jin Lian found it impossible to get comfortable in her expansive nest littered with plump cushions and tangled sheets. She curled onto her side and clutched the gold-brocaded coverlet in sweaty fists. Hong Yu, her brow knitted with worry, fanned her with rapid movements. Jin Lian attempted a smile, but failed.

Instead she concentrated on her breathing, as Royal Physician Wu had advised. Hong Yu offered cool jasmine tea and wiped her brow with a cold cloth scented with mint and cucumber. The smell soothed Jin Lian, until another pain seized her stomach and radiated across her lower back.

She grabbed the girl's hand. "Please ask Hei Po to come—" Unable to continue, Jin Lian closed her eyes to the pain. Time spiraled away from her. She was aware of nothing beyond the ragged sound of her own breath.

Then cool hands pressed upon her fiery belly, gently on top and along the sides. "He's in good position, dropped low, ready to enter this world, mistress," Hei Po said. "He arrives early."

Four weeks early.

Jin Lian did not open her eyes. She'd recognize her old nursemaid's voice anywhere. Her breath came in short bursts now, but she managed, "You said he."

"Merely a guess, child. It will be time to push soon."

Hei Po motioned to Hong Yu. "Girl, prepare the water as I instructed." The handmaid scrambled, as if afraid the baby would drop out at that very moment.

The pressure became unbearable. Jin Lian heard herself moan and gasp, unable to control the physical responses of her body. Improper. Unladylike. She should be embarrassed. These inner thoughts trickled, became muted.

Hei Po stroked her hand. "The pain brings your baby into this world. Just breathe and push when the moment comes." The midwife's words tumbled against her ear.

Jin Lian did not know how much time passed. The agony washed over her now in waves.

"It's time," Hei Po said.

Hong Yu stood behind the midwife. When had she returned?

"Bear down when you feel another constriction, Xiao Lian," Hei Po said. The childhood pet name surprised Jin Lian, comforted her.

She pushed. She felt the baby twist. Felt it move through her body. Emerge. There was a tremendous sense of release. An insistent wail filled the room. Jin Lian's heart swelled and ached all at once.

"Is it a girl or a boy?" Jin Lian finally found her weak voice.

Her chest seized when she saw the expression on Hei Po's face. "What is it? Is something wrong?"

"No, he's perfect."

A boy.

His hair was light brown, with a golden tint under the

blazing lanterns. Blood thundered in her ears. He opened his swollen eyes, as if sensing her. They were golden, too, tinged with a dark tea green.

He was one of mixed blood, half Xian and half foreign. Not the Emperor's son.

What have we done?

Jin Lian sobbed as she clutched her son. But she couldn't allow herself the luxury of crying long. Master Zhong checked on her progress daily, anticipating the birth of a son—the Emperor's son. He kept spies everywhere. She needed to act fast if she wanted her baby to live.

"Hei Po, stay within my quarters. No one expected the babe to arrive this early. No one can know."

The gray-haired woman nodded. Her wizened face betrayed nothing. Jin Lian knew she tested her old nurse-maid's loyalty. Hei Po could be killed for aiding her in this deception. But this was the woman who had brought her into the world with loving hands, who had cared for her as a child. Who could Jin Lian trust if not her dear beloved Hei Po?

"Hong Yu, find Master Wen."

Despite her youth, Hong Yu knew enough of Palace intrigue to understand the danger. Could Jin Lian trust this girl with her son's life? With her own? She had no choice.

The handmaid scrambled to the door.

"No. Not that way."

Jin Lian pressed one of the lotuses carved upon the intricate camphor-wood headboard. A hidden door eased open by her side. "Through here. Keep straight, you'll pass three openings before you make a right on the fourth. This will take you into Master Wen's quarters. Knock once, pause, then knock three more times at the passage door. Bring a lantern."

The secret panel shut behind Hong Yu without a noise.

The babe's face screwed up. He was intent on wailing again, as if he felt his mother's anxiety. She guided him to her breast. His head wobbled as he nudged his pink face against her chest. He found her nipple and began to suckle, making small contented noises as he nursed.

Hot tears fell on his chubby arm, unhindered. Jin Lian knew this was the last time she would hold him, stroke his smooth cheeks, and breathe in his sweet scent. Assuming either of them survived the night.

CHAPTER ONE

The book lay heavy in Ai Ling's lap, so massive it covered her thighs. She pressed her knees together, for fear the tome would crash to the ground otherwise. Bound in a brocaded cover of rich crimson, characters embroidered in gold read *The Book of Making*. She didn't want to open it.

"Take a look." Mother inclined her head. Black hair spilled over her shoulders in thick cascades, and the subtle scent of gardenia oil drifted with her every movement. Ai Ling rarely saw her mother's hair loose. She looked beautiful.

Ai Ling let the book fall open to a random page. Her face flushed at what she saw—a man and woman stark naked, their limbs entwined. THE DANCE OF THE CRANES was printed neatly above in black ink.

"Mother . . ." She could not bring herself to meet her mother's gaze.

"Keep looking, Ai Ling. This book is informative, with all the things you need to know about the bedchamber and what it takes to pleasure your husband."

Her mother put a gentle hand over hers. Ai Ling had always admired her mother's slender fingers, so deft in embroidering and playing the lute.

"It's soon time for you to wed. It's been one year since your monthly letting began." Her mother flipped the pages, and more nude figures filled Ai Ling's vision. "It tells you how to gauge your most fertile days, which positions are best—"

"But you didn't have me until you were twenty-four years!" Ai Ling wanted to slam the book shut, even as she was riveted to the drawings on the page. The only color came from the lotus pink of the woman's lips and the tips of her breasts.

"I married late, my heart." Ai Ling's mother stroked her hair, tucked a strand behind her ear. "It wasn't that your father and I didn't try. We lost one before we were blessed with you. He was born still—without spirit."

She could have had an older brother. Her mother's light brown eyes were bright with remembered sorrow.

"I didn't know," Ai Ling whispered.

"Now you understand what a true joy you are to us." She

touched Ai Ling's cheek. "Keep the book. Look through it. I'll visit in the evenings before bed so we can talk." Her mother rose, stepped delicately from the platform bed, and bade her a peaceful night.

Ai Ling remained sitting with the book in her lap. Its weight on her legs did not compare to the thoughts which weighed on her heart. After a few moments, she rose, placed *The Book of Making* on her writing desk, blew out the lantern, and slipped into bed.

Rest did not come quickly that night. When she finally drifted into slumber, her dreams were of couples etched in black, moving in jerky motions, passive smiles painted upon their faces, an emptiness within their eyes.

Ai Ling jostled against the plush silk cushions of the sedan seat. Father had hired it for the occasion. She had suspected her parents' intention when Mother shared *The Book of Making* last month, but she wasn't prepared for a betrothal so soon. She would be given away, traded off like cattle, fortunate to see her parents perhaps once a year—if her future mother-in-law allowed it.

Her empty stomach turned. She wished she wasn't alone, being presented as if royalty, under just as much scrutiny. What would her betrothed look like? With her luck, he'd have squinted eyes and not reach past her chin.

Despite it being in the tenth moon, the days were still hot. She fanned herself, feeling stifled, wishing protocol allowed her to draw aside the heavy drapes. Muffled shouts from vendors offering their wares reached her ears. Ai Ling peeled back the corner of the drape and peered out, spying a cobbler bellowing from his stand. A mother pulled her toddler son by the hand past the sedan, promising a candied fruit if he behaved. Ai Ling was whisked down the main street and allowed the curtain to drop once more, isolating her in a hot muted red.

The sedan stopped too soon. She wasn't ready. She brushed a nervous hand over her hair, where Mother had placed the delicate jade hairpin from her betrothed among the coils piled on her head. She had always worn braids until today. As a married woman, she would never be able to wear loose braids again. Her stomach clenched, and she fisted her hands tight to gather courage.

"Mistress Wen arrives!" shouted a deep sonorous voice.

Ai Ling wilted against the cushions. They had hired a master of ceremony? The Goddess of Mercy help her.

The curtains were swept aside, exposing her to the harsh light of midday. She blinked a few times and saw her mother and father, along with, she assumed, Master Wong, Lady Wong, and her betrothed, Liao Kang.

The master of ceremony, a rotund man with a fringe of hair circling his scalp and plump red cheeks, bowed low with surprising grace and proffered one hand. She took it and stepped into the empty street. She dared not look around but wondered if they had somehow cleared the area.

She walked past her parents and immediately went to Lady Wong, her future mother-in-law, as protocol dictated.

The petite woman raised one arm, clad in a lavender silk sleeve banded in gold. Ai Ling took the woman's cool hand and pressed it to her lowered brow.

Not a bad-looking girl. Good hips.

Her stomach seized as if someone had hurled a rock at her middle. She nearly reeled but managed to remain standing. Ai Ling lifted her head in shock, felt the blood drain from her face; but no one else indicated they had heard Lady Wong's comment.

Lady Wong regarded her with calculation. A palpable sense of disdain poured toward Ai Ling. The woman flicked her gaze up, then down.

Too tall.

She heard it as if it were spoken aloud, but Lady Wong's rouged lips remained pursed, never moved. Her future mother-in-law inclined her head, and Ai Ling quickly dropped her hand. The tightness within her immediately eased. Had she heard the woman's thoughts?

She fought to quell her trembling as Liao Kang stepped forward and extended his hand. He was a bamboo of a boy, the barely green type, with large almond eyes in a pale face. Would this boy see her hair unbound on their wedding night? Her mind flitted to *The Book of Making*. Heat suffused Ai Ling's cheeks. She took his hand, feeling the damp of her own palm, and allowed him to lead her into the restaurant.

* * *

The three-storied restaurant opened into a lush court-yard filled with orchids and fruit trees. Liao Kang led her to a round lacquered table with six matching chairs. He stepped to the space across from her. They remained standing, waiting for their parents. The men seated themselves first, next to each other, followed by their wives, also side by side.

The master of ceremony stood behind their table, announcing in his deep voice the names of both families and the betrothed, wishing them fortune, marital joy, and seven sons in seven years. After what seemed like an hour, the plump man bowed and retreated. Only then did Ai Ling and Liao Kang seat themselves. The server immediately placed the first dish on the table, cold cuts of beef tongue, pig ears, salted silver river fish, and marinated quail eggs. Ai Ling's mouth felt dry, as if stuffed with raw silk.

She sipped on the cool tea and pretended to eat.

It was after much laughter and reminiscing, when a contented silence fell between the two men, that Lady Wong spoke. "We want to make sure that Ai Ling is a good match for our Liao Kang. He is a sensitive, intelligent boy—our baby."

Ai Ling caught the smile about to break on her lips. She sneaked a glance at Liao Kang, but he was intent upon pushing the meatball pearls on his plate with his silver eating sticks.

"I'm concerned about your family's reputation, Master Wen." Lady Wong's pleasant tone did not match the menace of her words. "My husband withheld information from me when we accepted Ai Ling as a daughter-in-law." She cast a cutting glance at her husband. "Weren't you thrown out of the Emperor's court in disgrace?"

Master Wong slammed his wine cup on the table. Hot anger rose within her, and she looked toward her father. But he appeared unmoved by the accusation.

"I served the Emperor well, Lady Wong. For many years."

The woman sniffed. Master Wong lifted an open hand to his wife in appeasement. "Dear wife, Liao Kang and Ai Ling are betrothed. We're almost family. Master Wen and I are longtime colleagues and friends; we couldn't possibly find a better match for our son."

Her defiant look made her husband sigh too loudly. "The final decision is up to Liao Kang," Lady Wong said.

The server placed a deep dish of sizzling scallops before them, bowed, and retreated.

"The food is delicious. If only I knew the recipes," her mother finally said after an awkward silence.

"Our chef's dishes are far superior," Lady Wong replied, actually turning up her nose.

"You've come a long way, Lao Wong, from eating rice porridge and pickles at every meal," Ai Ling's father said, patting his old colleague on the back. But Master Wong stared at his dessert, a strained smile on his face.

Avoiding her father's eyes, Master Wong waved a server over. "More chilled wine here!"

Liao Kang had not spoken a word during the entire meal. Now his mother looked at him expectantly. After prodding the chilled yam in sweetened mare's milk without taking one bite, he dropped a piece of sky blue satin on the table, took his mother's waiting hand, and escorted her out of the restaurant.

Ai Ling's face grew hot, then cold. A gift of gold was given, usually a bracelet or ring, in acceptance of the girl chosen. The piece of discarded satin meant the very opposite. She did not doubt that Lady Wong had orchestrated this public refusal.

She kept her head bowed as Master Wong sputtered apologies, waved his manicured hands, and assured them that everything would be sorted, that it was merely a small misunderstanding.

But it was clear to Ai Ling. Her family was not good enough. She was not good enough. She fought the shame mingled with anger that filled her. She had tolerated this farce to please her parents, abide by tradition, but she had only managed to bring disgrace on her family. Gossip would follow, for an unmarriageable daughter was a bad daughter.

She walked home that day in silence, trailing behind her parents, refusing to speak to them. The elaborate clothing made her feel foolish. She pulled the jade hairpin from her hair and cast it aside on the deserted country road, just as her betrothed had cast her aside. But as she walked part of her thought—wasn't this what she had wanted?

Five months had passed since the disastrous Wong betrothal. It was the beginning of the third moon. The plum blossoms emerged early in the front courtyard, their delicate pink petals scented like rice tea. Ai Ling pressed her nose to the tiny buds. She loved the flowers for their scent as well as their herald of spring.

Her father had tried twice more to arrange a betrothal with prominent families, without success. She would either never marry or would be given to the butcher or cobbler, a family that didn't have the pretenses of the scholarly class.

Shame and frustration welled within her. Her parents wanted the best for her, a good family to marry into and a comfortable life. Instead she'd been made to feel unworthy. I'm not ready to marry anyway, she thought. But would she grow old as a spinster?

She heard their servant, Mei Zi, clanking away, preparing breakfast. Her mother was usually the first to rise, but she had not seen her in the main hall nor heard her voice in the kitchen. Perhaps she was resting.

She sensed someone and turned. Her father stood before her, dressed in royal blue robes. Ai Ling saw a hint of something she didn't recognize in his dark eyes.

"What is it, Father?"

"Ai Ling, there is something I must tell you." He rubbed his face with one hand.

She didn't like the tone of his voice. Even less so the look in his eyes. Was it worry? Resignation? She didn't know, and it troubled her. Ai Ling usually knew her father's moods like her own.

"I'm going on a short journey to the Palace," he said. "It shouldn't take more than two months."

This was entirely unexpected. Her father had never traveled for longer than a few days—and never so far.

"Take me with you!" She realized it was impossible even as she said it. Her father may once have been a high official at the Emperor's court, but she was no more than a country girl who could count on her fingertips the number of times she'd been outside their little town.

"You know your mother needs you here." His smile was kind. "Keep her company. Don't elope in my absence."

She would have laughed any other time, the suggestion was so ridiculous. "But why do you need to go? Why for so long?"

"Difficult questions, daughter. I'll tell you everything when I return." Her father drew closer, retrieving something from the satin pouch tied to his gray sash.

"I have something for you. A small gift for my favorite daughter." Ai Ling smiled for him. She was his only child.

He opened his palm, revealing a jade piece in the clearest green. The pendant nestled on a thin gold chain. "Father!

It's beautiful." Her father had always been a man who gave gifts of books, paper, and calligraphy brushes.

"Let's put it on." He looped the delicate chain around her neck and closed the clasp. Ai Ling held the pendant in her hand.

"Spirit," she murmured, recognizing the word carved into pristine green. The pendant was oval, shaped like a thumb-print, with the character carved on both sides in relief.

"It was given to me by a monk, years ago. Before I met your mother." He took the jade piece between his fingers. "I helped him transcribe a book of religious text in exchange for board at his temple."

He ran a fingertip over the raised character, his face pensive. "Before I left, he gave me this. He told me to give it to my daughter, if I should ever leave her side for long." A small smile touched at the corners of his mouth. "But when I said I had no daughter, he merely waved me away."

Ai Ling's father let the pendant drop and patted her shoulder. "This monk was wise. He saw much." Ai Ling met his gaze and realized the look she had not been able to identify earlier was sadness.

She blinked back the mist from her own eyes. "We'll miss you so." She threw her arms around his neck, and his body tensed for a moment. She had not embraced him like that since she was a little girl. He enveloped her with strong arms, but pulled away sooner than she was willing to let go.

"We have had our difficulties over your betrothal," her father said. Ai Ling looked down at her feet, not wanting these last moments to be about her failure as a daughter.

He lifted her chin with a gentle hand. "In truth, my heart was never in them either. They are fools not to see what a priceless gem I offer. People think I spoil you, dote on you. Perhaps I do. But I did not become one of the best-known scholars in court for my shortsightedness or poor judgment."

He caressed her cheek for one brief moment. "You are special, Ai Ling. Beyond what you mean in my heart. Remember that."

Her mother arrived late to breakfast, her black hair pulled back, impeccable as ever. But her eyes were red and swollen, even as she gave her daughter a reassuring smile.

Her father left that same morning.

CHAPTER TWO

Life slowed in Father's absence. There were no more lessons, no more discussions of poetry, history, or philosophy. No patient teacher guided her hand, showing her the strength needed for the bamboo stroke or the delicate dance of orchid leaves on paper. Each day, Ai Ling practiced copying her favorite passages from classical texts to improve her calligraphy. Often she sat in the front courtyard and found a muse—a peony in bloom, a bird pecking at seeds strewn before her—and painted, Father always in her thoughts.

Spring gave way to summer. The longer days dragged. Father had been away for three months, and Ai Ling and her mother had received no letters from him. This wasn't unusual, as it was difficult to find a messenger willing to carry word to their far-flung town. Still, her mother worried, even as Ai Ling reassured her while hiding her own concern.

But by the seventh moon, not knowing how far she would have to stretch the family savings, her mother dismissed their two house servants. Mei Zi and Ah Jiao waved and smiled on their last day, trying to feign cheer. "We'll come back as soon as Master Wen returns," Mei Zi said. The two women were like family. Ai Ling saw her mother surreptitiously wipe away tears as she prepared dinner that evening.

Without the house servants, Ai Ling and her mother began visiting the market square to buy fresh produce and other necessities. After several trips, she ventured out alone, entrusted with a list of items to purchase, while her mother stayed home to manage the household books.

Ai Ling's first foray from home without a chaperone was short. She hurried to buy the items she had listed on the thin sheet of rice paper. But as each week passed, she became emboldened. She took the time to explore her little town—the side streets with fried fish cake and sticky yam vendors, the old woman with a hunched back and three missing teeth displaying intricately embroidered slippers. Ai Ling discovered that she enjoyed this independence, this newfound freedom.

She was examining a fine slipper stitched with butterflies

one summer morning when someone tugged on her braid, then swept a palm across her back. She leaped to her feet to find Master Huang standing behind her, much too close. The merchant smiled, a smile that did not reach past his thin mouth.

"Your single braid caught my eye, Ai Ling. Should you be wandering unchaperoned?"

She stepped back. Master Huang was a successful merchant by trade, but ruthless and cruel as a person. Ai Ling knew the town gossip. The man was near fifty, and all three wives had failed to give him a son. He had three daughters, two from his first wife, one from the second, and nothing but tears and threats of suicide from the third. The last wife was seventeen years, the same age as she.

"Mother trusts me to do the shopping." Ai Ling lifted her chin.

"Surely your house servants can manage such menial tasks?" His leer broadened. A small breeze carried the scent of liquor and tobacco to her nose. She fought the urge to take two more paces back, even as the merchant leaned toward her. "Ah, yes. How rude of me. I heard your servants were let go. When will your father return from the Palace, Ai Ling?"

Furious, she bit the inside of her mouth. One could never be rude to an elder, no matter how loathsome. She simply shook her head.

"He was very brave to return to the Palace, considering he

barely escaped execution twenty years back," he cooed.

Father nearly executed? Her face tingled as the blood drained from it.

"You didn't know?" Master Huang reached out a hand to steady her. The cruel slant of his mouth betrayed his show of concern. At his touch, Ai Ling felt a tightening in her navel and a dizzying sense as if she were hurtling toward him.

I wouldn't mind seeing this one in my bedchamber.

She heard it as if he had spoken aloud, then felt a hard snap as she fell back within herself. She shuddered. The merchant squeezed her wrist, and she pulled hard, stumbling backward.

"Don't touch me," she said in a shrill voice.

The older man's eyes narrowed for one heartbeat. Then he threw his head back and laughed. She turned and ran, not caring which way she went.

The days melded into one another. Mother and daughter established a routine, and Ai Ling found that she had become used to her father's absence. That fact disquieted her.

Most nights, after dinner, they pulled chairs from the main hall into the courtyard, and worked on embroidering or sewing by lantern light. Ai Ling enjoyed this time the most, with the long day behind them, perhaps bringing Father closer to his return.

A sliver of moon shone the night she asked her mother about her own betrothal. Her mother smiled into her embroidery. Her fingers danced over a delicate pattern of lotus flowers with a dragonfly hovering above. Ai Ling worked on a new sleep outfit for herself. She chose a soft cotton in celadon from the fabric shop, perfect for summertime.

They sat amid potted dahlias in deep purples and brilliant oranges, brought to bloom by Ai Ling. She had clapped in delight when the first bud unfurled, revealing its gorgeous color.

"It wasn't arranged," her mother said.

That much Ai Ling knew, but never the details of their romance.

"Your father had just left the Emperor's court."

"The scandal," Ai Ling said.

Her mother inclined her head and continued with her tale.

"He was thirty years and still unmarried, refusing to take a wife while at court. After leaving, he came to my city in search of employment. He offered to tutor the children of families willing to hire him." Her mother paused to thread emerald green for the dragonfly.

"What happened to Father in court? Will you never tell?" Ai Ling furrowed her brow as she stitched her nightshirt. She had the right to know.

"That is something you need to ask your father," her mother said.

Ai Ling didn't reply. Her mother was right.

"My mother died giving birth to me and my father not

long after, from illness." Her mother bent closer to her embroidery.

"My grandparents took me in. But I grew up with the weight of my parents' deaths on me." She paused and lifted her elegant head to admire the moon. Ai Ling felt her sorrow, smothering the exquisite scent of jasmine, dimming the starlight above.

"My mother was considered bad luck, a poor wife, having died in childbirth, but even worse, taking her young husband to the grave with her. I grew up believing I was the cause of such ill fortune. Nobody made me think otherwise." The crickets chirped their familiar song as her mother sipped cool tea. Ai Ling quickly rose to refill her cup.

"At twenty-one years, I was still unmarried, never having been promised to anyone. I wasn't a priority among the grandsons who needed to bring home good brides and the granddaughters who needed even better husbands and families to be sent to."

Ai Ling imagined her mother as a spinster. The bad-luck girl no one could be rid of. Her heart went out to her mother. It wasn't fair. It never was fair.

"I took on the role of second mother to many of my little nieces and nephews. So I was there the day your father came to interview for the tutoring position, bringing the children in to meet him. He was very good with them. I knew then he would be a good father." Her mother smiled, her features illuminated by the flickering lantern light.

"He proposed the betrothal to my grandfather three months later."

"But what happened in between?"

Her mother laughed, throwing back her head so the silver ornaments in her hair tinkled. "That is between your father and me."

"You fell in love." Ai Ling said it almost accusingly.

"Yes, we did. It happened under unusual circumstances. I suppose we were both castoffs, me the unlucky orphan girl and he the scandalous scholar ousted from court. Grandfather hesitated; he did care for me. But I spoke to him and gave my consent. We were wed and left my family six months after. I was already with child."

"And you moved to Ahn Nan?"

"To this very house."

"What about Father's family?" Ai Ling spoke from the side of her mouth, a sewing pin between her lips.

"We stopped there first before coming here. But no one would answer the door when we knocked, even as we heard whispers from within."

Stunned, Ai Ling looked up from her work. "Yes. The Wen family disowned your father, believing the gossip from court. It broke his heart. He hasn't spoken of it to this day," her mother said.

Her kind, intelligent father cast out by his own family? This was why she grew up without doting grandparents, isolated from relatives. Why her mother hushed her whenever she asked why they never visited. How could they believe the worst of the gossip, whatever it may have been? Did they not know their own son?

"And then you had me?" Ai Ling asked.

Her mother threaded silver now, accent color for the dragonfly wings. Her face softened. "Yes. When we lost our firstborn, I blamed myself, believing that the curse of ill fortune continued. And then we were blessed with you."

"Did you want more children, Mother?"

"Of course we did. You were such a joy. Your father used to tote you around in a silk sling to show you off. I still have it tucked in a drawer somewhere."

"That's a funny thought!" Ai Ling chuckled, forgetting the pin clasped between her lips.

"We tried but without luck. After two years, I implored your father to take a second wife. But do you know what he said?" She leaned in close as if sharing a secret. "He said, 'Why would I want another woman in the house? I'm already outnumbered as it is.'" They laughed together, loud enough for the crickets to cease their song.

Her mother wiped her eyes. "He teased, of course. And always kissed me after." She smiled and laid her craftwork down. "This wears on me. I think I'll retire." She rubbed her brow with slender fingers.

Ai Ling bade her mother good night but remained sitting in the courtyard, head tilted toward the evening sky. Her cat, Taro, emerged from behind the jasmine, leaped across the stone floor in one breath, and twined his lithe body about her ankle.

She petted him, felt his rumbling purr even before she heard it. Her mind wandered to the image of her parents in youth, both outcasts, alone until they found each other. She couldn't imagine the same fate for herself—couldn't fathom the fortune of ever falling in love.

Ai Ling pulled the heavy courtyard door open to find Master Huang, stroking his long gray beard. She almost cried out at the sight of him. She had spent the evening after their encounter the previous week shut in her bedchamber, too queasy to eat, unable to speak of it with her mother. When asked if she felt ill, Ai Ling blamed it on her monthly letting, which wasn't entirely a lie.

"Is your mother in?" Master Huang asked without smiling.

She pressed her palm against the wooden door, stopping the trembling of her hand. She cleared her throat before speaking.

"Yes, she is. I will call her." She refused to address him by name.

She hated the thought of allowing this man into their home, but there was no way of turning aside someone of his stature. She stepped inside the main hall. Feeling the weight of his leer on her back, she straightened her frame even taller.

"Mother? Master Huang is here to visit."

Her mother emerged from the kitchen area, patting her hair with one hand. She was dressed in gray cotton house clothes, but managed to look regal.

"Master Huang. What brings us this honor?"

"No, I was rude to arrive unannounced. I met Ai Ling in the market and thought I would pay a visit."

"Please, sit." Her mother gestured toward an elm-wood chair. "Ai Ling, some tea." The pause before she answered him was not lost on Ai Ling. She should have told Mother what had happened—but how could she have explained hearing Master Huang's thoughts, if they were his thoughts?

Ai Ling retreated into the kitchen. She could see the back of Master Huang's head and her mother's profile through the arched doorway. Her mother looked uncomfortable, sitting with her back rigid and her hands clasped before her.

"Master Wen being gone for so long has been a burden, Lady Wen. Is there any news?" Master Huang asked.

Ai Ling held her breath, a jar of loose jasmine tea leaves in one hand.

Her mother studied her hands. "You are kind in your concern for our family. I know my husband will return in good time." Her mother's voice grew softer as she spoke. So soft that Ai Ling had to lean toward the doorway to hear. She swallowed the knot that caught in her throat.

Master Huang pulled something from his robes—a scroll. He unfurled it. "I regret having to do this. Your husband owes me a great sum. And I need to collect on it now."

"This can't be, Master Huang. My husband never mentioned borrowing from you."

The merchant rolled up the scroll, knowing full well that her mother could not read what was written on the paper. "Husbands don't divulge all matters to their wives, Lady Wen. What your husband was involved in was part of the man's world. Nothing he would have shared with you."

"My husband told me everything."

Master Huang shrugged. "I'm afraid it's my word against yours. This scroll contains your husband's signature and seal. It's a large sum."

He leaned forward and whispered close to her mother's ear. Ai Ling bit her lip to see him behave with such familiarity. Her mother remained composed, but blanched at his murmurs. Master Huang leaned back, the smug look on his face clear even to Ai Ling.

"There's a possible solution." Master Huang rubbed his hands together. "I'm aware there have been failed attempts in arranging a suitable marriage for your daughter. I believe she just turned seventeen? Not a young girl at the most desirable age to prospective families . . ." He trailed off, allowing the words to sink in. "I'm offering to take Ai Ling as my fourth wife in exchange for the money owed me. She's a pretty girl. And seems agreeable and intelligent enough."

Ai Ling dropped the jar. It thudded and smashed. Tea leaves scattered as she burst into the main hall.

"No, Mother, no!" She realized too late that she had shouted.

"Ai Ling!" Her mother's pale face jerked toward her just as the merchant's did. Ai Ling ignored him, and instead knelt in front of her mother and took her hands in her own.

"You can't. You mustn't. Not without Father here. Not to him."

She knew she was breaking every rule of decorum. But if she thought her failed betrothals were wretched, being sold to this brute for birthing purposes was an infinitely worse fate.

"Ai Ling, this is unacceptable. Apologize to Master Huang."

Ai Ling looked into her mother's face and saw for the first time how tired she appeared, how much she had aged in the six months Father had been away. Ai Ling realized with shock that her mother's hair was now more gray than black.

Her chest tightened with love and pain. She rose and turned to the merchant. "I'm sorry for my outburst, Master Huang. I just don't want—"

"It doesn't matter what you want," Master Huang interrupted. "You're a financial burden to your mother. An extra mouth to feed. An extra body to clothe. You are an embarrassment to your family, loitering about at seventeen years when other girls your age have already borne children."

Ai Ling's face grew hot; the fire spread to the tips of her ears and roots of her hair. But Master Huang was not finished.

"Your only saving grace is that pretty face. You're too tall for my taste, but I can overlook this fault. I held your father in high esteem, despite the scandal at court. I offer you my home out of generosity and in fondness for an old colleague. Consider yourself fortunate. That face won't be pretty forever."

Ai Ling felt rooted to the floor, unable to turn her gaze from the merchant. Master Huang misunderstood and smiled, revealing teeth stained from pipe smoking. He winked at her.

"You have a temper. But nothing that can't be tamed. One suckling babe at each teat should do the trick." The man threw his head back and roared at his own wit.

Ai Ling jabbed her nails into tight fists, clenching her teeth until her jaws ached.

"Consider my offer, Lady Wen. I'll give you two days. It is I who is doing you a favor." Master Huang rose and snapped open his fan before stepping out into their courtyard, unescorted. He did not look Ai Ling's way again.

That evening, they dined in strained silence. Ai Ling knew her mother would not succumb to Master Huang's coercion. She was certain he lied about the debt, and although she could have read everything written in that scroll, it would not have changed the situation. Master Huang fraternized with all the officials in their small town, plying them with wine and gifts. It was his word as a powerful merchant against theirs, two helpless women. Without Father, there was no one to protect them.

Master Huang was rich and did not need more money. He wanted her . . . to make a son for him. The thought brought a sour taste to her mouth, a mixture of panic and fury. She would leave home before ever stepping into his bedchamber. She could go look for her father and bring him back. She wanted to both laugh and cry—the idea was ludicrous. But she refused to stay, to suffer that brute's bullying.

Mother would be so worried . . . but it would free her from Master Huang's manipulations. He knew they had no money. And there would be one less mouth to feed.

In the late hours, as the crickets chirped outside her window, Ai Ling sat on her bed, a packed knapsack beside her, and surveyed the cozy room by lantern light. Taro climbed in to join her. He nuzzled her hand, tilted his head to have his chin scratched.

"I'm leaving, Taro, to bring Father back. You'll have to look after Mother while I'm away." She stroked the short gray fur down his back and trailed her fingers along the tail. "I'll miss you." She kissed the spot between his pointy ears.

Yet she didn't move from her bed, feeling her heart hammer wildly. She grasped the jade pendant in her hand. Was she doing the right thing? Should she be the dutiful daughter, offer herself to Master Huang, and take the burden off her mother?

Ai Ling couldn't do it.

She picked up her ink stick and slowly ground it against the square stone. What could she say to Mother to make her understand? After a few moments, with a trembling hand, she dipped her brush and wrote two sentences in clear, simple script.

I have gone to search for Father. Do not worry for me.

She signed her name and placed the ink stone over the small note. She hoped her mother could decipher the simple characters. And if she couldn't, Master Huang would.

She blew out the lantern and slid the lattice panel shut behind her. The flat-faced mutt next door erupted in wild barks, and Ai Ling froze, her nape damp with sweat. Silence returned as she hurried past her mother's dark quarters, the tears flowing freely now.

Forgive me, Mother.

She eased the courtyard door open and stepped into the silent alley. She dared not look back; Ai Ling walked as fast as she could toward the moonlight. And away from everything she had ever known and loved.

CHAPTER THREE

Ai Ling traveled onward through the night, guided by the half moon. The evening air was pleasant, still warm from the heat of the day. Yet she walked with her arms folded tightly around her, the hairs on her neck rising each time she heard the rustle of leaves or soft scrape of dirt. Ai Ling did not have the courage to look back, imagining dark shapes following her—Master Huang on a horse in pursuit or even lost ghosts, seeking the warmth of a living being.

She cursed herself for ever reading *The Book of the Dead*. She had found it just before her thirteenth birthday, hidden near the back of her father's desk drawer, while searching for a new ink stick. Father had discovered her crouched over the enormous book, riveted. He had slammed it shut, forbade her to read it. She had never seen him so angry. Ai Ling had stumbled across the book again months later, this time tucked on the highest shelf, hidden behind other volumes. She pulled it down, knowing her father wouldn't be back from his tutoring for hours. It was filled with tales of strange creatures. Truth or myth, she knew not. But the descriptions fascinated as much as revolted her. She'd studied it on the sly for years, and was being punished for her transgression this shadow-filled night.

She trudged on until the world began to take shape, dawn defining her surroundings. Her feet ached and her head throbbed. Exhausted, she finally curled up behind a hedge on the side of the dirt road and fell asleep, just as all else was waking up around her.

The sound of clopping hooves woke Ai Ling. She sat up and saw the rear of the powerful animal. A man was astride the horse's back, and Ai Ling crouched behind the hedge until the road was deserted. She brushed off her clothes and followed him. He was most likely headed to the next town.

Her stomach rumbled. By the height of the sun, it was near midday, and she hoped for a hot meal. She had a handful of coins saved. Mother had surprised her with birthday cash wrapped in a red satin pouch. She had found the gift resting against a sweet bean bun by her pillow on the morning of her seventeenth birthday.

She guessed it would take at least eighteen days to reach the Palace of Fragrant Dreams, assuming she did not become lost along the way. Ai Ling took a long swallow of water from her sheepskin flask and quickened her pace, imagining the dishes at the restaurant where she would soon dine.

Within the hour, she caught sight of the tall mud-colored walls surrounding Qing He. The gates to the city were wide open and kept by two guards. The tall one with a beaklike nose studied her with curiosity, while the other, more rotund guard did not bother to glance up. She released a long breath after she passed through the gates.

The main street clamored with throngs of people. There were other girls alone among the crowds. Their simple dress and unadorned hairstyle—braids wrapped tight on each side of the head—were clear indications of their servant status. Ai Ling had dressed plainly as well, her one long braid tucked inside the back of her tunic.

Qing He was bigger than the town she had grown up in. She jostled against others as she took in the storefronts of textile shops, bolts of silks and brocades gleaming in the sunlight. She ran her fingers along the smooth materials, imagining what her mother would create with the fabric.

She walked past the stationery store and quelled the urge to wander through it, knowing there would be endless rolls and sheaves of rice paper, bound books and journals, and elaborate seals to add to her small collection. Her father had taken her to the stationer in their town on many occasions. For her thirteenth birthday, they had selected a rectangular chop made of soapstone with a dragon perched on top. Her father had her name carved on the bottom. It became a tradition, the day of her birthday, to visit the stationer with Father and choose another seal. She had received one for each birthday thereafter, except this last one.

Turning a corner, she nearly collided with a woman balancing two baskets of eggplants on each end of a pole slung across her shoulders. The path immediately narrowed, and the noise of hawkers selling their goods simmered to a hum. The smell of steamed buns and dumplings drew her. The wooden sign hung above the restaurant doors read LAO SONG. She climbed the stone steps and went inside.

The enormous size of the place surprised her. It was two stories, and many patrons sat above on the second-floor balcony. A rowdy midday crowd crammed the first level. She had difficulty finding a table but finally chanced on one tucked in the back corner, with a view of the entire dining area. Dishes from the previous patron's meal remained.

A server girl who looked her own age approached to clear the dirty dishes. She wore her one braid coiled on the top of her head and a plain pink tunic over gray trousers.

"What'd you like?" The girl barely flicked a look at her.

"Steamed dumplings, please. And some tea." Ai Ling pressed her palms to her empty stomach.

Her server wiped the table clean with leftover tea and

hefted the bowls and dishes away with graceful ease. Ai Ling watched her retreating back and wondered what her life was like. Was she Lao Song's daughter? The girl was not wed, by the way she wore her hair.

Ai Ling came from the privileged scholarly class, yet she wouldn't mind working in a restaurant if it meant she could stay close to her family. She fingered her red satin pouch.

It was not long before the girl came back with a plate of steaming dumplings. She placed a dish of chili paste and ginger in front of Ai Ling, as well as two small ceramic jugs. "Soy sauce and vinegar," she said. "I'll bring your tea."

Ai Ling fixed her bowl with the condiments, just so. Lots of vinegar, light on the ginger and soy sauce, with a dab of chili paste. She swirled the concoction with her eating sticks and bathed the first dumpling. After making sure every bit of it was soaked, she took her first bite. Perfect.

Her server returned with a pot of tea, which she poured into a small chipped ceramic cup.

Ai Ling finished the dumplings too soon. She sipped her tea, observing the other patrons. They were mostly men, and the women who were present were accompanied by men. She was grateful for her corner seat.

A song filled the air. She looked toward the enchanting voice and spotted the singer a few tables down. The woman stood facing an audience of five men, her hair swept up in elaborate loops and adorned with red jewels. They winked in the sunlight that filtered through the open shutters above. She wore a flowing sky blue dress with wide sleeves. Ai Ling had guessed she was of high status, an official's concubine perhaps. Then she noticed that the woman's top was sheer, very clearly revealing three breasts.

Ai Ling's empty teacup clattered to the wooden table.

A Life Seeker.

She remembered the drawing from *The Book of the Dead*—a beautiful woman elegantly dressed, her gossamer top showing the contours of her three breasts. The caption below had read:

> *Emperor Shen of the Lu Dynasty issued a mandate which forced all Life Seekers to wear sheer tops, denying them the right to bind their breasts, and therefore baring their identity to the world. It served as warning for most, but an enticement for some.*

She had reread the paragraphs so often she'd memorized the passages. It was as if she held the book in front of her.

> *The Life Seeker can be easily distinguished by the extra breast on her sternum. The tips are dark blue, as are her tongue and womanhood. Legend has it that the extra breast was given to replace the heart she does not have. The creature is not mortal and maintains life through copulation with men. Each*

time, she steals a breath from her victim. Her lovers will find
her highly addictive, and most will die without intervention. A
monk is needed to bless the concoction given to the victim, who
must be locked in his own chamber and guarded for sixteen
days and nights. If he breaks free to meet with the Life Seeker,
the cycle begins anew. The creatures never grow old as long as
they are bedding a mortal on a daily basis. If for some reason,
access is denied to the Life Seeker, she will age near a decade
each day she goes without, until she finally withers.

The Life Seeker stopped singing and sashayed back to her audience. The men thumped the table with their fists in approval and lifted their wine cups in salute. One man pulled her into his lap, nuzzling her neck, then holding out a string of gold coins. The seductress took the gift and whispered in his ear. Blue tongue flicking, her eyes locked with Ai Ling's for one brief moment. Ai Ling wrenched her gaze away, both enthralled and embarrassed.

The man turned his head, and she caught a glimpse of his face. Master Huang! Ai Ling twisted so her back was to him. With an unsteady hand, she fished a silver coin from her satin pouch and put it on the table. She weaved her way through the crowd of diners, her chin tucked, stumbling once over her own feet. She slipped through the carved double doors and nearly slammed into someone.

"Hello, pretty. Where are you rushing off to?" A man blocked the way. He was squat, with broad shoulders and powerful arms. He leered up at her, a gaping hole where one front tooth should have been. She could smell the liquor on his breath.

"It isn't safe for pretty ladies like yourself to travel alone, you know. You need a friend with you. A friend like me." The man wiggled his unkempt eyebrows, his face twisted in a lewd sneer.

Ai Ling tried to keep her features blank. "I do have friends, sir. They are inside. I stepped out for some fresh air." She smiled and hoped her lie was convincing.

"Is that so? I better stay and guard you until they come out." He squinted at her. "Why don't we take a nice stroll while we wait? Are you from up north? So tall and pretty . . ."

The man reached out one filthy hand, making a grab at her wrist.

Such a tasty morsel.

She heard him. But he hadn't spoken aloud. Ai Ling stumbled back, her stomach seizing as if she'd been kicked. Warmth flared at her breast, and she looked down—the jade pendant glowed so bright it appeared white.

The man lurched toward her, but stopped to slap his neck. He grimaced in surprise. She heard an insistent buzzing. A large insect hovered between their faces.

"Curse of a rabid—oww!" More wasps appeared from the eaves above, flying straight toward him.

Flailing his arms about his head in panic, he ran into the restaurant, leaving Ai Ling wide-eyed, standing alone in the alleyway. Then she bolted toward the main street, one hand clutching the pendant, hot against her skin.

Ai Ling spent her second night in a shed. Two pigs and a few chickens kept her company, their scratching and snuffling noises comforting her. She removed her shoes and winced from the blisters on her toes. Her hand searched for the jade pendant in the dark, and she ran a fingertip over its ridges. It had burned bright, sent the wasps to her attacker. She couldn't have imagined it. Had the monk blessed it before giving it to Father? She closed her eyes and saw her father's face. She wrapped her arms around herself and fell asleep with her back pressed against the pigpen.

The crowing of a rooster startled her awake. She had not seen the creature last night, his chest puffed out now as he strutted among his hens. Light filtered through the cracks of the wooden shed.

She rummaged through her knapsack and retrieved a slice of dried mango and two salted biscuits. Everything tasted stale. Her empty stomach rumbled. But all she could do was fill it with the last swallows of water from her flask.

She eased the shed door open. The morning air rejuvenated her as she scanned the horizon. The rays of the sun were just beginning to wash the skyline. She reeked of farm animals and damp hay. Ai Ling scratched her itching scalp and wished for a mirror, then decided it was probably better she didn't have one.

She found a well on the other side of the shed and cranked up the heavy wooden pail with stiff arms. The water was biting and cold. She drank half a flask and refilled it. It was time to continue on her journey.

After she'd marched for two hours, the trees thinned, and she caught a glimpse of an expansive lake, a calming sight. The sky was cloudless. Birds swooped overhead, at times dropping like lightning into the water.

The lake's surface was still. She walked to the shore, sat down with care on the dirt embankment, and removed her worn cloth shoes. Never before had she walked as much as she had in the past two days. She wiggled her toes, and then massaged the arch of one foot with her thumb.

Ai Ling relaxed, a small sigh escaping her lips. Her shoulders dropped as she pressed her chest against her knees. She dipped both feet into the water. The coolness felt delicious, and she reveled in it, her toes tingling.

She reached for her knapsack and pulled out a small cotton rag. She soaked the cloth in the lake, wrung it dry, and wiped across her brow and cheeks. Her mind drifted to home, a world away now. How was Mother coping? Would she be taking her midday meal?

The water rippled in front of her.

Something slithered and tugged on her right foot.

Startled, Ai Ling recoiled as the thing grabbed her other foot and pulled harder. The force of it slammed her flat on her back.

She flailed her arms but found only air as she was dragged into the water. She clawed the embankment. The loose dirt provided no hold, and with another tug, she was below the surface. Whatever gripped Ai Ling pulled her down through the murky depths fast.

She could do nothing but watch the sunlight on the lake's surface grow dimmer. The last small breath she had drawn dwindled to nothing, even as she willed it to last. Fighting her terror, she looked down and saw dark, slithering shapes beneath her. Hundreds of shapes skulking below, tittering. She could hear them. That was the worst part. Worse than drowning.

Suddenly her descent ended, and she was left suspended upright in the dark depths. The pressure in her ears made her head throb. Her ribs felt crushed, her lungs compressed with the burning need for air. She struggled against drawing one breath, knowing there was nothing but fetid water if she did so.

The sinister thing writhed, like a massive eel, its body as thick as a man's, its length endless. Luminous eyes, glowing emeralds, stared at her, unblinking. She thought it had a long snout, but she couldn't be sure.

The creature's tail curled up and around her until her entire body was captured in its sinewy lengths. Yet those eyes never moved, floating in the water a short distance away.

Ai Ling. Your family is in ruins because of you. Because of your selfishness. Your pride. Your stubbornness. Your mother has not stopped weeping since you left.

It spoke without speaking. She struggled against its powerful grip, but the effort was lost, as if she had never tried. Her lungs spasmed for breath. Water seeped through her vision, filled her nostrils, her head. She refused to succumb to the darkness, to the monster that clutched her.

But she must breathe.

Just as she was about to surrender, to draw a mouthful of water, Ai Ling felt a hotness below her throat. Her lungs filled with air. She looked down at the pendant, burning like a star.

Images emerged in the depths, clear and bright, one object at a time. She blinked, focused. First a four-legged washstand holding a white ceramic bowl, followed by a rectangular desk stacked with books. Then her bed on the raised carved platform. Ai Ling's throat clenched at the sight of the familiar and beloved objects from her bedchamber.

Her mother appeared last. She was sitting on the bed, head bowed as she sobbed into her hands. She looked so small, frail, and dejected.

Tears escaped from Ai Ling's own eyes, bled from her core. She tasted the salt of them in her throat, even as the pendant flared hot against her skin and replenished her with breath once more. She cried with her mother until the fathomless lake was filled with her tears.

You have left her with nothing but a broken heart. With a debt that cannot be paid. You could have married Master Huang to help your family. But instead you shirked your duty and ran away.

The voice was like glass shards coated in honey.

The slithering forms, all murmuring their disapproval in some ancient tongue, shifted in the abyss around her. But Ai Ling understood. *Selfish. Ungrateful. Useless.* She wanted to tear off her ears, gouge out her eyes, anything to stop the voices inside her head.

And your father. He loved you so well. A useless daughter. Your father said you were special. Your father lied. The last word seemed to snicker and shriek. It tore through her mind, reverberated in her skull, and echoed into infinity.

Her father appeared, wearing his favorite dark blue robes. He raised one hand toward his daughter, a look of love and concern on his face. Ai Ling wanted to speak, reach her hand to him.

Then the whites of his eyes began to move as hundreds of maggots squirmed, falling from empty sockets, until his entire body was a writhing mass. His skin peeled away to expose raw flesh, then decayed to mere bones. The skeleton dissolved to silver wisps of dust, streaked away before her horrified eyes.

Your father is dead. Go home.

Ai Ling bit her tongue so she would not scream. You lie, she shrieked in her mind. But part of her believed it.

Go away. Go back.

The muscular tail squeezed tighter, smothering the precious

air she had been given. It crushed her until she was nothing. Nothing but darkness and hot salty tears.

Ai Ling felt someone tap her cheek. She opened her eyes and winced, her sight seared by the bright blue skies. A young man's face appeared above hers.

"Are you all right?"

She gazed into his strange amber eyes—a color she had never seen. They were filled with concern.

No, she wanted to say, I'm not all right. My father is dead. I may as well be dead to my mother.

She wanted to curl up and cry. And sleep. Forever. She shivered, even as the strong afternoon sunlight warmed her wet clothes and damp skin.

"Get me away from here," she whispered. It was all that she could muster.

Ai Ling felt herself gathered into strong arms as the stranger lifted her.

She leaned into him, trusting him completely in her grief and exhaustion. She shut her eyes and once more lost grasp of the world around her.

❦

CHAPTER FOUR

Ai Ling awoke to the sound of twigs crackling on a fire. The orange glow licked beneath her closed lids. She didn't want to open her eyes.

A shuffling noise to her left. Curiosity overrode fear. She peered from under lowered lashes and saw the young man kneel before the fire, stoking it with a stick. The fire fed and grew. Ai Ling basked in its warmth.

What had she said to him? Ai Ling couldn't remember. She tilted her head, wanting to see his face. Her movement caught his attention, and their eyes met.

Strange amber eyes. She remembered now.

"You're awake," he said.

Ai Ling looked toward the fire. Dusk neared. She could tell by the light and the birds singing above them. Cheerful. Just as they had been before she was pulled into the lake. Had she dreamed it? She touched her still-damp clothes and didn't answer him.

"I found you on the water's edge," he said. "You were half submerged. When I tried to pull you out—it was as if something was pulling you in."

He stirred the fire again, and the flames leaped. His brow furrowed.

"The water was clear. Shallow. There was nothing at your feet. Yet I used all my strength to drag you out." He sat down on the ground and rested his arms on raised knees.

"You saved me. There is no proper way I can thank you," Ai Ling said.

He leaned forward and smiled at her. It altered the lines of his face. "She speaks."

Ai Ling shifted with care and sat up, drew herself closer to the fire. She reached for the jade pendant without thinking. She squeezed it tight in her palm, remembering the breaths of life-saving air that had filled her lungs.

"You're shivering. Do you have more clothes?"

She shrugged, caught off guard by his concern. Her hand found her worn knapsack, which she had been using as a pillow. Could she trust him?

"Yes," she said.

"I'll turn around."

Ai Ling saw his back before he even finished the sentence. Under different circumstances, she would have sought privacy in the thickets, but she was in no mood to leave the safety of the fire as daylight ebbed. She pulled out a blue cotton tunic and trousers, sewn with care by her mother, then peeled the clothes from her body. Her gaze never strayed from the young man's back as she changed. She laid her wet clothes down flat near the fire.

"I'm done," she said.

He turned toward her, and she studied him. He had a high brow, tall nose, and a proud, serious face. His clothes were travel worn, but well made. She guessed him to be about eighteen or nineteen years. He had saved her life. Perhaps it would be safer to stay with him, at least through the night.

"I am called Ai Ling," she said.

"I am Chen Yong."

It was like a trick of the light, how his features appeared Xian from one angle, and then quite foreign with a half turn of his head. He wasn't fully Xian, she realized with shock. The idea had never crossed her mind before. You were either Xian or not.

"Are you hungry?" he asked.

She had not thought about it but heard her stomach growl at his question. She was starving.

"I bought some pork buns at the inn. They must be cold by now, but still tasty."

Chen Yong passed two large buns to her. The breading

was thick and a little sweet. The stuffing was savory, and the broth ran down her chin and fingertips.

"You're hungry, then." He smiled, stating the obvious.

Ai Ling nodded, abashed. The buns had disappeared like a conjurer's trick.

"You travel alone?" he asked.

The skin on her arms prickled, reminding her how alone she truly was, how vulnerable. One glance at Chen Yong told her he didn't realize the weight of his simple question. She looked away.

"I'm searching for my father." Ai Ling felt her throat clench. She swallowed hard. "But . . . but I think he may be dead." Sobs overcame her, even as she tried to suppress them. She wiped a hand across her face in frustration. As if it wasn't bad enough that she had been carried like a babe in the arms of this stranger, now she'd become a blubbering fool before him.

"We travel for similar reasons," he said, making no mention of her tears.

They didn't speak again that night. Ai Ling laid her head back down on her knapsack and watched the dancing flames. Chen Yong's profile, bent over a book, was the final image she carried with her into sleep.

Ai Ling's eyes flew open, and she sat up, confused.

"Good morning," Chen Yong said. He was sitting by the spot where the fire had been. All traces of it were gone, swept away. He held the same book in his hands. Had he even slept?

"I made some tea. It may be cold now."

He poured from a small silver kettle. She nursed the cup in cold hands, turning it. It reflected a distorted image of her curious face across its smooth plane.

"It's made of eng. From abroad. A gift from my father when he learned I was traveling."

"It's foreign? Is your father . . . ?" she asked.

"No. My adoptive parents are Xian. I don't know who my birth parents are."

She sipped the lukewarm tea, not knowing what to say. It soothed her, and the fragrance of jasmine reminded her of home. She rummaged through her knapsack and fished out a small bundle wrapped in a deep purple handkerchief. She untied the twine with care, revealing a heap of walnuts.

"My mother cooked them in sugar." She passed some to Chen Yong.

He popped one in his mouth. "Delicious. Walnuts are a rarity."

"They were a special treat. For my birthday." Had it really been less than a week ago?

"How many years?" Chen Yong crunched on another walnut.

She sipped her tea before replying. "Seventeen."

"Seventeen years? And wandering on your own?" He raised his dark brows.

Ai Ling felt anger and guilt rise within her. "I am searching for my father. There's no one else but me. My mother remains at home."

"It's dangerous for a girl to travel alone." He studied her, not having to mention how he had found her.

"I do what I must. Just because most girls are sequestered within the inner quarters does not mean I have to be." What was she saying? She had abided by the rules like every other girl until two days ago, when she'd decided to leave home. But Chen Yong's admonishing tone irked her.

"You speak as if I made the rules of decorum," he said, and did not reach for another walnut, as she clutched the bundle to herself now.

"No, you didn't make the rules. But I would wager a silver coin that you think a girl's place is sweeping the front courtyard and spoon-feeding her husband dinner broth each evening." She glared at Chen Yong, not caring that she spoke so forwardly.

His eyes widened, and then crinkled with a wry smile. "I admit that doesn't sound so bad right now."

Somehow his confession didn't feel like a victory.

"Are you not betrothed?" She couldn't stop herself. Anything to provoke a reaction.

The humor was wiped from his face. "No."

She allowed herself a small sense of triumph. It was short-lived.

"Are you?" he asked.

Chen Yong waited, vexing her with his deliberate silence. "I ran away to avoid a betrothal," she said after a few moments. There was nothing to hide. She had made the right decision.

Chen Yong paused for a moment before speaking, the surprise obvious on his face. "Our first duty is to our parents." His words brought back the hissed accusations from the dark abyss: selfish, ungrateful, useless daughter. She blinked, unwilling to shed more tears in front of him.

"My father would not have wanted it. Nor my mother." She stood, pulled the knapsack over her shoulder. Chen Yong rose with agility. He stood a hand taller than she.

"I should go," Ai Ling said. She owed him thanks. He had saved her life, after all.

He remained silent, looking down at her, his face never betraying his thoughts. His golden eyes were tinged with green. She dropped her gaze, hating herself for noticing.

What was he thinking? Without conscious effort, she cast herself toward him, threw an invisible cord from her spirit to his. She felt it waver like a drunken serpent, fumble, and then latch. The sudden pulling and tautness within her navel surprised her.

She remembered watching her father fish once. He'd offered her the bamboo rod when a fish took the bait, tugging so hard against the line she was afraid the rod would break. It felt like that.

She felt an irresistible draw toward her hooked target,

followed by a strange snap sensation. She was within Chen Yong's being.

Ai Ling noticed his higher vantage point immediately. She had always been told she was tall for a girl, but she didn't look so from his eyes. His body was more rested than hers. There were no knots of anxiety in his shoulders; no soreness in his neck. A power and strength unfamiliar to her coursed through his limbs, a litheness coiled within him.

She stared at herself. She stood in a stance of defiance, arms folded across her chest. Did she always look so childish, so stubborn?

Was that Chen Yong's thought or her own? She quieted her spirit, eavesdropped within his mind. *Feisty.* She plucked the one word that flitted to her from his thoughts. It emerged with a sense of amusement and surprised admiration. Suddenly she felt ashamed that she was intruding. She was curious, but it felt wrong. She drew herself back reluctantly, felt the snap as she returned to her own being.

The world tilted for a brief moment, and she tried to cover her unsteadiness by fussing with her knapsack. She blinked away the black spots that floated across her vision. What was happening to her? Had he felt her trespass? She glanced up at him. His expression had not changed. She straightened.

"I can never repay your kindness. Thank you." She spoke from the heart. He deserved that much.

"And to you, Ai Ling. Take good care."

She blushed, turned so he would not see, and walked away. She looked back once, to find him still standing in the same spot, and waved. He lifted one hand in farewell. Ai Ling hoped he would follow. She quickly cast the thought aside as if the desire had never existed.

CHAPTER FIVE

It was midday. Ai Ling wiped the sweat from her brow and touched the top of her head. Her hair felt on fire.

Two boys squatted in the middle of the road. A tan mongrel wagged its tail beside them. They clutched red firecrackers, heads bent together, and whispered in conspiratorial tones.

Her stomach growled, reminding her that she had not eaten anything since the walnuts at daybreak. She took two final swallows of water from her flask, savoring the last drops.

The bang of firecrackers startled her. Ai Ling looked back. The two boys scurried toward her with the dog in tow, their mouths wide in surprised fright.

"Wah! I didn't know it'd be so loud. It nearly took my fingers off!" the taller one shouted.

"You said you knew what you were doing!" His friend hopped angrily from one foot to the other.

"You made me do it." The lanky boy looked somewhat apologetic and tugged on his queue.

"I almost lost my nose!"

The acrid smoke from the firecrackers dissipated while the two argued. Ai Ling turned and walked back toward them.

"Are you all right?" she asked.

Afraid they were in trouble, the two nodded in unison. "No problems here, miss! Everything's fine!"

She smiled. "You need to be careful." She'd always wished for younger siblings. The short one seemed quite taken with her and grinned, his eyes nearly disappearing into round cheeks.

"They're good for scaring away evil spirits, you know. The firecrackers," he said.

"So they say."

The lanky boy tucked the remaining firecracker into his dirty tunic.

"Do you know a place where I can rest and have a nice meal?" she asked.

"Yes, miss! My uncle owns the best noodle house in town. It's this way." The chubby boy trotted down the dusty street with his lanky friend beside him while the dog trailed behind. Ai Ling followed the trio down the road.

The boys led her to a crowded one-room shack at the end of a narrow alleyway. The noodle house décor consisted of a few rough-hewn mismatched wooden tables and stools. No panels covered the two small windows looking out into the alleyway. Ai Ling wondered how the establishment kept cats and other critters out at night. She examined the room's edges and corners for scampering things. Seeing nothing that darted or crept, she sat down at one of the rickety tables. The scent of scallions and sour wine hung in the air.

Despite its coarse appearance, the noodle house indeed offered delicious fare, at least by Ai Ling's ravenous standards. Her disheveled appearance and dusty attire did not draw much attention in the busy establishment. She devoured her large bowl of beef tendon noodles in peace.

She was wiping the sheen from her face, brought on from the steaming soup and chili paste, when a roar of laughter drew her attention.

"Why don't you go back to whatever barbaric country you sailed from?" The man who spoke was nearly as wide as he was tall, and he waved a hand at the object of his derision.

Chen Yong stood next to a table of men, obviously not a part of the group from his defensive stance. When had he come into the noodle house? Had he followed her here? Ai Ling made a face at her own foolish thought. She watched him speak in a quiet tone and turn away.

"I doubt our illustrious Master Tan needs another mutt in

his manor." A dark, gaunt man with a hard mouth snick-
ered. His friends laughed, spewing wine on one another. "Be
gone, half-breed!"

Chen Yong half turned back to the group, his fists
clenched. Ai Ling's pulse quickened. He could not possibly
fight so many men. She waved her arms as if she were on a
sinking boat to draw his attention. But Chen Yong did not
see her. She stood too quickly and her stool tilted, clattering against the floor.

Chen Yong took a step back in surprise when he saw her.
She beckoned with a tiny twitch of the hand, mortified that
every eye was on her. He turned, ignoring the whistles and
foot stomping, and pulled a stool to her table.

"What are you doing here?" he asked, his demeanor calm
once more.

"Eating, of course. Their beef tendon noodles are delicious." She nodded to the large, empty noodle bowl. "What
are you doing here?"

"I'm in search of a Master Tan. He lived in this town,
at least twenty years ago." He jerked his head toward the
group of men continuing with their drink and gambling. "I
haven't had much luck getting directions to his manor."

She wrinkled her nose in obvious distaste, and Chen Yong
laughed. He waved a serving boy over and ordered.

Ai Ling drummed her fingers on the splintered wooden
table after his noodles arrived, trying not to stare while
he ate.

"Will you tell me what happened at the lake?" he asked as he captured thick noodles in the large soup ladle.

"You wouldn't believe me. You'd think I was crazy." Ai Ling wished she had enough coins to splurge on something sweet—sticky rice with candied persimmons, perhaps. . . .

"Try me." He stopped eating and studied her with such intensity she leaned in without realizing. Ai Ling then sat back so abruptly she almost fell off the stool.

She didn't want to talk about it, so she kept her voice low, for fear it would tremble otherwise. "I was dragged into the lake. Down deep. It wasn't the lake anymore. It felt . . . ancient. Evil. This black slithering thing held me. There were hundreds more. I could hear them . . . in my head." She stared into her bowl, unable to meet his gaze.

"What did they say?" he asked.

She wished he'd start eating again, before the noodles went oversoft or the broth cooled. "That my father is dead. That I broke my mother's heart. That it was all my fault—"

"Do you believe it?"

"No." She lifted her chin, daring him to say anything to the contrary. He did not laugh or accuse her of madness.

"I wouldn't believe you, if I hadn't found you on the water's edge myself. I was going to take a different route, but . . ."

"But what?"

"Something drew me toward the lake. A feeling. I can't explain it." He leaned closer, and she caught herself holding her breath. "Do you know why this happened?" he asked.

"No."

"I'm not one to discount the unexplainable—I've read enough of it in the ancient texts." He picked up his soup ladle. "Where are you headed?"

She released a small sigh, glad to be free from his scrutiny. Besides, limp noodles were not worth eating. "To the Palace. That was where my father went, six months past."

"That's a long journey by foot." He wiped his mouth with a handkerchief and waved the serving boy over again. "Bring some tea and dessert," he said.

Ai Ling beamed.

They ate the tricolored flower—named for the pale chestnut, red date, and purple yam layered into the sweet sticky rice, steamed in a flower-shaped bowl—in silence.

"Will you accompany me today?" he asked, breaking the silence after the dessert was devoured. "To look for Master Tan?"

Ai Ling stopped mid-chew and swallowed the sticky rice too soon. She reached for her teacup and took a quick sip. "Why?"

"I know it's a strange thing to ask."

She studied the thick topknot on his lowered head. His hair was near black, with deep auburn accents. Like his eyes, it was a shade she had never seen.

"My younger brother insisted on joining me for this journey. I wanted to be alone. But now . . ." He looked up.

"You're the first friendly face I've seen since leaving home."

"If you'd like, it's the least I can do," she said.

Chen Yong smiled at her, his serious face turned boyish. "I'm glad I followed you here."

Her eyes widened, and he laughed.

"I'm jesting. I didn't, truly. But somehow I wasn't surprised when I saw you again," he said.

He poured more tea for her. She wondered what he was thinking, but kept her spirit within herself this time.

They obtained directions to Master Tan's manor after speaking with people in the market square. But information was difficult to gain. Most of the men stared at Chen Yong with suspicion. Ai Ling avoided the glances cast her way. She had drawn less scrutiny traveling alone. Was this how life was for Chen Yong? It took hours walking around the narrow streets to find Master Tan's home. The directions they were given proved to be wrong, more than once.

"This must be it," Chen Yong said finally. They stood before a thick wooden door. Two faded paper door gods with fierce expressions and drawn weapons were plastered on its surface. Dusk neared.

Chen Yong thudded on the dark wood with a heavy fist.

The huge door swung open immediately.

"What do you want?" A sullen-faced servant peered out, his thin mouth drawn into a frown.

"I'm here to see Master Tan," Chen Yong said.

"Who're you then?" The servant spoke as if he suspected Chen Yong was there to ransack the place.

"I am Li Chen Yong," he replied in a strong voice.

"It's late for such an intrusion," someone interjected from behind the ill-tempered servant. "But I can always make time for the son of an old friend."

"Master Tan!" The servant bowed low and stepped aside, revealing the man who had spoken. He was tall, as tall as Chen Yong, and although his hair was gray, his face was youthful.

Master Tan grasped Chen Yong's shoulder with one hand. "I've wondered all these years if we would meet. I see your father in you."

Chen Yong's stoic demeanor was fractured by the mention of his birth father. Emotions Ai Ling could not identify flitted across his features before he nodded, without speaking.

Master Tan turned to Ai Ling, allowing Chen Yong time to gather himself.

"Is this lovely lady your wife?" he asked.

"Ai Ling? No," Chen Yong said, the surprise evident in his voice.

The older man's eyebrows shot up, his turn to be taken aback. Aware of her discomfort, Master Tan waved one arm toward his manor. "Come in. Welcome." The old servant pulled the door wide open.

Ai Ling drew in her breath at the sight of the expansive courtyard. Her family's courtyard could fit in one corner.

The lattice panels to the main hall were drawn open. Ai Ling and Chen Yong followed their host across the courtyard and into the hall. A long ancestor altar, laden with fruit, rested against the back wall, and the faint smell of incense wove through the air. Opalescent lanterns, already lit, hung in each corner, reminding her of giant sea pearls.

"Please, sit." Master Tan indicated the carved blackwood chairs across from him. She and Chen Yong both did so in silence.

"Would you like some tea? Have you eaten? You must be travel worn."

"Tea is fine, Master Tan. You're kind to complete strangers. We've already eaten." Chen Yong spoke for them both, even as she wondered what food Master Tan had to offer.

She smiled and nodded.

Master Tan raised a hand and winked at her. "Lan Hua!" Within seconds, a young woman near Ai Ling's age was by his side. She wore her hair as did many girls of the servant class, the black braids coiled on either side of her head. But her clothing was finer than anything Ai Ling had ever seen on a servant, a silk tunic and trousers in pale blue, embroidered with pink cherry blossoms.

"Please bring tea for our guests. And dinner as well."

"Yes, Master Tan." She retreated with quick steps.

Ai Ling grinned. She looked toward Chen Yong, but he was oblivious. Master Tan enquired after her companion's adoptive family, his studies and recent travel experience.

She hid her interest in Chen Yong's replies by studying the calligraphy on the walls, lines from Bai Kong's classic poetry. The scrolls of landscape paintings reaching the dark wood beams of the ceiling especially intrigued her.

Suddenly a face appeared behind a lattice panel, and Ai Ling half rose in fright. It quickly vanished. Probably a servant, she told herself.

Still, she was glad when Lan Hua interrupted them with a tray bearing teacups. The familiar warmth and feel of the cup calmed her. Ai Ling inhaled the rising steam—chrysanthemum, with a hint of something like mint.

"I sent a letter to the Li manor in Gao Tung last year. I never received a reply. It was your family, yes?" Master Tan asked.

"I apologize, Master Tan. I was unsure when I would be able to make the trip in person," Chen Yong replied.

They sipped in silence for a moment. Chen Yong cleared his throat.

"Master Tan, you said you knew my father. . . ." His voice trailed off.

Their host did not let him flounder. "It has been years since I've seen him. He traveled back to his country soon after you were born. I think about him often. We were like brothers."

"Where was he from?"

"Jiang Dao. A diplomat sent to the Emperor's court to open communication between the two kingdoms."

Already on the edge of his seat, Chen Yong leaned forward. "And my mother?"

Master Tan placed his teacup back on the lacquered tray. "Chen Yong, perhaps you would like to eat first, rest? It's a . . . complicated story." The older man's brow creased, his concern obvious.

Chen Yong sat back. He examined his hands without speaking for a few moments, then raised his face. Ai Ling admired the firm lines of his nose and cheekbone, the curve of his brow and mouth.

"I've wondered my entire life who I truly am. You can't tell me soon enough," he said.

Master Tan nodded. "Your mother was a concubine to the Emperor. No one knew you weren't the Emperor's son until you emerged with yellow hair and golden eyes. Before the eunuchs became aware, you were smuggled out of the Palace. They would have killed you. And your mother, too."

Chen Yong shook his head, his face taut with disbelief. Ai Ling fought the urge to reach over and touch his arm.

Master Tan leaned forward, his hands clasped together. His demeanor reminded her of Father. "Your father left court that next morning. He sent a letter and told me that someone had promised to place you with a family who would treat you well. I would have gladly taken you as my son, Chen Yong; my bond with your father is that strong.

"But the Emperor knew it as well. I was never told of

anything more than you existed. And your name. Your mother named you."

Lan Hua interrupted with rice and an assortment of hot and cold dishes, then retreated from the room. The familiar scents of savory sauces, garlic, and scallions wafted from the lacquered serving trays. But Ai Ling no longer had an appetite.

Chen Yong sank into the silk-cushioned chair. He rubbed his face and covered it with his hands. When he looked up, his amber eyes gleamed.

"How?"

"Your mother was interested in languages. She was educated. Being a favorite of the Emperor's, she was allowed to be tutored. Your father was one of her tutors. This went against all rules. But it showed how high she was in the Emperor's favor. Your father never mentioned the romance, but I suspected. They were foolish. They fell in love." Master Tan raised one palm and spread his fingers, as if it was all he could offer.

Chen Yong was quiet. Ai Ling sipped her tea, trying to quell the thundering in her own chest.

"Are they alive still?" Chen Yong asked.

The older man shook his head. "I've not received correspondence from your father in more than fifteen years. As for your mother, I know nothing. I wish I could tell you more." He spoke with regret.

How would an imperial concubine survive such a scandal? Ai Ling kept the foreboding thought to herself. Chen

Yong's face was a mask now, devoid of all emotion. He sat straight-backed against his chair, hands clutching each armrest so tightly his knuckles were pale. Ai Ling looked away, filled with sympathy for him, not knowing how to help.

Master Tan rose. "Please, I insist that you stay for the night. We have plenty of room. Please eat. Don't be modest."

A young man of twenty years stepped into the main hall and greeted their host.

"Ah, Fei Ming. I was just going to visit you and the little one. This is my son," Master Tan clapped the young man on the back. "And he just had one of his own. My first grandson."

Ai Ling and Chen Yong both offered their congratulations.

"Chen Yong is the son of an old friend. And this is Ai Ling."

Fei Ming made no reply. He avoided looking at either guest. Ai Ling's scalp crawled. Was his the face she'd seen peering through the lattice panel earlier?

"Lan Hua will take you to your rooms when you're ready. We can talk again tomorrow morning, Chen Yong. I kept your father's letters. They are yours if you like. I bid you good night."

Master Tan and Fei Ming stepped out of the main hall.

Chen Yong was terse, withdrawn. Although Ai Ling had felt hungry earlier, she yearned for sleep now. The world seemed askew. She was grateful when Lan Hua led her to her room. It was spacious, with a large bed hidden behind silk drapes. She was too tired to change. The servant girl helped her climb into bed. So kind, Ai Ling thought somewhere in the haze of her mind as she fell into a deep, dreamless slumber.

CHAPTER SIX

Ai Ling woke on the hard ground. She looked around, bleary eyed, unable to sit up. Her wrists were bound together in front of her with rough rope. She wriggled her fingers, the rope chafing her skin; her hands responded to her will as if from a distance, both tingling and numb.

"You're awake."

She jerked her head toward the voice. Fei Ming towered over her.

"Why—"

But before she could continue, he yanked her to her feet. She swayed, light-headed and nauseated. He held her with strong arms, and she leaned into him despite herself.

"You got something special in your tea. Lan Hua did what she was told."

"Where are we?" Ai Ling asked. She tried to swallow, and her stomach heaved.

"Somewhere private." Fei Ming's reply was guttural.

It looked like an abandoned temple. A bright lantern cast a cone of light about them. The moon's rays spilled through the paneless windows. The night was quiet.

"Enough talk. I've been hungering for a taste of you."

She tried to scream, but her throat felt too constricted, her tongue too thick. Glowing green eyes stared back at her. Just like the lake. Ice-cold terror shuddered through her.

Fei Ming spun her around and shoved her down onto the dirt floor. He had unbound her hair, and it swept across her face. He grabbed a handful and pulled her head back.

"I want you to be awake for this," he whispered in her ear. His breath was cold on her neck. Ai Ling tensed, prompting him to yank harder, his fingers digging in her scalp.

"No!" She tried to shout, but could not draw enough breath. Her vision blurred.

He pushed her face onto the floor, and her jaw clamped shut. The taste of warm, metallic blood filled her mouth. Hot tears escaped from the corners of her eyes. Dirt smudged her lashes, and she felt the grit of it between her teeth.

Fei Ming ripped at her trousers, and she banged against the ground like a rag doll. He fondled her bare skin. She struggled in terror, but was pinned beneath the bulk of him.

Her head spun as she fought off waves of nausea, made worse by the taste of blood and soil in her mouth.

Fei Ming raised himself for one brief moment. She gasped for breath, horrified. She tried to push herself off the ground; in an instant, he was gone. The jade pendant blazed hot against her chest.

Seconds later, there was a heavy thud and the creaking of tired wood boards. Confused and filled with fear, she rolled onto her side to find Fei Ming slumped on the ground, his chin on his chest and his lower half exposed. An aura of white sparks enveloped him.

Before she could look away, he flew into the air and slammed with a sickening crack against the ceiling. Pinned there, the glow that shrouded him cast leaping shadows across the derelict temple. Her pendant flickered brightly. She was doing this. And she didn't know how to control it.

Fei Ming crashed to the ground. Blood dripped from his nose, then dribbled from the corner of his mouth.

"No," Ai Ling whispered.

A green mist began to coalesce, rising from Fei Ming until it took on the shape of something monstrous, twice taller than any man. Its head was huge, its face as flattened as an angry bull's, the lower incisors jutting out. Red streaked across its features, reminding her of the opera masks that had scared her as a girl. Frost plumed from the flared nostrils. It lunged toward Ai Ling in one stride, its green eyes ablaze.

The demon moved into her. Consumed her. It caught her breath and heartbeat, plunged her in ice. A chaos of screeching overwhelmed her mind. The demon's spirit pulsated within her, attempted to expand like an ink spill in her mind. Horrified and sickened, Ai Ling resisted. She closed herself to the evil, folding her spirit into a slippery wisp. The demon shrieked and slashed through her being.

Then it was gone. Her head felt split open. A stench like burned hair hung in the air, and her ears were ringing. She gulped for breath. Her heart thudded against her chest like a fist.

With great effort, she lifted her head and saw Fei Ming sprawled on the floor by the wall, his bloody face turned toward her. He was alive, but struggling. A gurgling sound escaped from his throat with each ragged breath.

The rope fell from her wrists, untwining like a snake in the air. Ai Ling tried to stand but pitched forward instead. And the world collapsed to pinpricks of light until her vision failed her entirely.

Ai Ling groaned when she woke. Unable to focus, she blinked several times, feeling the ache and tremble of her body. Bright sunshine filtered through the windows of the abandoned temple.

She rose to her feet with effort, stumbling once and scraping the heel of her hand on the rough floor. Wincing, she slowly walked over to Fei Ming, who had not moved.

Dry blood crusted his nose and mouth. His eyes were half closed, his pallor like the naked skin of poultry offered at the butcher's, but he was still breathing.

She kneeled on bruised knees, pulled down his black tunic with a quivering hand to cover him. Her breath came in short gasps, and her stomach lurched. She grabbed her pendant, drawing comfort from the grooves etched in the stone. Fei Ming terrified her, even though he must have been possessed.

She laid a light hand on him. She hesitated, her trembling fingers trailing from his slack arm to his barely rising-and-falling chest. Ai Ling did not know what she searched for, allowing instinct to guide her. She stopped as her palm hovered over his heart. She closed her eyes and lowered her head, tangled black hair fanning across her face. She waited.

There was nothing at first. Just the sunlight behind her eyelids and the feel of the man's silk tunic beneath her fingers. She cast her spirit toward his, a weak, wobbling cord. It dissipated without reaching its target. She drew a deep breath and tried again. Her navel tightened as her spirit entered Fei Ming's.

She delved into his body, and his pain slammed her. Struggling to breathe. Struggling to live. A part of him wanted to give up; give in to the darkness. Ai Ling unfurled her mind to him. She searched for his being.

It cowered, as if shoved into a corner. Fei Ming was aware

he had been possessed. He had watched everything, a prisoner in his own mind and body. His spirit was traumatized, damaged, and afraid. Yet he still fought for each breath that seared his lungs. His heart fluttered, tapping out a faint and erratic beat.

Ai Ling willed her own spirit over his wounds, glided across broken ribs, the cracked collarbone, and the punctured lung. She knew nothing. She'd never studied anatomy or medicine, but she went where she felt his pain. She wrapped his injuries within her healing essence, coated and covered them until she felt his heart beating with a strong, regular rhythm. Until he took a deep breath without wincing, even as he lay unconscious, crouched inside his own mind.

Suddenly Ai Ling was aware of hurried footsteps. The sound came to her as if through a deep tunnel. She withdrew from Fei Ming's body, snapped into herself, and turned her head sluggishly. Master Tan approached like thunder, followed by Chen Yong and two manservants. He ran to his injured son and kneeled down beside him. Fei Ming remained unconscious but stirred and groaned.

Chen Yong dropped by her side, his dark brows drawn together. "Ai Ling, are you all right?"

"What happened here?" Master Tan demanded.

Ai Ling clutched at her torn clothing, feeling weak, depleted. Chen Yong cradled her elbow, as if afraid she would fall over otherwise.

What was there to say, except the truth?

"He laced my tea with poison. I woke and found myself here." Her voice, unfamiliar to her own ears, croaked with thirst.

"What?" Master Tan shook with fury. "Beware of your accusations, Ai Ling. I know my son."

"He—he was possessed," she whispered.

Master Tan's expression hardened, the color draining from his face. He pounded closed fists together and spat at the ground before her.

"Witch! Sorceress! How dare you come into my home and bring such evil on us?"

"There must be a misunderstanding," Chen Yong said. "We should send for the physician. Fei Ming can tell us what happened when he recovers." There was a strain in his steady voice she hadn't heard before. What did he think? Who would he believe?

Ai Ling lowered her head. It was her fault that Fei Ming was in this condition. Was it her fault as well that he had been possessed?

Master Tan gingerly touched his son's cheek. "Quickly! Bring the litter and fetch Physician Shen. Go!"

The two manservants rushed off without a word, panic on their faces.

"Leave, before I fetch the magistrate." Master Tan waved one arm at her and Chen Yong, his wrath unable to hide the tears of concern for his son. "I don't ever want to see your faces again. Go!"

Ai Ling met Chen Yong's eyes for the first time. They were

unreadable, his face taut and without expression. "I'll get our things," he said quietly, and he turned to go.

Ai Ling scrambled to her feet to follow. Her chest ached until it felt numb—like the rest of her.

Chen Yong walked with long strides, his posture stiff. "What happened?" he asked without looking back at her.

"It's as I said. Fei Ming poisoned my tea. I woke in the temple." She propelled herself forward so her legs would not buckle beneath her. "He was possessed." It was difficult to talk and half run, to keep her gaze on Chen Yong's rigid shoulders.

"Why is he unconscious?" he asked, again without turning. She felt like a rejected pet, scurrying after her master. Pride and anger would have surfaced under normal circumstances, but Ai Ling had no energy for such emotions.

She walked more than a few strides in silence.

"I think I did it," she finally said.

Chen Yong halted and turned to her, his features hard, his eyes dark like a stranger's. "You mean you don't know? Were you possessed as well?"

"No. I don't believe so."

"He was going to give me my father's letters. Now I can never speak with Master Tan again—the only man who knew him."

Tears welled in Ai Ling's eyes.

"I can try and speak to him." She stared down at her exposed legs, her trousers in tatters.

Chen Yong shook his head, his mouth pressed in a hard line.

They arrived at the Tan manor just as three servants rushed out the main gate with a litter.

"Go get your things. Hurry," Chen Yong said as he turned away from her.

Ai Ling entered the bedchamber she'd slept in the previous night. The bed was made and the silk drapes drawn back. She braided her hair with trembling fingers, picked up her knapsack and hurried back to the front gate. Chen Yong was waiting for her.

"Where to now?" she asked.

"The nearest inn."

They returned to an inn they'd passed twice while looping back and forth in search of the Tan manor the previous day. The building stood tall and narrow, with wide windows on each floor and a sloping red-tiled roof. Chen Yong swept aside the dark blue cloth covering the doorway, and she followed him.

The bottom floor was a tavern. Small and intimate, the room consisted of a few bamboo tables and chairs, the far side dominated by a long bar. The barkeep flicked a look toward his new patrons. His head was completely shaved except for a thick topknot of three braids that fell past his shoulders.

Chen Yong strode toward the barkeep, undeterred by the

man's scowl. "Where is the proprietor? We need a room."

"Do you now?" He cast a knowing glance from Chen Yong to Ai Ling. "I don't think you'll get much wear out of her, sir." The man snorted, his stare meandering from her tattered tunic to the ripped trousers.

"What're you doing? Why are we here?" She colored at the barkeep's innuendo but lifted her chin despite her embarrassment.

The barkeep propped both elbows on the bar, listening intently.

"You need to clean up and rest," Chen Yong said. It sounded more like a command than a concerned suggestion.

"We should go." She did need rest, but she didn't want to take it here.

"I'll leave. You can stay," he said.

Ai Ling felt the blood drain from her face. "What do you mean?"

"It was a mistake to ask you to accompany me to Master Tan's. We should go our separate ways." He spoke without looking at her.

The numbness remained. Good. She willed her features to stay composed.

"Get her a room." Chen Yong threw two gold coins on the bamboo counter. They clinked and rolled in opposite directions before the barkeep's large palms stopped them both.

"Oh. She'll get the best in the house at that price," the barkeep said, grinning widely at them.

"I don't need your alms," Ai Ling said, her heart thudding in her ears.

Chen Yong turned without saying another word. He shoved the dark blue cloth aside and vanished.

He meant nothing to her. A stranger she'd barely known for one day. And obviously she meant nothing to him.

"How long can I stay with that much?" Ai Ling nodded at the two gold coins.

The barkeep rubbed his hands together. "At least a week, miss. In our best room."

Ai Ling plucked one coin from the counter. "I won't be staying that long. Have someone draw me a hot bath. The hotter the better."

The man opened his mouth to argue, but her hard-edged glare stopped him short.

"Right. I'll get someone to do that. And show you to your room."

A boy not older than ten years ran into the tavern after the barkeep hollered his name twice. "Bao Er, show the miss to our best room. And tell the kitchen to start a hot bath."

"A bath!" The boy's head bobbed with excitement. Baths were rare, it appeared.

"You heard me."

"Yes, sir! This way, miss."

Ai Ling walked behind Bao Er, following him up steep wooden steps to the second floor, then up another flight to the top floor. She pressed her hands against the uneven walls of the staircase, feeling the onslaught of wooziness and exhaustion she had suppressed earlier. The boy skipped down the hallway, scratching the top of his head, his queue wagging like a donkey's tail behind him. He stopped at a wide door at the end of the cramped passage. He flung it open with a flourish. "Our best room, miss."

Ai Ling entered with caution. The best room was big enough to hold a narrow bed pushed against the wall, a black wooden table set under a window, a washstand, and a chipped cobalt basin. She ran a finger along the window ledge. It came away clean. The window offered a view of the alley below, as well as a skyline of colorful tiled roofs with expansive blue skies above them.

"Thank you, Bao Er." Ai Ling gave the boy a small copper coin. He broke into a toothy grin.

"Thanks! I'll go tell them about your bath."

Bao Er tore from her room as if his queue was on fire. She put her knapsack down and sank into the thick blankets on the bed, drawing her knees to her chest and resting her brow on them.

Ai Ling drew a shaky breath, and the room tilted. She staggered to the washbasin and heaved, bringing up bile that burned her throat. Tears mingled with mucus as she retched until her stomach cramped and nothing was left in her. She wiped the back of her hand over her wet face and mouth and dragged it across her torn trousers.

She crawled back onto the bed, laid down her head, and

curled up. She wished Taro was there to snuggle against. She wished her mother was there to smooth her hair and smile reassuringly, as she always did. But she had none of that now. She was all alone once more.

Ai Ling was awakened by a gentle shaking. "Miss. Miss."

She opened her eyes to find Bao Er's face peering down at her. "Miss, there's someone here to see you. A gentleman." Ai Ling's mind quickly flew to Chen Yong.

"Thank you, Bao Er. I'll be right out."

She knew she looked wretched, even without a glance in the tarnished round mirror on the wall. She pulled on a faded pink tunic and trousers. She examined the torn clothing; it wasn't worth mending. She could keep it for spare materials.

On a sudden whim, she climbed onto the wooden table and pulled the lattice panels back. The sun hung directly above her. She stuck out her head and looked below. The alleyway was empty. She bundled the torn clothes into a ball and threw them out the window.

CHAPTER SEVEN

Ai Ling climbed down the narrow stairs. She found Bao Er in the tavern standing beside a young man who looked familiar. She didn't truly believe Chen Yong would return, yet she hadn't expected a strange male caller, either. He was dressed in a black silk robe. Three silver pearls served as buttons on the stiff collar. Bao Er stared at him, his head tilted, reminding her of sparrows she had sketched.

"Mistress Wen?"

Ai Ling nodded, completely taken off guard.

"I'm Tan Hai Ou. I have a letter for you from my father."

Her pulse quickened. "Is Fei Ming all right?"

"My older brother is doing well." He pulled a scroll from his robe sleeve and began to unfurl it.

"I can read it."

Hai Ou masked his surprise in an instant and proffered the scroll.

The message was short.

Fei Ming insists that I apologize for my harsh words. He tells me you saved his life. Please come by at your earliest convenience.

The letter was signed by Master Tan with his stamp in red below it. She rolled up the scroll.

"Please tell your father I'll come today."

Hai Ou bowed and stepped out of the inn. Bao Er had listened to the entire exchange with interest.

"Master Tan has the grandest manor in the city, miss. I hear he has a fish pond with fish this big!" The boy threw his arms out wide.

Ai Ling laughed. "I'll ask to see it this time and let you know."

Bao Er beamed up at her. "Do you still want that hot bath you asked for two days ago, miss?"

"Two days ago?" she said, confused.

"You slept through the afternoon and all yesterday. I kept looking in because your bathwater was getting cold." Bao Er shifted from one foot to the other. "Auntie said I better

wake you when the master came 'cause it might be impor-
tant. Also to make sure you weren't dead." The boy nodded
in earnest.

She'd slept two days away?

"A hot bath would be wonderful. But first, what's good to
eat from the kitchen?"

Bao Er's face lit up like a festival lantern. "Oh, the braised
pork with rice is my favorite. With a tea-stewed egg."

He dashed back to the kitchen, and Ai Ling settled down
at a small bamboo table in anticipation of a much-needed
hot meal.

Refreshed from the hot bath and home-cooked meal, Ai
Ling stepped out onto the street with renewed energy. It
felt strange not to have Chen Yong by her side. She pushed
the thought away, chided herself for being so easily depen-
dent. She never truly knew him, even if it felt otherwise.

She found the Tan manor. The red-paper door gods
remained, but she noticed new slips of paper plastered on
the thick panel—bold characters she did not recognize,
written in black calligraphy.

She knocked on the door, and Hai Ou greeted her with
a slight bow. He was not as tall as his father, but he held
himself in the same dignified manner.

"My father is waiting for you in Fei Ming's quarters," he
said.

She followed his straight back through the manor, across

a courtyard and past halls she had not entered during her last visit. Hai Ou finally stepped inside a reception hall.

Brocaded cushions in a rich emerald rested on four carved chairs with arched backs and curved armrests. Landscape paintings spanned the width of each wall, framed in a delicate celadon silk. Sunlight glinted off the gold accents in the room—an oval vase displaying fragrant red roses, a cinnabar serving tray inlaid with gold designs. The reception room opened into Fei Ming's bedchamber. The lattice doors were pushed aside, allowing a full view.

"Ai Ling, you've returned. We are grateful." Master Tan stepped across the threshold to take her hand in his. "How's your health?"

She studied the genteel hands that clasped hers and was too embarrassed to pull away. "I slept for a long while. I'm better. How is Fei Ming?"

"I'm well, thanks to you." Fei Ming spoke from within his bedchamber. Ai Ling peered past Master Tan's shoulder and saw the young man smile. Anxiety twisted her stomach. She managed a weak twitch of her mouth.

"Please come in." Fei Ming indicated a rosewood stool next to his bed.

Ai Ling perched herself on it. Master Tan sat on the other side of the bed in a carved rosewood chair.

Fei Ming looked well. Completely different from the individual who had slouched with his head down, unwilling to meet her gaze when they were first introduced. Completely different from the man with crazed eyes and guttural voice who had attacked her. His dark, wide-set eyes were clear, the eyebrows above, strong and expressive. She felt foolish for her fear but could not look him in the face.

"I don't recall much from the other night, but I knew that I was not in full possession of my own mind or body."

Deep lines etched both sides of Master Tan's generous mouth as he listened to his son speak.

"I told Father as much and as best as I can remember. The part that I do know with clarity is when you came and laid your hands on me. I was barely conscious, it hurt to breathe—there wasn't enough in each breath. But you healed me."

Ai Ling stared at her hands, not knowing what to say. "It was a strange and awful night. I'm sorry that . . . you were hurt."

Hurt by me.

Fei Ming smiled at her. "Father, don't you have something to give to my heroine?"

Ai Ling blanched. This was too awkward, the situation too twisted about.

"Ah, yes. I'll get it." Master Tan stepped from the room.

She shifted on the stool, clutched her damp palms together, anxious that she was alone with Fei Ming again.

"Don't worry. Hai Ou is in the adjacent hall," Fei Ming said.

Embarrassed that her discomfort was so obvious, she

opened her mouth to apologize. Fei Ming interrupted with a shake of his head. "You remember it all. I recall little."

They sat without speaking for a few moments, the melodic twittering of the songbirds filling the silence. "Are you seriously injured?" she finally managed.

He shook his head, his eyebrows lifted in amusement. "The physician said I'm in perfect health. The dried blood on me worried everyone, but I was fine. Father assigned me to bed rest." He smiled, lighting his face with boyish charm. "I'll be an invalid today for his peace of mind."

She was unable to match his good humor. She needed to tell him the truth. Her stomach knotted, anticipating his reaction. "I have something to confess." She fidgeted on the stool, looked at her worn cloth shoes. "I was responsible for hurting you." Ai Ling met his gaze for the first time.

Fei Ming did not look angry. He tilted his head in puzzlement.

"I think I have some sort of protective spirit with me," she said. "I can't control it."

His face relaxed, and he examined her with a look of understanding. "I know what it's like not to be in control of yourself. You're no more at fault for what happened than I am."

Relief rose within her. She gave a wan smile in gratitude. Fei Ming studied her until she grew uncomfortable once more.

"How did you do it?" he asked.

Ai Ling considered the question before she answered. "I don't truly understand it myself."

He picked at the embroidered quilt with restless fingers. "Please don't tell my father about your protective spirit. He's a superstitious man and may not understand."

Master Tan returned to the bedchamber before she could reply. He held a bundle of papers wrapped neatly with dark blue ribbon. "These are letters from Chen Yong's father. We searched, but we couldn't find him. I regret my harsh words."

"Master Tan, I . . . Chen Yong and I have gone our separate ways. I'll not see him again."

"Nonsense. Chen Yong was as worried for you as I was for Fei Ming when we discovered you were both missing. You have the best chance of meeting him again and giving him this. Please, if you will."

Ai Ling didn't know what else to say and accepted the bundle.

"And for you, a small gift. A token of our appreciation for saving my eldest son." Master Tan handed Ai Ling a long blackwood box. She opened the lid and blinked with shock. Nestled within emerald satin rested a dagger, its blade the length of her hand. The short ivory hilt was encrusted with red jewels, the butt of it covered in gold.

"This is beautiful, Master Tan. I don't know how to thank you."

"Thank me by taking it to the Ping Peaks and my friend

Lao Pan. He can bless it for you, as you're the rightful owner. It will protect you in the future from evil spirits," Master Tan said, his face intent.

"What's this, Father? I thought we were giving Ai Ling a pretty bracelet or ring. A weapon is no gift for a young woman," Fei Ming said. He spoke what she was too polite to say.

Master Tan removed the dagger from the box, held it by its exquisite hilt. The sharp blade caught the sun and scattered diamonds of light across the bedchamber walls.

"I don't give such a dangerous weapon without much consideration, son." He placed the dagger in a black leather scabbard and handed it to Ai Ling. He indicated that she should put it on. She strapped the thin belt around her waist. It felt strange, yet comforting.

"You're both young and naive to the mysteries of our world—the wonder and danger that lurk outside our doorsteps, and sometimes within." His gaze swept them both. "What happened the other night was horrific. We can't know why either of you were targeted. Lao Pan blessed our home yesterday. You'll need protection, too, Ai Ling."

"If Lao Pan is not too far . . ."

"His home is on the way to the Palace," Master Tan said. "It would give me great peace of mind if you met with him." He clasped her shoulder with a warmth that made her think of Father, made her long for her own family. "Chen Yong told me about your search for your father. The fame of his intelligence, wise counsel, and kindness traveled far."

Embarrassed, Ai Ling knew full well that her father's infamy traveled even further.

As if reading her thoughts, Master Tan said, "I don't believe that anyone but an honest and brilliant man can raise a daughter like you, Ai Ling."

She could only nod.

"Will you rest here tonight?" Master Tan asked.

"Thank you, but no. I've already tarried long enough. I must find my father."

"Of course. I'll make sure you're given the best provisions for the rest of your journey. Please at least share a midday meal with us before you leave."

Ai Ling could never refuse a good meal, and agreed, smiling.

It was a feast more than a midday meal. Master Tan must have asked his chef to prepare the best. Ai Ling could not recall a time that she had indulged in dishes this extravagant: roasted pheasant, tender spring vegetables, hand-pulled longevity noodles, spotted porcelain river crabs, and emperor lobsters, named for their large size—dish after dish was brought to the table.

At the end of the meal, Master Tan stood to give a toast. "Ai Ling, we wanted to send you off with a full stomach. May you never go hungry, even during your travels."

At this, a servant entered bearing a package wrapped in

dark cloth and handed it to Master Tan. The older man opened it to reveal many small sacks tied with hemp rope. "I've made sure you have enough food to last you your entire journey to the Palace. And a little beyond that." Master Tan smiled. "It's not heavy rations. There's salted beef, squid, dried fruits, nuts, and biscuits. Also some fresh fruit if you're willing to carry the burden."

Master Tan gestured for the servant, who took the provisions away. "I've also had a detailed map copied for your travels. It shows the best route to take to the Palace. Lao Pan's cave is marked on it as well."

Overwhelmed by the generosity, Ai Ling struggled for the right words. "Master Tan, I can't thank you enough for your kindness. . . ." Her voice caught in her throat. Was Father even at the Palace?

Both Fei Ming and Master Tan saw Ai Ling to the front gate. "If ever you need anything, just ask," Master Tan said.

She remembered Bao Er. "Could the boy who helps at the inn come and visit your gardens? He has heard that the fish in your pond are very big."

Master Tan threw his head back and laughed. "They are indeed. We not only have fish native to Xia, but some collected from other lands. Your little friend is welcome to visit anytime."

Ai Ling waved good-bye, her heart full. She took a detour to the inn to pick up her knapsack. Bao Er skidded to her door.

"Leaving? So soon, miss?" His thin shoulders slumped as he watched her gather her belongings.

"Yes, Bao Er. But I leave with good news. Master Tan said you can stop by and look at his fish whenever you please."

The boy hopped about in glee before throwing his arms around her neck. "Thank you, miss! You'll come back and visit, won't you?"

She swallowed the knot in her throat and replied yes, not knowing if she would ever return. Her thoughts were on Chen Yong as she left the city. He blamed her for what had happened. What was the use of carrying his father's letters when their paths would probably never cross again?

CHAPTER EIGHT

Ai Ling walked at a brisk pace, already wondering where she would find a place to sleep. She had been frightened the first night she left home and walked through the darkness, but that was before she had encountered so much evil. It was as if the denizens of the underworld stalked her. Ai Ling shook that terrifying thought from her mind. But wasn't it true? From the monster in the lake who had told her Father was dead, to the demon that had possessed Fei Ming. She recognized it now as the red-faced Spirit Eater from *The Book of the Dead*. Was it possible?

Goddess of Mercy, had it only been five days since she left home?

The sun descended, streaking the sky with ribbons of vermilion. There was no farmstead in sight. Lush terraced fields reflected the light. The fields had collected recent rains, and the crops grew from pools tinted rose, gold, and green. Ai Ling followed the muddied path beneath these terraces.

Her legs ached and her worn cloth shoes chafed her feet. What wouldn't she sacrifice for a hot bath and meal. The comfort of the inn—for that spare room with the hard bed was a luxury in her tired mind now—and the extravagant meal at midday seemed a distant memory.

She needed to rest. A tree stump on the side of the road provided seating, and Ai Ling wondered how many other travelers had used it for this purpose. She unraveled one of the packets Master Tan's chef had prepared, revealing strips of dried squid. She chewed on a piece along with a salted biscuit, then retrieved the last of her sugared walnuts.

They reminded her of Chen Yong. She kicked at a rock near her foot, annoyed at herself for thinking of him again. She kicked another rock in anger at him, for abandoning her so unceremoniously. Ai Ling winced and rubbed her foot, cursing her own foolishness.

She washed the rest of her dry meal down with cold tea from her flask before rising to continue on her journey.

The sun slipped lower, half hidden behind the hilltop, slowly draining the world of color. She was taking another swig of tea when she saw a shape farther down the path. A man. Not within earshot, but definitely a man. He stood unmoving in the middle of the road. There was something familiar about him, and her arms prickled as if a cold breeze had blown through her.

Ai Ling stood frozen, didn't want to walk toward him. Even as she hesitated, the distance between them folded like a silk scarf, and she was face-to-face with him.

Chen Yong.

"I've been waiting for you," he said.

The voice was hollow. Before she could react, he grabbed her by the wrist. He drew her spirit toward him, and Ai Ling plunged into an endless void, without life and warmth. It drew her in like a whirlpool. Her spirit fought to stay within her body. But this thing was strong. Too strong.

Ai Ling stared into its eyes, and they weren't the amber eyes of Chen Yong. They were flat and opaque—swirling emptiness. The thing smiled as it continued to tug on her spirit, pulling her slowly now as if sucking through a reed dipped into a pond. She tried to wrench her wrist away but couldn't even twitch one finger.

A sudden slash of silver arced behind the demon, and its head thudded on the dirt beside her. Vile green curdled from the stump where the head had rested. Chen Yong stood behind his own headless image. She managed a small shake of her head, and a soft wheeze escaped her lips. Was this another demonic imposter? Chen Yong raised his sword and slashed the demon's hand with one stroke.

The fingers still held her in a death grip. Frantic, Ai Ling shook her arm, her entire body shaking. She sank to her knees, crouching over Chen Yong's decapitated head. It spoke. "It's futile to fight, Ai Ling." The head began to laugh, even as rancid curd frothed from its lips. She choked on the scream lodged in her clenched throat.

Ai Ling hunched over, rocking in terror.

The sword sank and split the high brow in half. The head cracked open like a rotten melon. Ai Ling covered her mouth as the curdlike substance bubbled onto the ground. It stank of vomit. She jerked a hand over her nose, trying not to retch, trying to suppress her hysteria. The body toppled forward. She scrabbled back on her knees, still caught by its fingers, shuddering as she tried to wrench her captured wrist free.

Chen Yong kneeled beside her, steadied her arm and worked to unclasp the clawed hand. Ai Ling flung her spirit toward him in panic—it was the only way she could be sure. She felt the familiar tightness within her navel, the snap as she entered his being. She saw herself through his eyes, stricken and pale, felt her slick trembling hand in his own firm grip. Concern mingled with relief within him. His stoic expression concealed the gallop of his heart, the furor surging through his limbs. *Thank the Goddess of Mercy, she's safe.*

She pulled back, the relief so overwhelming she wanted to throw her arms around him. Instead she struggled unsteadily to her feet.

"Are you all right?" he asked.

He seemed to ask that often.

Ai Ling willed her wobbling knees not to cave. She drew a ragged breath. "How . . ." She didn't know what to ask.

"I left the city the next day. That night, I made camp in the open. When I finally slept, I was plagued with horrific dreams." He still clasped her with a strong hand, and she regretted it when he let go. "I woke in the morning and knew something had been near. I could feel it moving away. I followed it."

Chen Yong looked down at the decapitated head, split in the middle, each half's mouth pulled in a grotesque grin. He considered it with horrified disgust. "Is that what I look like?"

Ai Ling wiped a sleeve over her face. "Why is this happening?"

"Let's move away from here—this thing. Do you need help?" he asked.

She nodded, wanting his touch. He sheathed his sword and offered his arm. Ai Ling rested her fingers on the crook of his elbow, feeling self-conscious and grateful.

"Your necklace was glowing," Chen Yong said.

She looked down at the jade pendant. It still held a wan light, so dim she thought she imagined it. "I think it protects me," she said.

He studied the pendant, dull now, his face betraying nothing.

They walked at a slow but steady pace. Neither spoke for a long time. She waited for her fingers to stop trembling, for her heart to stop fluttering against her throat. Chen Yong, in turn, scanned the horizon, often stopping to listen to the drone of insects and the rustle of grass and leaves.

Ai Ling concentrated on the steady feel of Chen Yong's arm beneath her hand. She forced her thoughts toward the mundane, pruning the plum tree in their courtyard, reciting poetry with her father. She suddenly remembered the bundle of letters she carried.

"I met with Master Tan again today. He wanted to apologize and—"

They turned at the same time toward the sound of galloping hooves approaching. It was near dark, and she could not clearly see the figure sitting astride the tall horse. Chen Yong stepped protectively in front of her, his sword raised. Her hand gripped the hilt of her dagger, her pulse racing. What now? She fought the panic that threatened to deluge her, the scent of it trickling from her pores, making her nostrils flare.

"Old brother!" A young man reined in the animal and smoothed its mane in an attempt to calm it.

"Li Rong?" Chen Yong asked, his dark brows drawn together, a hint of mistrust shadowing his face. His sword remained raised.

"Goddess of Mercy, did you pass the dead man on the road?" the young man asked. "Feng nearly threw me off in his fright."

"It was no man. But it used my image," Chen Yong said.

The young man dismounted in one fluid motion. He held the reins in one hand with the other arm thrown out wide. Chen Yong hesitated, but Li Rong stepped forward to clasp him in a hug, ignoring the raised sword.

"What happened?" Li Rong asked. The horse snorted, and Ai Ling approached to stroke its neck. It nickered, seemed to calm under her touch.

"The gates of the underworld have been flung open, it seems," Chen Yong said. His voice was grim when he finished his tale.

"It's the stuff of ghost tales and nightmares," Li Rong said. He paused to pull something from his travel satchel. He lit a small gilded lantern as the stars began to glimmer in the sky.

"Is it truly you, little brother?"

"Could this world possibly endure two of me?" Li Rong grinned. Ai Ling guessed him to be her age—seventeen years. He stood slightly taller than she did and was attired in dark gray riding clothes, the long-sleeved tunic hugging his chest with billowing trouser legs below. The lantern illuminated his mischievous expression as he cocked his head at his brother.

"Won't you introduce me to your beautiful travel companion?" Li Rong lifted the lantern and studied her with an open flirtation that made her ears burn. He was nothing like Chen Yong.

"This is Ai Ling. Ai Ling, my younger brother, Li Rong," Chen Yong said.

"Ai Ling." Li Rong swept his free arm with a flourish and bowed. His horse pranced. "If we were in distant kingdoms, I would kiss the back of your hand." He drew a step closer. It was obvious he enjoyed making her blush. "Father tells me that is the custom in the foreign courts, old brother. You should try it. I bet it'd work, what with your exotic good looks and all." He winked at Ai Ling as he nudged his brother in the ribs with one elbow.

Was he truly flirting with her after just passing a slain demon on the road?

"You fool." Chen Yong thumped Li Rong in the shoulder with an open palm. "What're you doing here? It's a long way from home." Chen Yong's hand remained clasped on his brother's shoulder.

"I've been trying to catch up to you ever since you left." He led his horse to a sparse patch of grass on the side of the road and released the reins. "It's fortunate you told me of Master Tan in Jiu Gong or else I'd never have found you. You travel too fast."

"Mother let you out to chase after me?"

Li Rong dusted off his sleeve with one hand, obviously avoiding eye contact with Chen Yong. "Not exactly. I told her I was going into the capital for my imperial exams."

"You lied to her?" Chen Yong thumped his brother on the

shoulder again in reprimand. "She'll have your hide when she finds out."

"Don't make me feel guilty now that I've finally found you! I was worried. I thought someone should be with you. And after your recent encounter, you definitely need my protection."

Chen Yong opened his mouth as if to retort, but laughed instead. "You've always been too impulsive. Journey with us; you've come this far already. Then Mother can have my hide as well when we get home."

"I take full responsibility, old brother." He rocked back on his heels, his smile wide.

Li Rong offered Ai Ling his horse. He helped her to mount, then led the dark brown steed down the road. Chen Yong walked beside him. Ai Ling had never ridden a horse, but she was relieved to be off her feet and fell into the horse's rhythm with ease.

"Have you discovered anything about your birth parents?" Li Rong asked.

"My father is a foreigner from Jiang Dao—"

"Jiang Dao! Where ice pellets fall from the sky and the people are as pale as mare's milk?" Li Rong interjected. "Don't they hunt spiked rats as big as piglets to eat?"

Ai Ling laughed despite herself.

"Don't encourage him," Chen Yong said, turning back to grin at her.

"And your mother?" Li Rong asked.

His brother allowed the question to hang in the warm summer air, long enough that Ai Ling wondered if Chen Yong had heard it.

"She was a concubine to the Emperor," Chen Yong finally replied in a quiet voice.

"Wah! Who would have thought my older brother was born in the Palace?" He shook his head in wonder, his top-knot swaying. Then the revelation hit him. "Your mother betrayed the Emperor? The heavens help her. Did she live?"

"I don't know," Chen Yong said. "The Palace is where Ai Ling is headed to find her father. And it's where I'm headed now. It would seem our goals have merged after a chance meeting."

Ai Ling's fingers seized Feng's thick mane. "I didn't think you wanted anything to do with me after what happened." She felt courageous for speaking this difficult thought aloud to him, garnering boldness from her tall vantage point astride the horse.

Chen Yong looked up at her, his features shrouded in shadow. He turned his head back toward the road before speaking. "I apologize for my actions, Ai Ling. What happened that night was terrible, and I shouldn't have deserted you. I acted out of anger and disappointment."

Li Rong tilted his head and studied her as a cat would.

"Thank you." She was grateful for the darkness that hid her hot cheeks. Why was she perpetually blushing?

The moon hung low over the horizon. The sound of the horse's steady hooves, an occasional bird call, and the rustling of leaves were all that accompanied their silence. Her shoulders tensed with each new stirring in the darkness. Chen Yong still clasped the hilt of his sword, while Li Rong strolled beside him in a jaunty, carefree manner.

Ai Ling finally broke the silence, speaking in a hushed tone, as if unwanted ears lingered close. "Master Tan mentioned a seer in the Ping Peaks. He said this Lao Pan may be able to help me . . . against the evil entities."

"You mean to say you've seen more than that dead thing lying in the road?" Li Rong asked.

"More than anyone should," Chen Yong said.

She simply nodded, not caring if they saw her. She did not want to speak of the events from the past few days.

"A seer's insight couldn't hurt," Chen Yong said, stopping. Ai Ling retrieved Master Tan's map from her knapsack and passed it to him.

He held it under the small travel lantern. "It's marked on the map. Very prominently as well." Chen Yong glanced up, the small flame highlighting his cheekbones and slicing shadows across his strong jaw line. "It appears only a few hours' travel from here." He leaned toward the parchment, put a finger on it. "Lao Pan's cave is nestled near the bottom of the peaks."

"Cave?" Li Rong said. "That's worth the trip alone."

They walked on until the moon rose directly overhead.

Ai Ling drifted toward sleep, listening to the two brothers catch up on family gossip in quiet tones. Chen Yong held the travel lantern in one hand, a tiny beacon in what felt like a vast world of dark shapes and fleeting shadows. Gradually the smooth lines of the terraced fields gave way to rugged hilltops, thrusting like gnarled fingers into the sky. They veered onto a path at the bottom of one such peak and started to climb slowly. The path soon narrowed, so they walked in single file, Chen Yong leading them while Li Rong guided Ai Ling on his horse.

Fully awake now as the ground below dropped sharply to her right, Ai Ling sat with her legs hugging the horse's warm sides. After a long time of walking in silence, the path opened to a large landing. She dismounted to stretch her sore thighs, offering the horse an apple that Li Rong gave her. The horse chomped on it with enthusiasm and whinnied as she smoothed a palm over its strong neck.

"According to the map, the entrance of the cave is just around the bend," Chen Yong said.

Ai Ling followed him while Li Rong led Feng behind her. She saw the two torches first, carved of a deep blue stone, reaching far above her head. They were on either side of the cave entrance, which was hewn in the shape of a tiger's head, its mouth gaping wide in a snarl. Dark green stones glittered above them, representing the cat's eyes. Fangs jutted from the ground and from above the entrance, formed from an unfamiliar milk white stone.

100

"This is the last thing I would've expected," Li Rong said, his head tilted up.

"Strangers approach!" A reedy voice spoke from near the cave entrance. Both brothers reached for their weapons. Ai Ling rested her own hand on her dagger.

A spray of water shot forth from one of the lotus-leaf fountains that stood on either side of the cave. The torchlight revealed water swirling in a rainbow of color. Ai Ling walked with caution toward the fountain and peered in. Multicolored stones rested at the bottom of the shallow bowl.

"A girl with raven hair," a voice said again. The sound came directly from the fountain.

"Stand back, Ai Ling," Chen Yong said. Even as she did so, another plume of water erupted, landing at her feet.

"They all have raven hair, you slippery twit," a voice warbled from the opposite fountain.

"Not so, not so," the first fountain replied. Ai Ling leaned over again. Another spray splashed her cheek. She yelped from the cold shock of water, then wiped away the drops as her face began to burn. Her hand tingled painfully where she had wiped her cheek.

"You got wet, did you?" Li Rong chuckled.

She covered her cheek with one hand. "The water stings," she said, unable to explain the pain beyond that.

Chen Yong gently pulled her hand aside to examine her face, while Li Rong held the gilded lantern close. "It bores a hole into the skin," Chen Yong said, his voice quiet with shock.

"What?" Ai Ling asked. Tears streaked down her face. The pain was so intense she could barely think. She was too afraid to touch the wound and turned her face from the young men.

"I see you have met my water pets," said a voice from within the cave.

A thin man approached with a torch in one hand. He wore his white hair in a single queue and a square gold cap on his head. He was attired in robes of the same color, a sash of bright crimson tied at the waist. Silk pouches in various colors hung from it.

"Come, Ai Ling. Let us apply the antidote to your cheek before you lose part of that pretty face . . . and more." His commanding presence discouraged any questions as they followed him into the cave. She stumbled as her tears blinded her, biting her lip hard to keep from sobbing aloud. Chen Yong took her elbow and guided her.

The man pulled a jar from the cave wall as if he had conjured it. He pinched something between two long fingers, stepped up to Ai Ling, and rubbed the substance into her cheek. "Did the water touch you elsewhere?" he asked.

She showed him her hand, and he pinched more thin flakes from the clear jar and applied them to her burning fingers. "The pain should cease immediately. And you will heal as if you were never hurt." He smiled at her, eye to eye. Even as he spoke, the searing agony faded. "I hope this teaches you to not look where you shouldn't."

"You knew my name." The realization hit her long after he had said it, her mind was so crushed by the pain.

"Master Tan spoke of you when I was called to his manor. I performed purity rites throughout the home," the seer said. Ai Ling's thought flew to the new writings and characters plastered on the Tan manor's main door. They must have been part of the purity rites, to ward off evil and cleanse the home.

"I am Lao Pan, an old friend to Master Tan. Please follow me."

Lao Pan's bright torch threw glimmers of light across the incandescent walls of the cave. After walking only a short distance, they were outside again.

It was a natural courtyard, oval in shape, nestled within the mountainside, with a small house tucked against the steep rock face at the back. A welcoming fire glowed in the middle of the wide-open space.

"We have no fresh grass, but there is hay for your horse." Lao Pan pointed toward what looked like a small stable. Li Rong led Feng there, speaking softly all the while. The seer swept an arm toward stone benches under a giant starfruit tree, and the weary travelers seated themselves.

"It's a breach within the mountainside. Nature shaped a perfect facade for my humble home," Lao Pan said. A boy of about thirteen years emerged from the house with a tray of tea. "My grandson, Rui. Also my apprentice."

"Did you carve the tiger head into the mountainside?" Chen Yong asked.

"Ancestors did. This place has been used by my family to pass on the art for many centuries."

Ai Ling wondered what he meant by "the art," but the seer spoke as if everyone should know, so she didn't ask. "Were those enchanted fountains at the cave entrance?" she asked instead.

Lao Pan chuckled. "No, no. My water pets are fish caught from the Sea of Zhen."

"Fish! That speak?" She touched her cheek. The skin felt smooth now, the pain completely gone.

"Indeed. They are mentioned in *The Book of Lands Beyond*. But scholars often read it as myth." Lao Pan smiled as if amused by the foolishness of it. "The Zhen fish spit venom. The poison will eat flesh to the bone, then spread if not treated."

A cool sweat broke over her brow. She could have died, slowly eaten away by venom until her entire body was nothing but agonizing pain and corrosion. As if reading her thoughts, the seer continued. "I keep the antidote at the cave entrance. It's the scales of the fish themselves."

"But I didn't see any fish," she said, her hand still pressed against her cheek.

"You wouldn't. They conceal themselves to their environs. It's why I laid colored stones at the bottom of the fountains," Lao Pan said.

Chen Yong shook his head in amazement. "I didn't know what to do when I saw that canker growing in Ai Ling's cheek."

She was glad she hadn't seen it herself. The image would have been nearly as frightening as the pain.

"Have you not heard the tale behind these creatures?" Lao Pan asked.

"I've read some from *The Book of Lands Beyond,*" Chen Yong said.

"It's not a tale Father ever shared," she said.

Li Rong joined them on the stone bench. They could hear Feng's contented snorts.

"It's a love story, as so many of them are." Lao Pan smiled. "Emperor Yeh, from many dynasties past, collected women for his pleasure as one would collect trinkets. He had more than one thousand concubines sequestered in his inner quarters, but it wasn't enough."

Rui returned with warm, wet cloths for the travelers. Ai Ling was relieved to wipe her face.

Lao Pan continued with the tale, his gaze intent on the fire. "One day an official near the borders visited. He brought his wife. She was sixteen years and of mixed blood—her mother from some frigid kingdom in the north, with hair so pale it was near white and eyes the color of warm seas."

Ai Ling sneaked a glance toward Chen Yong. He was leaning forward, relaxed, captivated by the story.

"The Emperor executed this diplomat and took his wife.

He went mad over the woman. Convinced that she would be taken from him, he exiled her to a small island in the Sea of Zhen. He asked the powerful sorcerers of his court to shroud the island in mist so no one could find her. And the fish of Zhen were created, to kill any person who approached. They were given voice so they could call out a warning to the Emperor as well as report to him when he visited.

"But the Emperor was so delirious for her he neglected his duties, instead spending all his time on this hidden island. When he finally returned to the Palace, he was poisoned by his closest adviser."

"What happened to the beautiful woman?" Li Rong asked.

"She was forgotten. Left on the small island hidden in mist to die alone. A victim of her own beauty and the Emperor's demented love for her," Lao Pan said.

"Ah." Li Rong sounded disappointed.

Ai Ling felt the same. This was no enchanted love story— it was too tragic and real. She felt immediate sympathy for the woman, kept prisoner because of the Emperor's deranged love. Why were women always seen as things to be possessed by men in these tales, never worth more than their physical beauty?

The seer clasped his hands together and stood, his golden robes shimmering before the flames. "Rest assured you can sleep in this courtyard in comfort and safety. It nears the thieving hour. I think it best we all retire for the night and talk more tomorrow."

Rui emerged from the house with three thin pallets. The tired travelers made their beds in a semicircle near the fire, like pack animals seeking warmth. The pallet was cozier than Ai Ling expected, and although she wanted to mull over everything that had happened that day, her exhausted body did not allow it. She fell asleep even before bidding a peaceful night to her companions.

CHAPTER NINE

Ai Ling woke with a start and sat straight up. The sky was a deep blue, and white wisps drifted past the jagged peaks encircling them. The whinnying of a horse had roused her. Her two travel companions had already risen. Li Rong tended to Feng while Chen Yong sat on the stone bench, his head bent over a book.

She stretched languidly and rolled her shoulders. Rui approached and asked if she would like to wash up inside. Ai Ling followed the lanky boy into Lao Pan's small house with its wooden porch and tall celadon-tiled roof.

Books lined the main room from floor to ceiling against two walls. A wooden ladder constructed of bamboo leaned upon one, allowing access to books out of reach. Jars and boxes filled the third wall's shelves. Most jars were clear, revealing their contents, but a few were murky or opaque. The room smelled of dry herbs and the must of old books. Lao Pan sat at a large black wooden table, the planks so worn it shone. He studied a thick tome, oblivious to their entrance.

Rui guided her past a small kitchen into a rudimentary washroom at the back of the house. He pointed to the ceramic basin and the narrow back door, which led to a well if she needed more water. Ai Ling quickly washed her face and rubbed her teeth with the coarse salt provided in a gourd-shaped bowl. She rummaged for her wooden comb, looked around the cramped washroom and saw no mirror. It was too much to hope for. She ran the comb through her hair. She wondered what Lao Pan would tell her. She plaited her hair with deft fingers and walked back to the main room.

This time, Lao Pan raised his head. He smiled at her, the lines deepening in his gaunt, sun-browned face. "Ah, Ai Ling. We can do a reading with the lunar telling sticks this morning. Perhaps they can shed light on what occurred that awful night."

She clasped her hands in front of her, feeling awkward. "Other things have happened, too. Evil things . . ."

"Tell me, girl." He waved for Rui to pull up a stool for her.

Ai Ling sat down and folded her hands in her lap, not

wanting to fidget. She described seeing the Life Seeker, how she was pulled into a lake and Chen Yong's discovering her. She spoke in short, choppy sentences about the attempted rape by Fei Ming and the demon who tried to possess her after. Lao Pan never interjected, letting her fumble for words. Finally she told him what happened the previous night, when the monster bearing Chen Yong's image had accosted her.

The seer stroked his beard in silence long after she'd finished her tale. Would he believe her? Pronounce her mad and a half-wit? Finally he stood and pulled a black leather-bound volume from the shelf. "I've read of similar demons in *The Book of the Dead*. But never before have I met an individual who has encountered so many and in so short a time."

He tapped the front of the book with long fingers. Ai Ling hesitated before speaking again. "I've seen that book in my father's study. I thought they were made-up tales to scare children."

Lao Pan pulled back, tense. "You've read this?"

She looked down. It was like being caught by her own father.

"It's not light reading . . . nor for the impressionable, young, or weak-minded." He rapped the leather cover hard, as if for emphasis. "Rui is never allowed to open this book unless in my presence. It's not to be read without guidance, girl."

Ai Ling stared at her clasped hands, feeling guilt mingle

with irritation. Father had warned her, and that was exactly why she had looked. "It's just a book." She raised her chin and met the seer's cutting gaze. "And I am not weak-minded."

He pursed his lips. "It's not make-believe, Ai Ling." He flipped through the thick pages as if searching for clues. "The demonic creatures described within these pages are summoned through the dark arts. You're fortunate to be alive."

He closed *The Book of the Dead* with a dusty thud. "Perhaps the lunar telling sticks can offer us a clue." The seer stood and, his thin arms straining with the effort, slid the heavy book back onto the shelf.

"But first, let us take our morning meal together. The mind and body cannot function properly without sustenance." Ai Ling rose to follow Lao Pan. She could not agree more.

Breakfast was hot rice porridge with salted fish, pickled carrots, and spicy bean curd. Chen Yong, Li Rong, and Ai Ling sat together on the stone benches, which were configured into a half moon underneath a starfruit tree. They ate without much conversation. Ai Ling enjoyed the quiet calm of the morning, the feeling of sanctity this small dwelling within the mountains offered.

Rui took the used bowls and utensils away after the meal and brought lukewarm tea. Lao Pan whispered something to him, and Rui hurried back into the house. He reemerged soon after, holding a carved ebony canister filled with bone-colored sticks.

"Have you used these before?" Lao Pan asked. Ai Ling shook her head. She had seen others use them at the temples but had never tried herself.

The seer pulled one stick from the canister. It was flat and wide as a thumb, rounded to oval points at both ends and polished until it shone like the moon. A phrase was inscribed on the stick in black. "Each has its own saying," Lao Pan said. "You ask your question and shake the canister until one falls to the ground."

Lao Pan demonstrated as everyone watched, holding the canister diagonally and shaking it in a slow rhythm. The sticks began to shift forward, clattering against one another. "I can interpret the saying for you. It may offer some insight to your situation."

He handed her the canister. Ai Ling stood under the shade of the tree, feeling awkward. "Ask the question in your mind. We can discuss it after a lunar stick falls in answer."

Feeling self-conscious and a little foolish, she closed her eyes. Will I be able to find Father? She began moving her hands up and down, the sticks clanking in a soothing cadence as they bounced forward. She continued shaking as five sticks separated from the rest, then three. Finally one escaped from the cluster and dropped to the ground.

Ai Ling heard a gasp and glanced toward Rui, who gaped at her feet. She looked down and saw that a lone stick stood poised on its rounded tip, as if hanging by an invisible string. Lao Pan rose from the bench and touched the perpendicular stick, and it fell to the ground.

"I've never seen the like. The fortune cannot be told unless the stick lies flat of its own accord. I never thought it could do anything otherwise until today." He picked up the errant stick and put it back into the canister.

"Try once more," he said.

She closed her eyes again. Ai Ling conjured her father in her mind, guiding her hand as she wrote calligraphy. Will I be able to find Father? She shook the canister steadily and watched the sticks move forward in a group, then the few that slipped ahead of the others. Two sticks fell from the canister at the same time. Both stood on end.

Everyone stared at the upright sticks until Ai Ling grew uncomfortable.

Lao Pan finally plucked them from the ground. "Your fate cannot be told. The Immortals must have a hand in this."

"The Immortals!" Li Rong exclaimed. "The Immortals do not interfere in the realm of man—if they even exist."

Lao Pan glanced at the young man, his expression austere. "Not unless they have to."

Everyone turned back toward her. Ai Ling tilted her chin and tried to appear unaffected. "So much for gaining insight," she said.

Lao Pan smiled. "I fear I can offer no help there. But I can bless the dagger Master Tan gave to you. It will take all morning but will be worth the wait." The seer gestured to Rui, who stopped gaping at Ai Ling and retreated with the lunar telling sticks back to the house.

"A blessed weapon can offer protection against the tainted and undead," Lao Pan said.

Ai Ling pulled the dagger from her waist and handed it to the seer. "I would be in your debt."

"It is my pleasure to help those who need it." Lao Pan bowed and disappeared into the house.

The three companions sat under the starfruit tree in silence. Finally, Chen Yong let out a low whistle. "It seems even the Immortals cast an eye on you from the heavens, Ai Ling."

Chen Yong's comment broke her reverie. There was too much to think about—too much she couldn't comprehend. "I just want to bring Father home."

Chen Yong studied her, then nodded in understanding.

Li Rong cleared his throat. "It'll be a while before Lao Pan is done with his incense waving and strange mutterings. How about you and I do a little sparring?"

Chen Yong grinned. "I haven't beaten you enough?"

"The presence of a beautiful woman"—Li Rong bowed toward Ai Ling—"will inspire me to fight harder."

She pretended not to hear him, but the now-familiar heat crept from her cheeks to the tips of her ears. Ai Ling pulled out her small sketchbook as a distraction. She could sketch Feng and use it as reference for a horse painting someday.

Chen Yong laughed. "Come on, then. This space is perfect."

She had never seen sparring before and did not know anyone who practiced shuen. She couldn't decide whether to continue the guise of drawing or simply put down the sketchbook and watch.

The two brothers faced each other in the oblong courtyard, warming up with some kicks and punches. Li Rong shook himself vigorously, like a wet dog, and she giggled into her drawing.

"Nothing but applause, please, lovely lady. Kisses are welcome as well." Li Rong winked at her with a wide grin. She was unable to pretend she hadn't heard this time.

Chen Yong coughed, which sounded suspiciously like a snort.

"Ready, old brother," Li Rong said.

They took a wide stance, their hands raised in loose fists in front of their torsos. Li Rong dropped to the ground and swept his leg out in an arc, kicking dust in the air. His brother simply danced out of the way.

"You're too slow to use that for your first attack." As he said this, Chen Yong jabbed one hand out toward Li Rong's chest, which Li Rong struck out of the way with his forearm at the last moment.

"You've been practicing," Chen Yong said.

Li Rong responded by punching him in the chest. But Chen Yong spun and vaulted, landing behind him. Ai Ling blinked, her sketchbook in her lap now, watching with open fascination. Chen Yong's hand darted like a viper and hit Li Rong in the lower back. She heard Li Rong grunt as he sprang on one hand and somersaulted out of the way.

The brothers circled, staring with unblinking eyes. Sweat glistened on their brows.

"I didn't hit with full force, little brother."

"I'm not six years still." Li Rong ended the sentence with a kick to Chen Yong's chest, accompanied by an exhalation of air that became a gruff yell. The next thing Ai Ling knew, Li Rong was on the dirt ground, with Chen Yong towering over him.

"You let pride distract you." He offered Li Rong a hand.

Li Rong did not take it, but leaped to his feet in one fluid motion. He loosened the sash on his tunic and shrugged it off, rolling his shoulders. He took the open sparring stance again.

Chen Yong turned to face him, and Li Rong met his gaze with a resolute intensity. Chen Yong untied the sash around his own tunic and tossed it to the side. Li Rong's frame was taut, wiry. Chen Yong was broader, his muscles dense and powerful.

Ai Ling gnawed her lower lip as she watched, the morning light glistening off of their slick bodies. Maybe it was time to start sketching Feng again, or the starfruit blossom. Instead, she admired the lithe forms of the two brothers as they danced around each other, kicking up dirt, limbs flashing so fast in combinations she was not sure she even saw. There was no sound but their heavy breathing and the scuffle of their feet.

The sun crawled overhead. She felt the sweat collect on her own brow and wished for a drink. But she did not stir from the bench.

Chen Yong suddenly thrust forward as if to punch Li Rong in the face, but instead he brought a leg up and kicked him square in the chest. Li Rong doubled over with an audible grunt and fell to his knees.

"No, you certainly aren't six years anymore," Chen Yong said.

Li Rong squinted up at him. Chen Yong offered his hand a second time. "You've improved tremendously. You kept your concentration and cast away your emotions." The admiration was clear in his voice. Li Rong took his hand this time.

The two brothers bowed low to each other, one hand clasped over a closed fist.

"Thank you, Chen Yong."

Ai Ling could see the respect Li Rong held for his older brother, even if they teased each other constantly. Li Rong tugged his tunic back on and wiped the sweat from his face with one sleeve. He then disappeared behind the house, where the well and washroom were located, and emerged not long after, looking refreshed, but still a bit flushed.

Li Rong joined her at the stone bench. "May I?"

They both watched Chen Yong go through his forms,

bounding into the air with grace and executing kicks and punches that made him look as if he were flying.

"You accompanied Chen Yong to see Master Tan?" Li Rong asked.

"He asked me to."

He turned and tilted his face. "To be truthful, I'm surprised. He must trust you. It hasn't been easy for Chen Yong, being half foreign. He's always on guard."

Ai Ling recalled the insults and scrutiny he had endured as he searched for Master Tan.

"I urged that I should go with him on this journey. I offered many times, but he refused. He's so stubborn. He said he had to do this alone. You reached him, somehow."

Ai Ling's heart soared, and she furrowed her brow to disguise her pleasure. "Chen Yong told me he was adopted."

"My parents took him in when my eldest brother, Tian Ren, was just one year. Father insisted. But my mother was always partial to her firstborn and the son of her own blood." Li Rong sighed, a seriousness passing over his roguish features. "She treated Chen Yong well enough but, in the end, insisted on arranging a marriage between my eldest brother and Chen Yong's childhood love."

Ai Ling glanced at Chen Yong, who continued through his forms, oblivious to all else. His face was serene, but she could hear his breath quicken with each movement. Did Chen Yong love this girl still?

"I didn't know," she said, her mood heavy now.

"He doesn't talk about it with anyone. It only made him more withdrawn," Li Rong said.

"And this childhood love . . . ?" Ai Ling felt compelled to ask. Was she beautiful, accomplished, and elegant? She looked away, trying to mask her interest.

"She loved Chen Yong as well," Li Rong said.

Of course she did.

"But she was the best match for the family, and Mother made sure that she married Tian Ren—her favorite. No one else had a say in it." He spoke quietly as he watched his brother. "Chen Yong was devastated. He tried not to let it show. But I know him well enough to know he suffered."

Ai Ling stared at her hands. "That's so sad."

"Ah, who weds for love anyway? We're bound by what our parents dictate when it comes to marriage."

Her stomach twisted. "My parents wed out of love," she said, surprised by her own vehemence.

"That's a rarity, isn't it?"

"I don't understand why it has to be. And Chen Yong is here because his parents were in love."

Li Rong scuffed the ground with his shoe. "I guess that's one way of seeing it. But out of love, they only managed to be selfish and create scandal, defying an entire empire for their own desires." Li Rong looked toward his brother. "Not that I would or could ever imagine life without him. I just wonder what Chen Yong himself would have chosen, if he could."

Ai Ling also turned her gaze toward Chen Yong. She didn't have an answer.

Li Rong slapped his thighs with open palms. "I think I've lost enough face today. It gives me incentive to practice harder and win back my honor." He shook his fist in the air, a look of determination on his handsome, boyish face.

Ai Ling laughed, her heart lightening with his good humor.

"Really, I've never been able to beat him. No one has. And my father's family prides itself on its knowledge of shuen. Even my sister was taught from a young age."

Li Rong turned to his brother and shouted, "Enough showing off for our lovely companion. You've made me look bad enough as it is."

Chen Yong finished with a final leap and kick, twisting around in a complete circle midair, arms flung over his head, fingers splayed wide, weightless before landing on his feet. He pressed his palms together and bowed.

"The mantis takes its prey," Li Rong said. He saw the confusion on her face and smiled. "It's the name of that last move."

Chen Yong also disappeared behind the house, emerging a few moments later. He strode toward them in long easy steps, as if he had not spent the last hour leaping about like a graceful leopard.

"He hasn't talked your ear off?" Chen Yong asked. "Are you promised yet?"

Li Rong thrust a pretend kick to his brother's shin. "You need to marry before I do, old brother."

Chen Yong's smile dropped, the humor wiped from his face. Li Rong blanched, obviously regretting his jest. He leaped to his feet and slapped his brother on the shoulder. "Next time, I'll win. Ai Ling is my witness, and I can't go back on my word to a beautiful woman."

"Let me know if he bothers you," Chen Yong said, amusement quirking the corner of his mouth.

But Ai Ling had not missed the pain that had pinched his features. Even if he had hidden the emotion in the span of one breath. He still cared for this girl, his childhood love.

She managed a tight smile and shook her head, hoping her mask was as persuasive as Chen Yong's.

Li Rong laughed.

"I see you've charmed another one, little brother. Impressive."

The midday meal did not disappoint. The steamed silk-thread bread was light and slightly sweet. This was paired with cold spiced lotus roots and bean curd mixed with a savory minced pork sauce. She watched the two brothers dig in to the meal, eating voraciously. Ai Ling wasn't used to competing at the table, but she filled her small porcelain bowl often, for fear the food would disappear.

But they need not have worried, as Rui returned with a second tray laden with filled plates.

"The food is delicious, Rui," Chen Yong said. "Did Lao Pan prepare this?"

The boy smiled shyly. His skin was dark, making his round eyes seem even brighter. He wore a black square cap on his head, similar to the seer's. "My grandfather does not have time to prepare meals. I do. I must learn everything as his apprentice."

Ai Ling clinked the eating sticks against her empty bowl in appreciation, and Chen Yong and Li Rong followed suit. "It was a wonderful meal, Rui," she said.

Rui bowed low, bobbing his head with obvious pleasure. He retreated back into the house and returned with a tray of fresh-cut starfruit drizzled in honey.

"Are these from your tree?" Ai Ling asked.

"The last offerings of summer."

She bit into the golden fruit, its five points tinged in green, savoring both the tartness of the fruit and the silken sweetness of the honey.

"I'm going to burst," Li Rong said as he shoved another piece of starfruit into his mouth. He reclined fully on the bench with a groan, forcing Chen Yong to sidle next to Ai Ling. She was acutely aware of him, thinking of the last time he had touched her and how she had entered his spirit. She edged away, fearing it would happen again.

She was grateful when Lao Pan emerged from his house. He walked stiffly and carried her dagger nestled in his two outstretched palms. He presented the weapon to her.

"I've imbued it with the most powerful chants of protection. It has also been bathed in an elixir to make it truly harmful to the undead. Any evil creature of this world can be hurt by it." He bowed his head, and she did the same, feeling that it was appropriate in this moment.

She took the dagger and examined it. Her features reflected from its silver surface, warped. The stones glittered in the sunlight, and the end of the dagger looked even more honed at its dangerous point.

"Thank you, Lao Pan—"

The thin seer raised a hand before she could continue. "You owe me your tale when it is fully told. It's unusual for a girl your age to carry such a dangerous weapon, but from what you have told me, from what the lunar sticks would not tell, my efforts will not go to waste."

Lao Pan clasped her shoulder, surprising her with his familiarity. "Take good care, Ai Ling."

"I'll send word to Master Tan when I return home with my father."

"I'm certain it will be a most interesting journey," Lao Pan said.

The seer and Rui saw them to the cave entrance. Ai Ling dashed through the tiger's gaping maw, past the fountain in two giant leaps. Chen Yong laughed, and she looked back at him, pursing her lips into a pout before she realized it.

"You'd do the same if the venom had hit your cheek," she said.

"It looks like you've learned your lesson." He smiled at her, ignoring her sharp glance.

Li Rong chuckled, and Lao Pan shook his head in amusement. "You weren't the first curious victim, Ai Ling. Nor will you be the last," he said.

Lao Pan and Rui waved farewell as they started down the path. The daylight provided a breathtaking vista of the terraced fields they had passed. Feng whinnied after he kicked a large rock over the edge, sending it tumbling. Ai Ling would be relieved when they walked on flat ground again.

CHAPTER TEN

Lao Pan's cave was at least two hours' walk behind them, when a shrill scream sent Ai Ling's heart into her throat. Chen Yong ran toward the noise; Li Rong followed with Ai Ling behind, astride the horse.

Four bodies lay in pools of blood next to an ornate over-turned sedan. A richly attired woman struggled with a man swathed in dark blue, who ripped at the jewels on her throat. The assailant turned glittering eyes toward them, the only feature revealed behind the hood pulled over his head. He took one look and bolted.

Chen Yong sprinted after him, only to be stopped mid-stride by a breathless protest from the woman. "Please, no! Let him go. No more bloodshed."

She swooned, and Chen Yong turned back and offered his arm to steady her. The lady sobbed, her face ashen. But somehow she remained alluring. Her rouged cheeks and black eyeliner did not smear. Her dainty rose-colored lips quivered prettily. Ai Ling suddenly felt very plain and dirty next to this woman, elegant even in her distress. She dismounted and stood next to Feng, stroking his neck.

"You came just in time," the woman said. Li Rong stepped forward and gallantly offered her a handkerchief. She dabbed at her eyes, holding the fabric gracefully in one ivory hand.

"He ambushed my attendants, then dragged me out of the sedan . . ." She paused dramatically as tears continued to stream down her face.

Ai Ling frowned. She remembered watching a similar scene in a play staged a few years back, only the distressed maiden wasn't so pretty, as she was played by a man.

"Are they . . . dead?" The lady swayed toward Chen Yong.

Li Rong approached the men, bent down, and searched for a pulse. Ai Ling sensed no life in them. Dark blood seeped through their tunics; her stomach turned at the cloying scent.

"They were so loyal. They would never have run and left me alone with that villain." She knelt trembling in the dusty road next to the bodies.

Chen Yong put a hand on her shoulder. "I'm sorry, lady, that you suffered through this, and that your attendants lost their lives. Can we escort you to the next town at least?"

She stood, looking ashen still. "I am Lady Zhou. I was headed to the city of Dai Ting to visit family."

"We were also stopping there. We should reach it tomorrow by foot. If you don't mind walking," Chen Yong said.

And would they tote her in the sedan like her attendants if she did mind? Ai Ling tried to suppress her irritation and jealousy. Must Chen Yong be so chivalrous? She was annoyed with everyone, but most especially herself.

Li Rong stepped forward in greeting, one palm pressed to his heart. "I am Li Rong, at your call, lovely lady."

Ai Ling contained her snort but could not stop her eyes from rolling.

Chen Yong looked embarrassed and introduced himself, and she followed suit.

"I would be so grateful to have you as escorts. A woman can't travel alone safely these days." Her gaze lingered on Ai Ling with that statement. Ai Ling raised her chin and looked down at her, drawing her shoulders back so she stood even taller.

Li Rong and Chen Yong righted the overturned sedan so Lady Zhou could retrieve her belongings. She pulled out a pink satin purse.

The brothers moved the bodies to the side of the road.

"We'll tell officials when we arrive in Dai Ting," Chen Yong said, "so they can retrieve the bodies for their families."

They bowed their heads, and Chen Yong led them in a short prayer. They decided to continue on, to reach the town as soon as possible.

"You've had such a shock, Lady Zhou. I'm sure Ai Ling wouldn't mind if I offered you my horse," Li Rong said.

Dung of a diseased turtle! Ai Ling tried to smooth the scowl off her face. She nodded imperceptibly and handed the reins to Li Rong.

"Oh, thank you so much," Lady Zhou breathed, still a little winded from her ordeal.

Li Rong offered an arm to help her onto Feng. But she had some trouble, falling into a close embrace with him on the first try. She blushed deeply, which made her prettier some-how. Ai Ling never felt pretty when she blushed. She always imagined her head turning into a bulbous red radish—the kind Taro liked to dig up and chew.

"I'm sorry. I've never been on a horse," Lady Zhou said.

Neither had she, but she didn't fall into anyone's arms try-ing to mount the beast. Ai Ling chided herself for these thoughts. How could she be so petty and mean?

But Feng did not appear to like Lady Zhou. The horse nickered and pranced, making it difficult for the woman to sit comfortably. Li Rong tried to placate him, to no avail. Feng's nostrils flared, and he continued his jittery dance, tossing his head.

"I'm distressed and making the horse nervous," Lady Zhou said. "Perhaps it's better if I walked, as long as you offered an arm?" Li Rong was back by her side before a cock could crow.

Ai Ling approached Feng with one hand outstretched and stroked his velvet neck just as he liked. The horse became calm and still, allowing her to climb onto his back. A part of her felt a smug satisfaction. At least Feng wasn't swayed by any pretty thing that sauntered by.

They walked until the sun faded behind the mountains. Li Rong strolled beside Lady Zhou, regaling her with funny anecdotes and silly jests. Her laughter tinkled through the warm air. Ai Ling pursed her lips. She and Chen Yong followed behind the merry couple, Chen Yong leading the horse by the reins.

They made camp that night against the hillside. Ai Ling's thighs and rear were sore from riding, but she was grateful she hadn't had to walk the entire way. She shared a sparse meal with the brothers. Lady Zhou had no appetite. She prepared for sleep. Chen Yong had already retired, while Lady Zhou and Li Rong sat near the fire, their amused faces lit by the flames. Each strand of Lady Zhou's ebony hair stayed in place. Ai Ling touched her own hair, most of which had escaped from her one braid, making a sweaty halo around her head.

They whispered, and Ai Ling was glad for it. She did not want to hear Li Rong's flattering blather. She wasn't jealous . . . but perhaps she had become used to being the only female in their little group. She admonished herself for acting so foolish. She was not interested in Li Rong, much as he teased and flirted with her.

Her mind wandered. She could see Chen Yong from where she lay. She still hadn't given him the letters. She didn't want to, in the presence of others. Especially Lady Zhou. She wanted to share the moment alone with Chen Yong. It was terribly selfish, she knew.

Ai Ling shifted on the hard ground, tucking her thin blanket beneath her chin. The fact that Chen Yong slept while Li Rong and Lady Zhou flirted by the fire made her feel even more alone. She thought about the first time she had entered his spirit. Could she do it again?

She flung herself forward, felt the tautness within her navel, extended her spirit and snapped into his being. His body was completely relaxed. He drew deep breaths, and he dreamed. She stayed with him, unable to pull herself back, wanting this closeness. She dreamed with him.

They sat in a beautiful pagoda set in a lush garden. The flowers bloomed in bright yellows and reds, without scent. The girl beside him laughed, peered up with adoration. She reached over to caress his cheek.

"I miss you, Chen Yong. I had no choice, please forgive me."

The girl could not have been more than thirteen years, but she spoke as a grown woman, with a regretful sadness. Ai Ling felt her heart, his heart, crush with an empty ache and longing, with such anguish it was difficult to breathe. . . .

The scene wavered, dispersed. He sat in the study grinding ink. A sheet of neatly written characters lay on the desk. I am going home, read the flowing strokes. Someone entered the study and looked over his shoulder, but he did not turn to see who. It no longer mattered.

He practiced forms in a wide courtyard. He whirled in the wind as if he had wings, his spirit soaring, free. He leaped in the air and was surrounded by galloping waves, on a sea that was unfamiliar to him, the waters a churning black. He landed on the deck of a ship, looking out to the endless horizon. The sun crept upward, bleeding crimson. . . .

"Help!"

Feng's agitated whinnying sounded almost like human screams.

Ai Ling bolted straight up and gasped as she snapped back within herself. She felt winded, unable to catch a full breath, and rose unsteadily to her feet. Chen Yong was already standing, his sword raised. The fire flickered low but cast enough light to reveal Li Rong struggling with a massive writhing thing just beyond it.

Chen Yong sprang toward his brother. The monstrous serpent raised its head and hissed. A long forked tongue darted out. Its scales were a stunning bloodred, the muscles beneath them moving in powerful undulation as it wrapped itself around Li Rong.

"Sssstand back or your foolissssh brother diessssss." The serpent turned its head, and she saw Lady Zhou's face, except her wide eyes were now vertical slits, glowing like golden lantern light. The face merged with the strong neck of the serpent, the pale skin of human flesh melding with the crimson scales.

Li Rong continued to struggle.

"You liked me well enough when we shared kisssssssesss." It flicked its tongue toward Li Rong, who jerked his face away in terror.

Chen Yong's legs were in a wide stance, his sword high. Ai Ling knew he would not attack while the serpent gripped Li Rong. Murmuring a prayer, she unsheathed her dagger, crouched and edged out of the circle of light cast by the dying fire. She steadied her trembling hands. Li Rong needed her help. She clung to this thought. She sneaked around the serpent demon's massive coils and twitching tail; Chen Yong saw her, she knew, but she dared not meet his eyes.

Taking a deep breath, Ai Ling vaulted through the air and plunged her dagger into the back of the serpent's head. The sharp blade sank in to the hilt, and there was a sizzling sound, reminding her of meats spitting above hot coals at the market. She tried to pull out the dagger to strike again but could not budge its glowing hilt, burning cold within her hand. The demon shrieked and slammed its tail on the ground. The pungent smell of burning flesh hit Ai Ling's nostrils; her stomach seized.

She saw Chen Yong grab Li Rong by the arms and drag him away from the writhing beast. The serpent's tail whipped toward her like an angry eel, knocking her off her feet.

Li Rong raced to Ai Ling, pulling her back. The demon lunged at Chen Yong. But he twisted out of the way. Chen Yong jumped forward and sank his sword into the thick body, right below its human face. The demon hissed and bucked as blood the color of pitch flowed from the wound. Chen Yong withdrew his sword and attacked again with a wide swing, and more of the thick ooze erupted as the head tottered on its thick coil. The demon shrieked in the throes of death, its mouth a red slash, the dark tongue lolling out.

Chen Yong raised his sword again, and the head thumped down at his feet. Dark blood splattered across the dirt. The shrieking stopped, but a faint ghost ring reverberated through the night. The thing convulsed violently before becoming still. Ai Ling's throat felt thick from the raw, potent scent of blood.

Chen Yong wiped his sword on the scales of the dead beast, smearing the brilliant red corpse with its own black blood. He turned to the fire and tossed the wood he had collected earlier that night into it. The flames leaped, illuminating the grisly scene. The serpent's body stretched out the length of at least five men, its width as thick as a man's torso. The powerful head with the porcelain face lay inert now, in a pool of black. The face was almost beautiful, if not for the forked tongue that hung limply from its mouth.

"The heavens help me," Li Rong choked out.

"What in the underworld happened?" Chen Yong asked.

"We were flirting. And kissed a little. Then she started moving lower . . ." He threw an embarrassed glance toward Ai Ling. She managed to keep her expression blank. "And the next thing I knew, there was a monster between my legs!"

Chen Yong snorted. "That'll teach you to keep your bird to yourself."

Li Rong's mouth dropped. He closed it, then opened it again, like a gaping fish out of water. She looked from Chen Yong's stern expression to Li Rong's look of incredulity, and burst into laughter. She bent over and laughed until the tears ran down her cheeks. The two brothers joined in, and soon the night rang with their hysterical merriment.

Li Rong grinned at her sheepishly. "This would never have happened if you had accepted my affections in the first place, Ai Ling."

She threw her hands up in the air. "Don't blame your failed romantic pursuits on me," she said. "You'd be her evening snack if it weren't for us!"

"You certainly know how to choose them," Chen Yong said.

"When do women turn into serpents but in the old ghost tales?" Li Rong managed to look even more chagrined.

"Lao Pan tried to warn me," Ai Ling said, barely above a whisper. "Perhaps the demons and monsters in *The Book of the Dead* exist after all."

Li Rong shook his head. "I wouldn't have believed it if I hadn't seen her change shape before me."

"There isn't much I wouldn't believe after what I've encountered these past few days," Chen Yong said, his sword still drawn.

They stood in silence, each staring at the carcass of the serpent demon. Then slowly, the crimson scales grew darker until they became ebony in color. The monstrous form collapsed on itself in a plume of black ash, leaving an outline of its length on the dirt. Ai Ling shuddered. They could have died this evening.

Something silver glittered in the ash. Her dagger. The blade was pristine, as if she'd never thrust it into the serpent demon's neck. She slid the dagger back into its sheath, saying a small prayer of gratitude to Master Tan and Lao Pan.

"The hilt glowed while it was in the serpent," Chen Yong said.

Ai Ling felt the excitement drain from her limbs. "I tried to remove it to stab her again, but I couldn't pull it out."

"Lao Pan's blessings seem to have taken," Chen Yong said.

"And thank the heavens for that," Li Rong added. "I will raise a cup of wine to you the first chance I get, wise seer."

"You should thank Ai Ling first," Chen Yong said.

Li Rong dropped to both knees, his hands outstretched toward her. "You saved my life, beautiful lady."

Ai Ling collapsed near the campfire. "It was probably my

fault anyway." She rested her chin in her hand and stared into the flames.

"How so?" Li Rong asked.

"These demons seem drawn to me. There have been too many attacks—and I'm always the target." She wanted to articulate her jumbled thoughts better, but her tongue would not cooperate.

"But she attacked me, not you." Li Rong rose and sat down beside her. "I only jested when I blamed you earlier, Ai Ling."

She tried to smile, but could not manage it. "What if . . . the demons are targeting my friends now?"

Chen Yong placed a light hand on her shoulder, nearly causing her to jump to her feet. "Rest, both of you. I'll keep watch until light breaks."

"You need sleep, too, old brother." But Li Rong must have recognized the expression on his brother's face, for he made no further protests and crawled under his blanket.

Ai Ling did the same. Sleep claimed her sooner than she expected, even as the image of the powerful serpent with a beautiful face haunted her.

CHAPTER ELEVEN

Ai Ling woke before daybreak, stirred by violent dreams. It was as if she hadn't slept at all. Feng was gone. Li Rong paced in frustration, pounding a hard fist in one hand. "I should have noticed last night. He must have been frightened out of his mind to bolt like that."

"You wouldn't have been able to find him in the dark. Let's search now," Chen Yong said.

The trio walked in wide circles, among the trees and along the path, calling Feng's name, but to no avail. Li Rong's shoulders sagged, his usual jaunty manner gone.

"He's a smart beast. Someone will find and take care of him." Chen Yong patted Li Rong on the back.

They ate their morning meal of salted pork, dried banana, and biscuits, accompanied by hot tea, in near silence.

Chen Yong pulled out Master Tan's map, which he had tucked in his knapsack, one finger tracing lines across the parchment. "We'll need to continue through the Sentinels' Grove to Bai Yun Peak. It isn't a tall peak, and it offers the shortest path to the Palace."

Ai Ling's legs quivered at the thought of climbing a mountain, no matter how small. Chen Yong rolled up the parchment and met her gaze. The skin under his eyes was dark, as if faintly smudged with soot. Weariness from travel had sharpened his features, making his amber eyes deeper set, his jaw line and cheekbones more defined. She blinked and half turned, embarrassed, when she realized she was staring.

Ai Ling scuffled behind her companions, forcing her sore legs to move, dragging her blistered feet. The sun was merciless. Each step brought her closer to the Palace, she told herself, and Father. She refused to ask for rest, willing herself to keep up. Finally, Chen Yong turned and stopped. The air hung still around them. Even the birds were too hot to sing. She took the opportunity to gulp down a few mouthfuls of water from her flask—it too was warm. She made a face.

"Do you want to rest?" Chen Yong asked.

Ai Ling shook her head, but something in her expression betrayed her misery.

"We're but a few hours walk from Sentinels' Grove. It'll be much cooler there," Chen Yong said. "We can make camp early tonight."

"Goddess of Mercy, what I wouldn't pay for a sedan to tote me along this very moment," Li Rong said, his face mottled from the heat. "With two women fanning me with palm leaves and another—"

"Save your breath, little brother," Chen Yong said.

Ai Ling giggled and surprised herself, amazed she had the energy.

They walked on. Finally, she saw tall shapes ahead—bamboo towering above them. They followed the path as it narrowed into the grove. A hush, punctuated only by the occasional twitter of unseen birds, fell over them when they entered the forest.

Ai Ling approached a stalk as thick as a man's calf. She ran her fingers over the ridges of its divided sections, the shell hard and smooth. Fading light filtered from above, illuminating the regal bamboo shafts that spanned as far as her eye could see. The air was cool, and she was grateful for the shade.

"This is magnificent," Li Rong said, his face turned upward.

"Bamboo is one of my favorite subjects to paint," Ai Ling said as they ventured deeper into the grove. A calm settled over her, a contentment to be traveling with good companions, a sense of freedom, a joy and wonder at being alive.

"You paint?" Chen Yong cocked his head, studying her with interest.

"It's always been a part of my studies. Writing calligraphy is like painting in a way."

"You can write?" Chen Yong asked, but it came forth more like a statement of amazement.

"My father was a top scholar in the Emperor's court," she said, her tone sharper than she intended. "And it may not be common, but yes, women, just like men, can learn to read and write if they are taught."

Two spots of color flared on Chen Yong's cheekbones. "I didn't mean to offend, Ai Ling. I'm traditional in many respects, but I never did understand why girls weren't taught the language like the boys. My sister was taught how to spar, but not how to read or write."

"I don't think An Xue would have been interested any-way," Li Rong said, chuckling.

"I'd like to see your paintings someday." Chen Yong moved to stand beside her. Her scalp tingled from his nearness. He turned toward her, lips curved in a smile, and Ai Ling for-gave him everything—much to her own chagrin.

"Chen Yong enjoys painting as well," Li Rong said.

"I'm not very good," she said.

"Me neither." Chen Yong tapped on one of the sturdy bamboo stalks with his knuckles. The sound came back solid and strong.

They made camp in a small clearing surrounded by the

majestic sentinels. The forest was aptly named, as the bamboo did remind her of those standing guard. Ai Ling felt safe. They gathered broken stalks and twigs, and Chen Yong started a blaze with an oval striker and flint. They clustered around the fire and dined on dried beef, papaya, nuts, and salted biscuits. Ai Ling fished out a fresh apple and pear to share, slicing the fruits with her sharp dagger.

She could not help but think of where the blade had been previously, jutting out of the powerful neck of the serpent demon. The pungent scent of burned flesh returned to haunt her. She did not eat any of the fruit and passed it to the brothers to enjoy. Chen Yong brewed tea for them, always a comfort.

"So what's so special about you, Ai Ling?" Li Rong asked, breaking the contented silence after their meal. He sat hunched by the fire, sharpening a long, thin bamboo stalk with a small knife, honing the end to a dangerous point.

"What do you mean?" She had been sketching the bamboo in her book and paused before speaking, annoyed by the interruption—perturbed by the question.

"We all saw the lunar telling sticks stand on end," Li Rong said.

Chen Yong sat with his elbows propped easily on raised knees, gazing into the fire. Li Rong grinned and winked at her, continuing to whittle away.

"I think there may be a spirit that protects me . . . inside this pendant," she said finally, raising her hand to the cool jade lying against her breast.

"I've seen her pendant glow," Chen Yong said to Li Rong. "But why didn't it work against the serpent demon, Ai Ling?" His face did not appear as taut as it had that morning; perhaps he too felt the peacefulness amid the bamboo.

"Maybe because I wasn't under direct attack?" Ai Ling shook her head. "I don't know how it works, but it has saved me several times since I began this journey."

"Who gave it to you?" Li Rong asked.

"My father did." She paused. "I also seem to have this . . . ability."

Both brothers turned to her; Li Rong's expression one of amusement, Chen Yong's pensive. "You mean the ability to steal the hearts of all men who lay eyes on you?" Li Rong asked, pressing a palm to his chest.

She twisted her mouth and ignored his comment. "I think I can enter others' bodies . . ." She did not know how to explain herself.

"Sounds rather—" Li Rong was interrupted by a thump on the shoulder from his brother.

Ai Ling drew a deep breath. "I think I can delve into other people's spirits." She lifted her face to see their reactions.

Li Rong had tucked his chin in surprise, his mouth slack. Chen Yong leaned toward her. "Can you explain?" he asked.

"Better yet, why not demonstrate?" Li Rong added.

"You mock me," she said, feeling her anger rise.

"Not at all. Delve into me, it'd be a pleasure." One corner of Li Rong's mouth slanted upward, his dark eyes twinkling.

She'd show him. "Think something. I can hear your thoughts when I'm within your spirit."

"Will I feel anything?"

"I don't know," she said. "You tell me."

Li Rong sat straight, crossing his legs in front of him. Ai Ling ignored the weight of Chen Yong's gaze and concentrated on the invisible cord within her navel. She cast it forward, felt the irresistible tug, and entered Li Rong's spirit.

Where Chen Yong was coiled with strength, Li Rong was loose, relaxed. Yet a power and vigor still dwelled in his limbs, an energy that could be summoned in a heartbeat. His hearing was sharper than hers, and Ai Ling heard the rustling of leaves far above, along with the quiet chirping of bugs which she had not noticed with her own ears.

She quieted her mind and listened to his.

Think of something . . . think. This is silly. I feel silly. Only for you, Ai Ling. When are you going to kiss me? That's a thought. When will I get my kiss?

His amusement bubbled and rose to her. Ai Ling would have shaken her head if she could, but instead she released her hold, relaxed, and drew back into her own body with a hard snap.

"How long will this take?" Li Rong asked.

"I'm done."

"Already? I didn't feel a thing."

Ai Ling put her brow against her knee, feeling woozy. Chen Yong leaned forward to fill her teacup, and she lifted it to her lips with a trembling hand. The warm brew steadied her, the scent of the tea leaves sharpening her senses.

"Did it work? What was I thinking?" Li Rong asked, his voice a mixture of curiosity and impatience.

"You wondered when we would kiss," she said, attempting to hide her face in the tiny teacup.

Chen Yong threw his head back and laughed, slapping his palms together.

Li Rong nearly rose to his feet. "That's an easy guess! You guessed."

"You also have an ache in your right shoulder. Perhaps it's bruised from the serpent demon or from sparring yesterday. Your left ankle is scraped. It smarts and bothers you."

Chen Yong stopped laughing, and Li Rong opened and closed his mouth. Both young men stared at her as if she'd sprouted a second head.

"Is this true, Li Rong?" Chen Yong asked.

His brother nodded without speaking. The crackle of the fire emphasized the long moments of silence. Ai Ling fought the urge to curl up and hide. Had it been a mistake to share her strange ability with them? They were only just beginning to feel comfortable together—becoming friends. How would they see her now?

"I can't believe it," Li Rong finally said.

"How did I look?" she asked, curiosity overriding her discomfort.

"Quiet. Like you were meditating," Chen Yong said.

"Try it on Chen Yong," Li Rong said.

Chen Yong leaned back. "No, thanks."

"How do you know she hasn't already? I didn't feel a thing," Li Rong said. "It's like spiritual rape, and no one would know."

Ai Ling blanched. She dug her nails into her palms.

"Ai Ling wouldn't do that," Chen Yong said in a quiet voice. "Mind your words, Li Rong."

Her neck grew hot. Chen Yong defended her when she had done exactly as his brother accused. She decided in that moment that she would never enter Chen Yong's spirit again. An instant sense of regret filled her. She remembered his dream, the ache and longing for a love lost, for something that could never be.

"I apologize." Li Rong turned to her. "You can do it to me anytime."

Ai Ling punched him in his bad shoulder, and he winced.

"Actually, don't. My thoughts will only bring me more trouble," Li Rong said.

"That's an impressive ability." Chen Yong added twigs to the fire. "Have you had it all your life?"

She propped her chin on one hand. "No. It started soon after I turned sixteen years. I thought I was imagining it at first." Ai Ling remembered hearing Lady Wong's words in her mind: *too tall, good hips*. "Since starting this journey, the ability has grown stronger."

"Do you know why?" Chen Yong asked.

She shook her head. "Do you think I'm . . . strange?"

Chen Yong stirred the firewood. She could tell he was thinking, weighing the facts by the way his brow furrowed. "I think you have this ability for a reason." He turned and smiled at her. "Maybe we'll find out why on this journey."

Li Rong nodded until his topknot swayed. "In the adventure tales I read, the hero always has a special ability."

Ai Ling laid a thin blanket on the hard ground and arranged her knapsack as a pillow. "The heroes in those tales are men," she said.

Li Rong rubbed his chin. "Hmm. You're right. The women are usually there to look pretty. Add to the scenery, so to speak."

She searched for something to throw at him. Finding nothing, she made do with a loud snort.

"But it doesn't mean you can't be one, Ai Ling!" Li Rong explained with boyish enthusiasm, and Ai Ling smiled despite herself.

She put her head down and drew her knees to her chest. She listened to them speak in low murmurs, allowing the dancing flames to coax her into slumber. That night she dreamed of wandering alone in the bamboo forest. But instead of a lush green, the bamboo was ink black with leaves in gradations of gray, like a painting by the old masters.

* * *

The next morning, Ai Ling awoke before the others—a first. The day had barely broken, its light too faint to penetrate the mist that swirled like phantoms among the bamboo. The fire had burned out sometime in the night, and the air was damp against her cheeks. Li Rong and Chen Yong lay curled close to the fire pit.

She drew the thin blanket tight about her shoulders, tucking the edge beneath her chin, and stared out at the silver mist. Her mind whirled, trying to make sense of all that had taken place since she left home. With the exception of the snake demon, the others had attacked her, tried to break her spirit. The writhing eel from the ancient lake had told her to go home, lied and said her father was dead. Yes, it must have lied. She couldn't trust its words, the heartbreaking images it had conjured.

They did not want her to go to the Palace, that much was clear. She wouldn't let them stop her.

Li Rong scuffled his feet and grunted—no doubt chasing a pretty maiden in his dreams—and woke his brother. Chen Yong sat up and stretched his arms above his head, yawning like a languid panther. She watched him from her thin cocoon, drank in his every movement.

"Good morning," Chen Yong said in a quiet voice.

Ai Ling wrinkled her nose. "How did you know I was awake?" she whispered.

"I could see the glint of your eyes." He climbed out of his makeshift bed with fluid ease.

"There's no light." She pursed her lips. Why did he have to be so observant? She stuck out her tongue.

"I saw that, too." Chen Yong grinned at her as he folded his travel blanket, his own eyes hidden.

Ai Ling snorted, quiet enough so she would not wake Li Rong, but loudly enough for Chen Yong to hear. She emerged from her cocoon in reluctant stages, first freeing her shoulders, then rolling the soft cotton down to her hips, finally wiggling her legs out. She rinsed her mouth and wiped her face with her damp cotton rag and also folded her blanket, tucking it back in the knapsack. Her fingers touched a bundle. The letters she had not wanted to share until they were alone. A twinge of guilt wormed its way through her—she had been so selfish to keep them.

Ai Ling withdrew the stack of letters bound in blue ribbon and walked over to Chen Yong, who was preparing to restart their campfire. She handed him the thick bundle. "I should have given these to you sooner. Master Tan asked me to deliver them. He didn't think he would see you again."

"My father's letters?" He was down on one bended knee by the remnants of the fire, his face tilted toward hers.

"Yes."

He clutched the letters for a brief moment before slipping them into his knapsack. "Thank you," he said in a thick voice.

She helped to gather more firewood, sat down, and watched him strike a small flint against the carved oval striker, creating sparks like tiny exploding stars. A pinpoint flame finally emerged, fed, and grew brighter.

Chen Yong retrieved the bundle and sat down next to the fire, removing a thin folded parchment with careful hands. The page was yellowed, the black calligraphy visible from the underside as he held it to the light.

Ai Ling watched as he folded each letter after reading it and opened another with gentle fingers. Li Rong sat up, scratching his head. He opened his mouth to speak, saw the expression on Chen Yong's face, and lay back down again.

So it went until the mist dissipated and sunlight shone through the bamboo leaves above them. Chen Yong sat hunched near the flames, his broad shoulders folded forward, in a posture of reverent prayer. He was oblivious to everything but the words written by a father he never knew. Ai Ling's gaze did not stray from his face. Faint lines creased between his dark brows at certain moments, crinkled around his eyes when he narrowed them as he read.

Finally he folded the last letter and tied the blue ribbon around the bundle once more. Having stayed silent longer than she would have believed was possible, Li Rong spoke. "What did the letters tell, old brother?"

But Chen Yong didn't reply and wiped the tears from his face.

CHAPTER TWELVE

The jagged peak towered over them, obscuring half the sky. Ai Ling's shoulders dropped in exhaustion when they finally arrived at its base. At least a path had been worn for them by the many travelers who made this trek before. They huddled in the shade of the rocks to take a midday meal. She sank to the ground and wished she could do anything else but climb this hill.

They rested for only a short while. Ai Ling rose to her feet with reluctance and drank another swallow of cool water from her flask.

They hiked in silence. Even Li Rong was quiet, the sweat trickling down his face. It was early afternoon when they reached the summit and saw what lay beyond—a vast sea rose, expanding within a heartbeat to surround them, until the endless water merged with the skyline. Ai Ling gasped. She turned to look back at the path from which they had come, but there was no path, no mountain. Only the piece of jutting rock they stood on and the sea that engulfed them. In the distance was the vague shape of land, an island perhaps, shrouded in mist.

"The heavens have mercy," Li Rong said under his breath.

"We're trapped," she said.

"We're hundreds of leagues from the sea." Chen Yong drew his sword from its sheath. "This must be sorcery of some kind."

"Even that island is too far away to swim to, if it is an island," Li Rong said.

The image of the island before them shimmered as the mist swirled around it. Ai Ling squinted, and thought she saw the reflection of something gold. It wavered and was gone.

"I would think I was hallucinating if you weren't both standing beside me," she said.

"What's that?" Chen Yong pointed. A shape seemed to be moving over the water toward them.

Ai Ling shaded her eyes with one hand. Whatever it was moved fast, almost in a blur. "It glints in the sun," she said.

The thing suddenly veered up into the sky, and she saw

the length of it in its entirety, the underbelly gleaming in shades of blue, turquoise, and green, just like the changing seawater itself. Its length was incalculable by sight, but seemed to stretch over half the distance between the island and where they stood.

No one spoke. They craned their necks to the sky and knew what they saw. A dragon flew toward them, wingless and ushered by clouds. It sliced through the air more gracefully than any bird. When it was above their heads, it began to circle, almost spiraling on its own length as if dancing. Ai Ling could see four feet and gold talons. It drifted downward, escorted by cloud wisps that clung around its tail and underbelly, until it was face-to-face with them. Ai Ling held her breath. She could sense, rather than see, Chen Yong standing frozen, his sword still raised.

The dragon snorted as if in greeting, bobbing lightly, riding the sea zephyrs beneath its belly. Its head was magnificent, the length of one man. Its eyes were luminous pearls; the eyebrows and whiskers flowed like kelp on its face, which was the color of a deep sea green. It grinned, revealing teeth as long as her dagger's blade.

Ai Ling shivered, fear and amazement ricocheted through her. She stood entranced by the beauty of the beast, not knowing if this would be the last thing she saw.

The creature tossed its head, and she felt its spirit tug at her own. Its touch on her was pure, good. It brought to mind the dragon lore she had read in *The Book of Lands*

Beyond. Dragons were companions to the Immortals and helped men in distress. But how much of the myth could she believe? Awed and hesitant, she extended her spirit into the beast—and the world took on an opalescent sheen. She looked at herself and the others. They were blurred, with bright halos surrounding their forms. An ancient strength coursed through the dragon, and it felt light to be within its body, despite its massive size. The dragon held a sense of protection and duty toward the three humans, who looked so diminutive and frail.

"Come. Ride." It spoke an ancient tongue Ai Ling could barely grasp. She saw an image of herself, Chen Yong, and Li Rong soaring with the wind. Her heart sang, felt utterly free.

She glided back within her own self, the experience a soft whisper, smooth compared to the jarring snap of previous times.

"It wants us to ride on its back," she said.

"What?" Li Rong asked. "How do you know?"

They looked at the magnificent dragon, and then turned their gazes to her as if she had morphed into a dragon herself.

"It told me," she said.

"You never cease to surprise me." Chen Yong sheathed his sword. "It seems as if higher powers intervene with our journey. We'll fly with the dragon."

"Wait! How do we know it's safe? We haven't been

153

welcomed by gentle creatures during our travels," Li Rong said. He stood with his hand on the hilt of his sword, his mouth pressed into a firm line.

The dragon undulated to its side, allowing Ai Ling to clamber on its back. Its scales were smooth and warm to the touch. She could feel the power of the beast beneath her palms as she steadied herself.

"I entered its spirit and know it is good. The dragon feels protective toward us." She graced Li Rong with—she hoped—a charming smile. "Please trust me."

Chen Yong climbed on behind her, leaving Li Rong standing alone on the jagged rock.

"The things I do for pretty women," Li Rong muttered before getting onto the massive beast.

The dragon swept over the waves, and Ai Ling hugged its back with her thighs, fearful she would fall into the water below. This was not like riding a horse. The dragon climbed slowly into the air. She glimpsed the gold horns on its head for the first time, next to ears very similar in shape to a deer's, but covered in rich green scales. They glided on smooth winds, and her spirit soared. There was pure joy in this flight, in this freedom, this world.

"Incredible," she heard Chen Yong breathe softly behind her.

He held her at the waist with both hands. Her pulse quickened. Ai Ling wanted to lean back into him but wrapped her arms around the neck of the magnificent dragon instead. She let the sea wind cool her hot cheeks.

They floated above the waves toward the mist-shrouded island. As they neared, its appearance grew and changed. The parting mist sometimes revealed a high fortress wall made of gold, which then disappeared behind opaque clouds. The clouds dissipated again to show tall trees on a rocky peak.

The peak collapsed upon itself, and parting clouds next revealed a pagoda set within a lovely garden, with fruit trees and flowers that she knew from home.

A dense fog pressed around them, cold in some spots and uncomfortably warm in others. The mist was so thick Ai Ling became disoriented, grateful for the glimpse of gold horns on the dragon and the feel of Chen Yong's hands on her waist, gripping a little tighter. Ai Ling lost all sense of time.

Finally light filtered through the mist, and the sky glinted cerulean, bright and endless. The clouds turned soft, pearl-like.

The dragon alighted on a tall mountain suspended in mid-air above the waves. Golden walls stretching endlessly into the sky blocked their view, and a giant door painted the color of cinnabar stood a short distance away. The dragon was still.

"I think it wants us to dismount," Ai Ling said.

She eased herself off, running her hands over the supple blue-green scales. Chen Yong and Li Rong climbed down after her.

"Thank you," she said to the dragon.

It lifted its head in acknowledgment, its kelp beard stirred by a wind she could not feel.

"We have come to where the Immortals roam," Chen Yong said, gazing at the towering golden walls.

"What do you mean?" she asked.

"The Golden Palace of the Immortals resides on the Mountain of Heavenly Peace," Chen Yong said. "It's surrounded by walls of gold—from *The Book of the Divine*."

Li Rong pulled a face. "I never did do my lessons for that."

"You didn't do your lessons for much of anything."

"I'm not the scholarly type. Besides, I thought that was ancient folklore—"

"Folktales of Immortals whom many Xian still pray to, offer fruit and burn incense for," Chen Yong said.

"But country folk, poor peasants, surely," Li Rong said.

"You judge the gods by who bows down at their altars?" Ai Ling asked.

"I didn't give it much thought. I . . ." Li Rong looked down and scuffed his shoe on the ground.

"We'll learn soon if there was truth to those folktales," she said.

They walked toward the giant doors. They towered so high she could not see their tops. Two creatures flanked them—a jade dragon, coiled like a snake, and a giant lion carved from jasper, with its head tilted back in a ferocious roar.

Ai Ling glanced back at the sea dragon, but it had curled up on the ground, seemingly in the midst of a nap. She jumped, startled, as the jade dragon by the doors reared its head. The red lion relinquished its roar into the sky, so loud and thunderous it left her ears ringing. A familiar warmth washed over her breast. She looked down to find her jade pendant glowing so brightly it looked like a white star.

"Goddess of Mercy," Li Rong said. His eyes darted from the jade dragon, extending itself to its full length, to the jasper lion, which had risen onto all fours and was shaking its unmoving mane. Two pairs of curious diamond eyes glittered at them.

"Don't draw your weapon," Chen Yong said. "Don't move."

"Are you mad? That was the last thing on my mind." Li Rong gulped audibly.

"I don't think they'll hurt us," Ai Ling said. "We were brought here by the dragon . . ."

"As their snack," Li Rong finished her sentence.

Ai Ling took slow, deliberate steps toward the two creatures. A cold-hot sweat collected at her temples. They wouldn't hurt her; she was brought by the sea dragon, which was good, protective. She opened and closed her sweaty palms, willing her arms still by her sides. Something drew her to the massive doors—she had been brought here for a reason. As she passed the magical stone beasts, both bowed their heads to the ground, making her draw a sharp breath.

"It's as if they welcome you." Chen Yong's voice behind her was higher than usual.

She reached the doors and examined them closely, forcing herself not to look back. They were carved intricately with beings she could not identify—three-legged people with two heads, horses with bird beaks, twisted serpents with human faces. Ai Ling reached out and stroked the etching. Was this the serpent demon they had slain? The doors slid ajar at her touch.

The dragon to her left snorted, stretching its four short legs and digging its jade claws into the mountain. The jasper lion rumbled deep in its throat and sat down on its powerful haunches once again, eyes never straying from Chen Yong and Li Rong. Ai Ling eased the massive doors open with a light touch and walked through.

She turned and motioned for the others. They stood immobile, gaping at her, the expressions on their faces making them seem like blood brothers after all. Chen Yong was the first to stride forward, and Li Rong scrambled to follow.

They stepped into an immense garden filled with fantastic trees that stretched to the skies. The air hung fragrant with the scent of honeysuckle and sweet ginger, distinct, yet not overpowering. A marbled path wound up toward a pagoda in the distance. Ai Ling stopped at the first tree, its trunk as thick as three men, the roots gnarled and spread wide, drinking deep from the ground. Its ivory leaves were shaped like the palms of hands, and it bore fruit—glistening human hearts that beat rhythmically on white stems. A jade placard set into the ground had the words Love Lost Tree etched in gold upon it.

What did that mean? She slanted a sidelong glance toward Chen Yong. Did his heart hang from the branches of this tree? Would hers as well, some day? The sound of a hundred heartbeats thudded against Ai Ling's ears, each pulsing to its own story of loss. She walked on, unable to bear the thrumming of all those broken hearts.

The next tree was slender and delicate compared to the last, its trunks and branches silver. It carried no leaves, yet bore red and green berries of ruby and emerald. They glittered in the sunlight and rustled in the wind with a pleasant tinkling. She looked for the name of this tree and found the jade placard with the words Eternal Berry Tree etched on it.

"The dragons eat the fruit from this tree," Chen Yong said.

"You mean they don't tear humans limb from limb?" Li Rong asked, only half jesting.

His brother lifted his shoulders. "It's what I recall from *The Book of the Divine*."

"Only the flying dragons," Ai Ling said.

Both young men turned to her. "Those who live in crevices

and mountains—the ones that can't fly—they all dine on different things."

"Another scholar in this group, I see. And much nicer to look at than you." Li Rong nudged Chen Yong in the ribs with an elbow.

"I don't remember that from *The Book of the Divine*," Chen Yong said, ignoring his brother's gibe.

"It's from *The Book of Lands Beyond*. Father didn't let me read from it much; he didn't consider it scholarly enough. I studied the book on my own," she said.

The only one that had fascinated her more was *The Book of the Dead*.

Ai Ling moved on to the third tree along the path. This one looked like an ordinary peach tree, lush with green leaves, but without fruit. She started at the sight of a six-headed vermilion hawk perched on one of its lower branches. The heads twisted in every direction, seeing everything, the six-pointed beaks as lethal as daggers. It flapped its wings, the span as wide as her own arms outstretched, but stayed on its perch.

A sudden movement from a higher branch revealed a nine-headed feline, a pantherlike creature with golden fur. All nine heads hissed in unison as it extended sharp claws and climbed onto a lower branch. Ai Ling backed away from the tree, but not before reading the placard partially buried at its roots.

THE TREE OF IMMORTALITY.

She turned and nearly slammed into Chen Yong. He stopped her with both hands and peered up at the hawk and the nine-headed golden panther.

"The most ordinary-looking tree is the most protected in this garden," he said, dropping his hands from her shoulders.

Her father had told her of the Tree of Immortality when she was a young girl—the tales always fascinated her. It only bore fruit once in many human lifetimes, but the mortal fortunate enough to eat from the peach would live more than a thousand years. She never understood why anyone would want to live for so long and continuously lose loved ones, to watch them age and die. But many stories were told of men and women who murdered and betrayed for a taste of the fruit—for the possibility of immortality.

They walked past nine more trees, simply observing, silent in their awe.

There was the tree with leaves that were giant eyes blinking in the wind. The irises were of every shade imaginable, pink, green, scarlet, and orange. The pupils were all shaped differently, from circles to squares and diamonds, swirls and stars. The eye leaves rustled under the gentle breeze of the heavenly mountain, all blinking, and all-seeing. THE OBSERVANT TREE.

"What do you think it means?" Ai Ling asked no one in particular.

"I don't know, but it makes the hairs on my arms stand on end," Li Rong said.

She felt the same way.

Another tree was subject to the change of seasons every few minutes—one moment in full bloom with ripe red fruits like apples, in the next all the fruits plummeted to the ground and withered. The leaves crumpled from brown to black until they decayed into nothing. The branches were bare before budding leaves appeared and red fruit began to form again. They stood watching the seasons change through two cycles, amazed by the speed, disconcerted by something so against nature in their world. The placard below read THE TREE OF LIFE.

The compression of the seasons haunted and disturbed Ai Ling, and she averted her face and walked on.

The winding path finally led them to the steps of the jade pagoda. Its sloping roof was hewn of gold, the pillars of white jade, and the rest, jade of the clearest green. Ai Ling climbed the steps, knowing in her heart that she had been summoned here. Chen Yong and Li Rong trailed behind her. They had followed her through the gates and into the garden, as if accepting her as their leader in this otherworldly realm. But she did not feel like a leader.

A long rosewood table stretched across the diameter of the circular pagoda. A silk screen embroidered with mountains and clouds shaded the sunlight from one side. The rest of the pagoda was open to the outdoors, with a view of the gardens and trees beyond, a glint of water visible among the flowers.

A Goddess sat regally behind the table, her three heads held high. One faced her audience directly, while the other two faced right and left. They looked to be identical in their features, ebony hair swept up in loops and adorned with pearls. The Goddess' faces were lucent, pale. Long, slender eyes lined in black examined them intently, making Ai Ling feel as if she stood in her underclothing. A fine, straight nose graced each face, above a curved mouth touched with a hint of lotus pink. Her features were perfect, yet the Goddess with her austere expression was remote, above them, beyond any measure of human beauty.

Four arms protruded from her torso, two on each side. One hand held a giant square-shaped chop carved from jade, another a calligraphy brush, while the third grasped an ink stick, and the final hand held a blank rice-paper scroll.

"Ai Ling, you and your friends are welcome in the gardens of the Golden Palace. No mortal has passed through those gates in countless centuries."

Why had they been allowed entrance? Ai Ling bowed her head, not knowing what else would be appropriate. Chen Yong and Li Rong both dropped to their knees beside her.

The Goddess set her brush down. "That is not necessary." She waved one hand imperiously. "Please sit."

Carved chairs of jasper and jade appeared. Ai Ling fell into the jade chair, her awe at this magic dampened by her anxiety. Chen Yong and Li Rong took the jasper seats that flanked her.

"You called us here . . . Lady?" Ai Ling did not know how to address her.

"I am the Goddess of Records, but you may call me Lady." Only then did Ai Ling realize that all six lips moved, each mouth speaking the words in unison. The combined voices were dreamy and soft, soothing. The Goddess placed the objects she was holding on her desk and clasped elegant hands in her lap.

"That jade piece"—the Goddess lifted one slender finger toward her necklace—"was a gift from me to you. Your father gave it to you before he left on his journey, as he was told to do. It was given to him by one of the Gods, disguised as a wise monk. Your father, being wise himself, took his advice to heart."

Ai Ling looked down at her pendant and saw that it was aglow, bathing her skin in a calming warmth. She clasped it in one hand, remembering the last time she had spoken with Father in private, by the plum tree in their front courtyard.

"Why is 'spirit' carved onto it, Lady?" she asked.

"The pendant carries a protective spirit. We feared you would be the target of strong enemies. Evil enemies." The movement of the Goddess' mouths became hypnotic. Ai Ling glanced at her companions; they were looking at the Lady with rapt expressions, as if unable to turn away.

"Protective spirit," Ai Ling repeated.

The Goddess nodded. "A powerful spirit to help guard you. You were chosen for this task before you were born. It seems you have also reincarnated with strong powers of your own—neither planned nor foreseen. The fates work in strange ways, indeed. These abilities will help you to kill Zhong Ye, who holds your father captive at the Palace."

Kill? Who was Zhong Ye? It couldn't be real. Her hand trembled on the jade pendant, and its light emanated through her fingers. The warmth washed over her again, and she felt calmer.

"Is my father all right?" Ai Ling asked.

"Yes. For now. Zhong Ye uses your father to lure you to him." The Goddess' mouths murmured, as if in condolence.

"I don't understand."

"Zhong Ye has played the guise of counselor to numerous emperors for over three centuries. As a mortal, he was intelligent and cunning; now, in his unnatural state of life, he is even more so. He fell in love with you in your last incarnation. But his plans to wed you were thwarted. Zhong Ye wants you still."

Her world reeled in dizzying circles. This man wanted her . . . loved her in a past life? Ai Ling felt queasy and lightheaded, sickened by the thought that Father was a prisoner because of her—revolted that Zhong Ye desired her for a bride.

She sensed both brothers turn to her, but she could not

look at them. Li Rong reached for her hand and squeezed her damp palm, bringing the sting of tears to her nostrils. Ai Ling sought Chen Yong's eyes as Li Rong withdrew his hand. His high brow was knitted in concern.

Ai Ling swallowed the knot in her throat. "How do I do this, Lady? Kill Zhong Ye?"

The Goddess stood and surprised Ai Ling with her height. She was taller than any person she'd ever seen, at least three hands taller than Chen Yong. The Goddess strode with regal steps toward her and revealed a crystal vial in one hand. "Take this. You must visit the Lady in White, and she will fill this vial for you. Its contents will aid you in casting Zhong Ye to the underworld."

Ai Ling took the vial. It was barely the length of her smallest finger and near the same width in diameter. The glass was elaborately carved with characters she did not recognize.

"If Zhong Ye wishes to have me, if you wish me to kill him, why have there been so many obstacles on my journey to the Palace?"

The Goddess smiled.

"You are perceptive. Zhong Ye does not wish harm upon you; he believes he loves you. It is the work of his current bride, who realizes her days ruling by his side are numbered if you do appear. After many centuries, she knows you have reincarnated, that you are on your way. She wants you dead."

Ai Ling felt the hairs on her neck rise. Finally things were falling into place, even if they were too incredible to believe. Who had she been in her last life? And why had she been chosen for such a horrific task? Ai Ling wrapped her arms around herself. She wanted to be back home; back in a time when her world was ordinary.

"She is powerful and cunning, a dangerous foe," the Goddess continued. "But it is Zhong Ye you need to be most leery of. He has managed to stay alive by devouring others' spirits, keeping them bound to him, so they are unable to truly die and reincarnate. Hundreds of spirits have been sundered from the Life Cycle."

The Goddess returned to her seat and sat down, her delicate eyebrows drawn together. "As the Goddess of Records, it is my duty to enter names in *The Book of Life* in crimson and in *The Book of Death* in black. Too many births have been recorded without souls to fill their human form—the babes are born without spirit." The Goddess raised her elegant heads, and her anger swept across Ai Ling like a lash of cold rain.

"Zhong Ye is playing god, when he is no god," the Goddess said.

Hundreds of spirits held captive, unable to become reborn and fulfill their destiny. Ai Ling thought about the older brother she never had, the one who was born still. Had Zhong Ye killed him? Stolen his spirit so he could not live? She gripped the jade armrests with tight hands. Was he the cause of her parents' grief—and so many others'?

Li Rong cleared his throat. "Couldn't you kill Zhong Ye yourself, Lady? Fling a lightning bolt at him? Turn him into a water buffalo?"

The Immortal shifted, her three faces turned to him. Li Rong tucked his chin, like a tortoise shrinking within himself—only he had no shell to hide in. Ai Ling would have smiled, but he asked a very good question.

"I cannot. I am bound by heavenly laws and duties. The Immortals do not often meddle in human lives." The Goddess turned now and regarded her. "I aid you for very selfish reasons, Ai Ling. You face a great nemesis in Zhong Ye. There is no telling what will happen if he continues to live through the consumption of others' spirits."

The Goddess rose. She raised one ivory arm, her stance reminding Ai Ling of the statues of Immortals hewn from white jade. "Roam the garden. Explore. You will find food and a place to rest." With that dismissal, her image shimmered and then faded completely.

After a long silence, Li Rong spoke first. "I've been a fool in my refusal to believe in the gods." He jumped from his chair and banged his head on the floor three times.

"You disbelieved? What did you think happened when we die?" Ai Ling asked, incredulous.

"I assumed there was nothing after death," Li Rong said, and then struck his brow against the luminous jade floor three more times.

"You've got your head too full flirting with pretty ladies to think about the mystic and otherworldly, little brother," Chen Yong said.

Li Rong stood, but not before bowing once to the goddess' empty chair. "There may be truth in that. Do you mean to say you believed in all the worship, the offerings, the incense burning?"

"I accepted it as our obligation, and I never questioned its truth. And I'll never have to question it, after this day."

"You were always the most traditional, Chen Yong, for being only half Xian."

Chen Yong rose from his jasper chair, but not before Ai Ling saw him wince. He turned from them, the brief hurt she'd glimpsed already masked. "We should look around the gardens," he said. "Not many mortals can say they had such an opportunity."

Ai Ling and Li Rong rose. The elaborately carved chairs shimmered and disappeared, just as the Goddess had. They walked down the gleaming jade steps of the pagoda and took the path that meandered beyond it, adjacent to a winding river rushing over smooth red pebbles.

"This must be the Scarlet River, which is supposed to run through the Golden Palace," Ai Ling said.

The path opened into a secluded garden. Chrysanthemums bloomed in orange and red, their faces turned to the sun; rare orchids bowed gracefully in their carved ivory pots. Ai Ling breathed in the scent of jasmine and sunshine.

"Look over there." Li Rong pointed to two birds strolling majestically by the pavilion.

"Phoenixes," Ai Ling whispered, afraid of startling them.

The birds reached taller than her waist, with long legs covered in golden scales. Their heads were white, with a vermilion comb on top. One phoenix stopped briefly to ruffle the crimson and gold feathers of its back with a pointed beak. They walked with dainty steps, light glancing off their hooked talons, the giant plumes of their red tails trailing behind.

"This is their favorite spot," said a lyrical voice.

A woman dressed in a pale green gown stood under a pavilion. She swept her arm to reveal the table behind her, laden with dishes. The smell of scallion and ginger and even more exotic scents assailed Ai Ling.

"A meal awaits. Eat at your leisure." The woman bowed, her black hair free flowing except for two braids coiled on top in loops. She vanished from view.

"I'll never become used to that," Li Rong said after she was gone. And, as an afterthought, "I wonder if a mortal can love the servant of a goddess?"

"Why don't you find out?" Ai Ling teased.

"You didn't have much luck with a serpent demon," Chen Yong said.

Ai Ling and Chen Yong laughed together. Li Rong threw a playful jab at his brother, which Chen Yong pushed to the side with a sweeping arc of his forearm.

"We're not all monks like you, old brother," Li Rong said. Chen Yong raised a brow but made no reply.

They settled down on the stools and watched the two phoenixes stroll to the river and dip their golden beaks into the rushing water.

"Do you think it's safe to eat the food of the Immortals?" Li Rong asked.

"I feel we're safe here," Ai Ling said, helping herself to rice, vegetables, fish, braised meatballs, and a steamed bun. "I'm afraid to return to our world."

Both brothers looked serious now, as they joined her in the meal. The food on their plates never dwindled, nor did their teacups empty. Each serving was more addictive than the last.

"Thank you, Immortals!" Li Rong said, unsuccessfully hiding a burp behind his hand.

Ai Ling laughed as Chen Yong shook his head.

"Have you considered all that the Goddess said?" Chen Yong asked.

"If I dwell too long, saving Father becomes an impossible task." She closed her eyes, hoping for silence.

"What Zhong Ye does affects all of us in a way. Who knows how he has skewed the Life Cycle by keeping these spirits trapped? I wanted to go to the Palace to find my mother, but I go now to help you slay this man as well," Chen Yong said, his voice quiet and steady.

"Me, too," Li Rong, head down, mumbled from behind his sleeve.

Ai Ling opened her eyes and found Chen Yong studying her with an expression she could not identify. She fought the urge to touch him with her spirit, just to glean his thoughts, but she had promised herself she'd never intrude on him like that again. She smiled instead, unable to express her gratitude.

"You must have been very strong in your past life to be chosen for this task," Chen Yong said.

She straightened, no longer drowsy. Her hand unconsciously sought her dagger's jeweled hilt. What was the use of being strong in a past life? Would she be strong enough in this one?

They spent the rest of the afternoon following the curve of the gentle river, exploring the lush garden. Ai Ling sketched the flowers; Li Rong stalked the phoenixes, until he came too close and got pecked in the thigh.

At dusk, they found three plush beds under the same pavilion where they had dined. A platter of fruit and some more lavender-colored tea were set on a low table.

Before the light faded entirely, Ai Ling decided to find a secluded spot and bathe in the river. She strolled away from the pavilion, feeling safe and at ease in the garden. She'd been so tense, so afraid these past few days. Thank the Goddess Chen Yong and Li Rong were with her.

Finding an area with soft grass along the riverbank, Ai Ling stripped bare. She loosened her braid, and threw a glance over her shoulder. Nothing stirred.

The water was warm. The rush of the current exhilarated her, and the elliptical pebbles pressed into her flesh, massaging knotted muscles. Her tension unfurled—Ai Ling imagined it rising to her skin's surface, being swept away by the flow of water. She slid a bit lower, propped herself up on her elbows, her entire body beneath the warm, gurgling river.

She threw her head back and wet her unbound hair. Her breath caught in her throat. The stars emerging from the deep indigo of early evening were endless. At first the sky was flat, but the longer she looked, the more bright specks leaped into place, until the darkness took on depth. Brilliant points of silver, white, bright orange, and cold blue blinked down from above.

She traced the Azure Dragon by the glimmering dots in the sky and had begun to search for the Agate Tortoise when she heard the brush move.

Ai Ling quickly sat up and drew her knees to her bare chest, bumps prickling her arms. "Who is it?" she asked in a quiet voice, quelling the unexpected panic that filled her.

A silver cat glided from the thickets, seating itself daintily near the river's edge. It was unlike any feline she had seen, with short, thick fur the exact color of a shiny coin.

"Hello there." She cocked her head at the cat, which raised a paw and began licking it. The action was so familiar it immediately brought Taro to mind. She ached for home.

"The water is very relaxing. Have you tried it?"

The cat paused in its cleaning and regarded her with silver eyes. It mewed as if in reply, the sound throaty and lyrical, taking her by surprise.

"No. Taro doesn't like baths either."

There was a rustle of steps on the path. She wrapped her arms around her breasts.

"Ai Ling?"

Chen Yong.

"Yes, I'm bathing."

"I thought I heard you speaking." His voice carried in the still night, even though Ai Ling could not see him.

"I was talking to myself." She decided that was easier than trying to explain why she was having a conversation with a silver-haired cat.

There was a pause before Chen Yong replied, "All right."

Embarrassed, she quickly braided her hair. It was time to dress and retire. Ai Ling reached for the thick towel she had brought, dried herself, and pulled on a clean tunic and trousers.

She bade the cat good night and headed down the path toward the pavilion. Their beds were arranged in a triangle formation. One glass lantern shaped like a lotus flower glowed in the middle of this makeshift nest until Li Rong extinguished its three flames.

The only sound was the soft rustle of leaves and the chirping of crickets. Even the Immortals have crickets in their garden, she thought, before she fell into a contented sleep.

CHAPTER THIRTEEN

Ai Ling sat up and rubbed her face, embarrassed to be the last one to rise.

"A peaceful morning." Chen Yong smiled. The dust of travel had been scrubbed from his face, his thick hair bound in a topknot wet and dark. Had he bathed in the river? He wore a new tunic, slate gray embroidered with hints of cerulean along the collar and sleeves.

"There's hot goat's milk for your morning meal, along with sticky rice balls with sweetened taro, rice porridge with pickled vegetables and salted pork, and the most amazing fruit you've ever tasted." Li Rong waved his arm in a flourish toward a lacquered tray laden with food at the end of her bed.

"We couldn't wait for you," Chen Yong said, although he didn't sound apologetic. She didn't mind. She wouldn't have waited either.

She scooted to the end of the bed and picked up a sticky rice ball and bit into it. Sweet things first. The chewy taro paste within had just the right hint of sugar. "Mmm," she managed with her mouth full.

"I'd be twice my size if I lived here," Li Rong said.

Ai Ling had another sticky rice ball already stuffed in her mouth. She washed it down with a sip of tea, and then realized both brothers were watching her. She gripped the teacup tight in her hands, not knowing how to express her jumbled thoughts and feelings. "I'm truly grateful you journey with me."

"This Zhong Ye who has captured your father must be defeated. Besides . . ." Chen Yong waited for her to raise her face before he continued. "I feel as if our fates are somehow intertwined. I've felt it from the moment I saw you lying on the edge of that lake . . . and when we met again at the noodle house."

She looked away. She felt connected to Chen Yong unlike anyone else she had ever known. Was it because he had saved her life? Or because she had slipped into his spirit? She only nodded, for fear she would squeak if she spoke.

"The Immortals are probably pulling the strings," Chen Yong said.

"We have control over many things, Chen Yong, but not

an individual's fate. That falls within the patterns of life itself. How one's path crosses or misses another's is beyond our control," the Goddess of Records said.

They turned to find the Immortal at the bottom of the pavilion steps. They leaped to their feet, the young men bowing low.

"But I thought you said I was chosen, Lady, to defeat Zhong Ye," Ai Ling said. She spoke without thought, and felt foolish for speaking as she would to her companions. She felt even more awkward with her mussed hair.

The Goddess smiled with all three faces. She waved one pale hand, indicating that they should sit. "It wasn't so much that you were chosen for the task, Ai Ling. But rather, you volunteered for it—more than two centuries past—while you dwelled in the underworld, waiting to enter your next life. This life."

Ai Ling closed her mouth after she realized it had dropped open. She turned to Chen Yong and he blinked, looking as surprised as she felt. Apparently, rashness transcended lifetimes.

"Two centuries?" she finally managed.

"It is an unusually long time in the underworld. I think your former incarnation was biding her time, gathering her strength," the Goddess said.

The phoenixes emerged from behind a flowering hedge and ambled toward the pavilion. The Goddess sat down gracefully on a jade step. "The sea dragon will take you to the Mountain of Eternal Prayer. It hovers in the clouds, between your realm and ours. This is where the Lady in White resides."

She stretched long fingers toward the two birds. Ai Ling saw that her fingernails were perfectly manicured, and that she wore pointed gold finger covers over the last fingers of her right hands. The Immortal leaned forward, the lavender silk of her gown cascading around her feet like liquid, and fed the birds purple berries, which had magically appeared in two palms. The stiff collars of the gown showed off her graceful necks, the material embroidered with a thousand blooming chrysanthemums. "The sea dragon awaits outside the gates, when you are ready. May good fortune keep you." She shimmered out of view.

"We should go. I don't know how long it'll take, but I would prefer not to arrive at night," Ai Ling said finally.

Chen Yong and Li Rong nodded in solemn agreement.

They gathered their belongings and wound their way past the pagoda where they had first met the Goddess of Records. No one was seated at the long table. They walked past the magnificent trees that had greeted them when they entered the gardens. The sun shone as brightly as before, the sky bluer than ever. Ai Ling glanced over her shoulder, feeling a heaviness as she walked closer to the red door. Why had her previous incarnation—she almost laughed at the thought—given herself to such a task? Should she take the word of the Goddess? She was in danger, and so were her friends.

Li Rong walked beside her, and Chen Yong strode a little ahead, as he always seemed to. "Thank you again for coming with me," she said.

His expression was serious. Then the boyish mischief returned and he grinned widely. "I wouldn't miss it for anything. Imagine the stories I can tell, the women I can impress after this fantastic adventure."

Ai Ling smiled. Li Rong could make even the task of sending someone to his grave feel lighthearted.

With a soft touch, Chen Yong pushed the massive red doors open. The sea dragon was waiting, stretched out to its full length. Its beautiful green, blue, and turquoise scales were dazzling in the sun. Ai Ling walked with lighter steps, as if she too had cloud wisps clinging to her feet. She approached the creature first, and it bowed its head, inviting her to climb onto its back. Li Rong and Chen Yong climbed on behind her.

The dragon ran on its short muscular legs, then bounded into the air, riding the winds. The blue of the heavens spanned forever.

"I hope it isn't too far away," Ai Ling said, not knowing if Li Rong, sitting with his hands on her waist, could hear her with the wind singing in their ears.

She looked down and saw nothing but a thick bank of storm clouds. She glanced behind, in search of the Mountain of Heavenly Peace, but encountered only sky. She would never walk in the Immortals' gardens again. The thought brought regret tinged with relief.

She could not say how long they traveled, but the next thing she knew, she woke with her cheek pressed to the spine of the dragon and a crick in her neck. She had fallen asleep, and the weight of Li Rong's head on her back told her he had done the same. Ai Ling slowly straightened and glanced behind her. Li Rong opened his eyes, yawning. Chen Yong's hands rested on his brother's shoulders as he scanned the skyline, alert.

The dragon began descending through the bank of ominous clouds. The air turned cold and dank, and she shivered. After a long moment, they emerged below the clouds, and she saw a jagged mountain. It appeared to drift in midair, composed only of rocks the color of tar. She had never seen a black mountain peak before—devoid of any living thing.

The Lady in White lived on this barren pile of sawtoothed rock? Where was her palace? Not even a small hut graced the summit. Her stomach knotted with anxiety, and she leaned back into Li Rong, seeking comfort. His grip around her waist tightened just a fraction, as if he sensed her fear— or felt his own. The warmth of his hands calmed her, and she smiled, grateful for his company.

Picking up speed, the dragon flew to the flat peak, the only even terrain on the entire mountain, and landed with a gentle glide. Ai Ling climbed off its back and stroked its sleek side in gratitude.

Chen Yong and Li Rong dismounted. The dragon bowed

its head low before leaping into the air and disappearing within the dark clouds. They were silent for a moment, their faces turned to the sky. Ai Ling wrapped her arms around herself. She wished the dragon had stayed.

"Where's this Lady we seek?" Li Rong said aloud what they all wondered. The air was damp with drizzle, and it was difficult to gauge the time of day.

"Look there," Chen Yong said, pointing, his body tense.

Ai Ling followed his gaze and saw that the light mist that swirled about seemed to leave a wide circular space empty before them. She squinted; something wavered, a sheen of white. She blinked, and the illusion was lost.

"I can't see anything," Li Rong said.

"There's something here, hidden from view," Chen Yong said.

Ai Ling walked toward the empty space, through the mist spiraling at its edges. A wall shimmered again, rounded and smooth like that of a tower, reflecting her image. She paused, stunned. Her figure warped and vanished. She reached out and walked to where she had seen her image. Her fingers touched cold, smooth stone.

"Ai Ling!" Chen Yong's voice was tight with warning.

She jerked her hand back. Clear crystal crackled where she had touched. The cracks spread like fissured ice, thrusting upward and around, until a giant tower glimmered before them. The tower's thick quartz wall was both clear and milky, revealing nothing within.

She turned back to her friends, lightheaded from fright. Li Rong let out a long whistle.

"I see no way to enter," Chen Yong said.

He withdrew his sword and began to walk the circumference. Ai Ling pressed a hand to her breast as he disappeared around the curve of the shimmering tower. She drew a long breath when he reappeared from the other side, after too many heartbeats.

"I counted nearly three hundred strides. I saw no windows or doors, no way of entering the tower."

"I don't understand," Ai Ling said.

She laid tentative fingers on the sleek wall again. And the next moment, a surge of cold rushed from her fingertips through her entire body; everything flickered, and she was within the tower.

The stench assaulted her. A monster loomed over Ai Ling, the smell of death pluming from its gaping mouth. She fought to remain standing, not to crouch and heave the contents of her stomach. The thing turned its sunken eye on her, black and circular, like a wound in its head. Fetid arms hung to the ground and ended in sharp black claws.

She realized then that it was composed of corpses—arms and legs jutted from the top of its head instead of hair. Its naked mass was formed of human torsos, more limbs, and worse, heads and sagging faces. Some of the eyes were so decomposed only empty sockets peered from a putrefied skull. Ai Ling barely reached its knee, which bulged with human spines and sharp shoulder blades.

The monster lurched and turned to face her fully. She tried to step back, but her limbs failed; tried to scream, but found no voice.

Chen Yong materialized facing her, right below the thing, his sword gripped in one hand.

"Behind you!" Her voice sounded muted, her need to warn him dislodging the words from her clenched throat.

He bounded to her side in an instant, his face distorted by the stench that assailed him. "Mother of the heavens," Chen Yong breathed when he saw the monster.

Li Rong appeared on the opposite side of the tower. He drew his sword and looked at Chen Yong and Ai Ling with wide-eyed terror. The monster took no notice, his eye boring down at her and Chen Yong. It dragged its black claws on the crystalline floor, making a horrific screeching noise. Ai Ling saw that the stone floor was etched with deep grooves.

"Stand back!" Chen Yong yelled. He vaulted forward, slashing his sword into the monster, cutting through a face and torso with flaccid breasts. The beast roared, a deep boom, and its cadaverous arm swept down like falling timber, but Chen Yong had already twisted away. They now formed a triangle around the beast.

Ai Ling stepped back, her knees shaking. A familiar warmth gathered against her breast, and she looked down to see the glowing jade pendant. It flickered, grew hot, and a white blaze enveloped the monster. Please let it kill the thing.

The monster continued its attack, oblivious to the bright light surrounding its body. The heat around her throat cooled. She looked down. The pendant had dimmed; the intense glow faded from around the monster. Ai Ling's heart dropped to the hollows of her stomach. How could it fail her now, when she needed its powers the most? She reached for the dagger tied to her waist and pulled it from the sheath, gripping the hilt too tight. She wanted to throw it but didn't trust her aim.

Li Rong crept up behind the monster. He slashed a trunk-like leg with his sword. The beast roared again and turned toward him.

Chen Yong sprang, leapt off one decomposed heel, and stabbed the back of a thigh. He let the blade sink in, and he dangled like an acrobat from the hilt. The monster thrashed and lurched toward Ai Ling. She managed a small step backward, her entire body trembling. Chen Yong landed light on his feet, like a feline.

The beast blinked its black eye once, and in the next moment, she was behind the monster, where Li Rong had stood. They had switched places. She saw Li Rong where she had been. His eyebrows climbed so high from shock they nearly met his hairline.

"Its eye, it blinked . . . ," Ai Ling said, knowing she made little sense.

"Curses on the Devil's daughter," Chen Yong said.

Li Rong stood in a fighting stance before the beast, legs wide, both hands gripping his raised sword.

The beast thrust its claws at Li Rong. His blade met one with a resonating clang. He rushed forward and between the sweeping arms. He plunged his blade into its pale shin, then sprinted back to the side of the tower opposite Chen Yong and Ai Ling.

"Ai Ling, touch the wall!" Chen Yong shouted, his voice sounding too far away.

She laid both hands on the stone, and her fingers tingled with cold—but that was all. They were trapped.

The beast had turned its eye back to Chen Yong and her. Chen Yong jumped away from Ai Ling, making himself the target by brandishing his sword. The monster stomped after him. Cornered, Chen Yong attempted to dodge the creature's claws as he slashed.

"Watch out!" Li Rong shouted. He ran toward the back of the monster, his sword extended.

Chen Yong crouched low against the wall as the creature lifted its arm high, ready to strike. It blinked its sunken eye once. The hunkered figure of Chen Yong vanished, to be replaced by Li Rong, upright, exposed, with his sword raised. Frantic, he lunged forward.

The monster's sharp claws crushed down, puncturing Li Rong through his chest. Li Rong's dark eyes widened with shock, and his mouth slackened. Then his head lolled forward, and his sword clattered to the scarred stone floor.

Ai Ling screamed.

"Little brother!" Chen Yong roared.

Chen Yong attacked the back of the beast in a fury. Over and over he raised his powerful arms and hacked at its dead flesh. Ai Ling watched, helpless, as the monster turned toward Chen Yong. Li Rong slumped over, almost as if he were resting in the monster's palm.

Ai Ling threw a searching cord out to Li Rong but could grasp hold of nothing to anchor herself. Utter rage erupted within her as she ran after the beast. It lunged toward Chen Yong, not bothering to shake Li Rong from one hand as it thrust with the other.

Ai Ling stabbed her dagger at a rotting ankle, an elbow sprouted from the wound. The hilt glowed bright blue beneath her fingers, shockingly cold to the touch. She withdrew the blade and plunged again as deep as she could in its thick calf, but the monster continued to lumber forward. Desperate, she placed one hand on the creature and leaped inside. There was no spirit, merely a deep pit of furor.

She saw Chen Yong through its eyes. His features hazed, his body was outlined in a blurred red. The need to seek and kill overwhelmed her. Then to absorb. The beast flicked one hand in impatience, flinging Li Rong's body across the tower. *Kill. Absorb. Grow.* They were not spoken words, but amorphous images forming ideas. The thoughts thudded with each beat of its booming heart. That was how she found it. A large lump composed of dead hearts, drumming an inhuman rhythm.

Her spirit surged. She concentrated on the immense cadaverous heart, focused her grief and ire. What she could heal, she could also destroy. Her spirit whirled around it in a frenzy.

The heart erupted and splattered.

The beast howled once before it fell to its knees. It toppled, nearly pinning Chen Yong beneath its rotten bulk. She snapped back into her own body, woozy, her head bent over the cold floor, her trembling hands barely able to hold herself up.

Strong arms pulled Ai Ling to her feet. "Are you all right?" Chen Yong asked. He took her dagger, still clutched in one hand, and sheathed it for her.

She shook her head. "Li Rong . . ."

She crumpled against him, and he held her. Frustrated by her own weakness, she shoved herself from him and staggered toward Li Rong. He lay like a broken puppet, arms flung out, legs askew. Blood had pooled around him. His eyes were closed, his face ashen and taut.

She laid her hands on him, above where the claw had gored his sternum. The wound was ragged, wider than her palm. She tried to enter his body but could find nothing to grasp. Tears blinded her, spilled hot against her cheeks. But then she felt it—something was still there—barely clinging, just about to let go. She lunged for it with her own spirit, seized it, and began to move across his wounds. There was nothing to see or feel. Just this wisp she clung to, refused to release.

From a distance, as if watching from above, she saw her own limbs start to shake. Sweat beaded at her temples, but she felt ice cold within, frozen and empty.

Li Rong's eyelids fluttered, revealing unseeing orbs beneath. An unnatural grunt escaped from between his pale lips, and then the jaws clenched. Even as she held on to the thin thread of his spirit, she could not truly enter his being.

She felt a touch on her wrist and saw Chen Yong crouched beside her. "Ai Ling. Don't."

She snatched her hand away as if scalded, and lost the grip she had on Li Rong. The wisp flitted off, slipped into the ether.

Li Rong was dead.

Black circles burst across her blurred vision. She stumbled away and slumped to the floor, not caring that the corpse of the monster was but a few arms' lengths away. Sobs shook her. She lifted her head, and through the haze, saw Chen Yong crouched over his brother, holding one slack hand in both of his.

The Immortals didn't care, she thought, the bitterness rising like bile in her throat. They sent us here. They knew this would happen. They let this happen.

She felt a light touch on her shoulder and jumped. A

warmth zinged through her, easing her. The scent of honeysuckle filled her nose. She turned to find that the corpse
of the decaying monster had vanished. A woman stood in
its place.

"You have freed me," the woman said.

The Lady in White.

Ai Ling scrambled to her feet. "My friend died. He—he
was gored." The tears came again, and she put her face in
her hands. She felt the Lady stroke her hair. Something her
mother used to do. The Lady lifted her chin with soothing
fingers and touched the wetness on her cheeks. The tears
dropped like glass into her palm.

"The Goddess of Records gave you a vial," the woman
said.

How did she know? Distrust mingled with the anger and
grief, making her stomach clench. Ai Ling pulled the small
vial from the hidden pocket within her tunic. The Lady in
White carefully put the tears in the vial; they clinked like
diamonds as they dropped.

"Consume them when you need strength. You will know
when."

Ai Ling nodded, not understanding and not caring. She
turned and saw Chen Yong still with his brother, but looking toward her and the Lady.

"Can you bring Li Rong back?" Ai Ling asked.

She inclined her head. "The dead should stay dead," she
said.

The Lady gazed down at her. She was as tall as the Goddess of Records. Her smooth porcelain skin made the jet black brows that much more dramatic. She wore her raven hair in two braids, looped on either side, with clear crystal jewels woven through the locks. A gossamer gown floated about her like a cloud, pale and white, revealing shimmers of blue with each graceful movement.

"But it was my fault." Ai Ling wiped her nose with the back of her hand. "And she knew! The Goddess knew he would die, and she sent us here. Without warning—without . . ." She scrubbed the tears from her cheeks, hiccupping.

"Li Rong chose his own course in life," the Lady said.

Ai Ling turned toward Chen Yong, helplessness and grief smothering her breath. He was bent over Li Rong again. She walked to them, the true friends she had made on this journey. She put a hand on Chen Yong's shoulder, but he did not turn to look at her. He blamed her. She was certain of it.

"We can't take him with us. We need to give him a proper funeral." Chen Yong whispered, his face still turned to his brother.

"We need wood to make a pyre. There's nothing here," Ai Ling said.

"I can help," the Lady in White said.

Chen Yong rose to his feet. "Thank you."

"I will need your strength, young man." She glided through the tower wall.

"Will you prepare him?" Chen Yong finally asked, his voice low and hoarse.

The tears rushed into her eyes and stung her nostrils once more. He approached the smooth fissured wall, placed a hesitant hand on it. And vanished.

Ai Ling crouched over Li Rong's body. She slammed her fists against the cold stone floor until her hands bled. Why did the gods allow evil men to live, and care nothing for the innocent? She could not believe he was gone, despite the pool of dark blood fanning beneath him. She reached out and stroked his face and smoothed his hair, intimate acts that she would never have dared were he still alive.

Finally she reached for his knapsack and searched through it, feeling intrusive. She selected his best tunic. It was made of gray silk with simple gold embroidering along the collar and sleeve edges. She unhooked his buttons with trembling fingers, lifting him to pull off his sleeves, cradling his head as she lay him back down. Sweat stung her eyes, and she swiped a bloodied hand across her face.

His wound exposed, Ai Ling saw the startling white of jagged rib bones and his shattered sternum. Nestled within, something glistened. His heart. Hope surged to her throat. She could still bring him back. The Calling Ritual from *The Book of the Dead*. She could try. She had to try.

"Forgive me, Li Rong. I will make it right again."

She *had* to try.

Ai Ling freed her dagger and reached into Li Rong's gaping wound. Sharp bones scratched her arm. His heart was still warm, wet. Ai Ling felt removed from herself. She could not think about what she was doing. There was no choice. She had no choice.

The heart shifted but would not pull free. She grasped it, took the dagger and made one cut. The hilt glowed blue, became as cold as ice. Ai Ling lifted the heart free. It was the size of her fist and lay like a sacrificial offering in her shaking hand. She needed to preserve it—one month to bring him back, with her own blood. Most other components were common. But the empress root was banned. She would find it. She would not fail Li Rong.

Ai Ling closed her eyes, forcing her mind to see the page, to remember the words. She muttered them in a low voice, verses she didn't understand. The heart turned ice cold, felt like heavy glass in her hand. She opened her eyes. It glowed slightly, but her blessed dagger had turned a dull black. Ai Ling frowned, sheathed the blade. She grabbed one of Li Rong's cotton tunics and wrapped the heart carefully within its folds, then tucked the bundle in her knapsack.

Ai Ling poured water from her flask over her bloodied forearm and hands, watched it slide in red rivulets onto the ice white floor. She licked her cracked lips, tasting the salty mucus that ran from her nose, and wiped her face with a dampened rag cloth. She gently dressed Li Rong's body, pulling the tunic over his head, holding his hand to guide the sleeves. After he was clothed, she wiped his face clean with tender care. She did the same with his hands.

His wound had already stained the new tunic, like a crimson flower blooming across his chest. But at least he would not be sent into the next world in the tunic he was slain in.

Chen Yong and the Lady appeared again within the tower, emerging like apparitions from the crystalline walls. "Thank you," Chen Yong said simply.

Ai Ling could not look at him. She was out of breath and clutched her knapsack with tight fists. Chen Yong kneeled down and cradled his brother as if he were a child. His eyes were swollen and his nostrils red, but he no longer wept.

"The body will transport through the wall with you," said the Lady.

Ai Ling walked to the gleaming wall and placed two timid fingertips on it. The tingling cold rushed through her, and she was outside on the black peak once more.

The Lady and Chen Yong had built a pyre on the rocky landing. A dark blue cloth was spread neatly on a wood platform, with black twigs and branches filling the space beneath.

"I couldn't conjure much, under the circumstances," the Lady spoke apologetically. "But it will be a proper funeral— as best as we can make it."

Chen Yong carefully laid Li Rong on the platform and arranged his arms alongside his body.

At the end of the platform was a small altar, with incense

burning and a pile of spirit money—gold and silver-foiled coins. The flame from one white candle flickered in the wind. "I am unable to conjure food," the Lady said. Was she a goddess as well?

Ai Ling carefully searched through her knapsack and pulled out a packet of nuts and dried mango, given to her by Master Tan so long ago. She also found the last two strips of dried beef, Li Rong's favorite.

"I can offer these," she said.

"And I have rice wine," Chen Yong said. He placed a finely carved gourd on the altar.

The Lady began chanting the song of mourning in a sing-song voice as Chen Yong bent down and started the fire. He looked up at Ai Ling. "Help me."

She joined him and fed the spirit money into a bronze bowl. The embers fluttered around them. There was a chill in the air and the skies were overcast, the day darker and colder than before. She did not know how much time had passed, how long they had been on the mountain.

She felt again Li Rong's reassuring touch when they had first descended on this mountain. No, he shouldn't be dead. Not when someone like Zhong Ye lived. She would bring him back—even if she needed to use the dark arts to do it. Li Rong had died because of her. She would do anything.

The Lady's chanting was soothing and hypnotic. She clapped her hands at certain points, swaying like a delicate orchid. "The body wears to sand," she sang. "Yet the teaching of goodness will always linger. . . ."

The spirit money burned bright, and then dimmed to a few points of glowing red.

"Place his belongings at his feet. It is time," the Lady said. She gently laid a yellow cloth over Li Rong's face and placed a sky blue one over his body. She touched the platform, and the black sticks beneath roared into bright flames.

They crackled, spread, and illuminated Li Rong's face, making him appear lifelike again. Soon the flames engulfed him. Ai Ling and Chen Yong stepped back from the pyre as the wind blew across the barren mountaintop, feeding the fire.

She caught glimpses of him still. He shimmered and wavered until he was lost, and she turned her face away.

Chen Yong stood beside her, their shoulders touching. She looked toward the Lady, who faced them, standing close to the fire, unaffected by its heat. Their eyes locked, and her arms prickled despite the roaring flames. The Lady's gaze pierced through her. Ai Ling looked back to the pyre, willing her face to betray nothing.

A low wail erupted from Chen Yong as he fell to his knees. He hugged himself and banged his brow against the ground, the keening never stopping. It flooded her with grief. She too collapsed to her knees, allowed her sorrow to voice itself in a piercing cry. She banged her brow against the black rock of the mountain, giving herself to physical pain until her vision swirled with orange flames.

They remained prostrate until the fire burned itself out, until darkness fell and a sickle moon shimmered down on them. The air was frigid. The stars were distant, indifferent—so unlike the sky that had comforted Ai Ling the evening before, when she had bathed in the Scarlet River.

"It was a proper funeral for a hero," the Lady said.

Suspicion coiled within Ai Ling. Why hadn't the Immortals prevented this?

"Are you a goddess, Lady?" Ai Ling asked, her voice quiet.

"It's been so long that I've been held captive—I do not know anymore. Come, you can rest in my sanctuary tonight."

Ai Ling recalled the Lady's light touch on her shoulder, the warmth of her healing mingled with the scent of delicate honeysuckle. She knew the Lady was good, but a part of her did not know if she could ever fully trust her or the Immortals again. Not now.

The Lady in White led them down a path through jagged black rocks, a path that had not been there when they first alighted on the mountain. The ice tower was gone, and in its stead, a white circle hewn into the ground gleamed in the moonlight.

The Lady's gown emanated a silver sheen that made it easy for Ai Ling and Chen Yong to follow her. She led them to a small, simple hut built into the side of the mountain. A pine tree the same height as Chen Yong grew by the wooden door. Wild honeysuckle nestled beneath the window ledges. Their hostess pushed the door open, and they followed her inside.

The small room was rectangular in shape, cozy for one person and crowded for three. The wooden beams above were high, allowing for the Lady's tall stature. A square lacquered table dominated the room, and a lantern sat on it, a bamboo pattern etched in the glass. Two other lanterns hung from the high beams, casting a warm glow.

"I regret I have no food to offer. But there is a well at the back of the house, and its water is refreshing. I do believe I have a jug of wine hidden somewhere, if you'd like," the Lady said. She looked like she needed neither refreshment nor rest. Incredible, if she had been held captive as long as she claimed. Unease curled around the edges of Ai Ling's grieving heart. Perhaps they had been used by the Immortals to rescue this woman.

"It would warm me up, I think," Ai Ling said. She had never drunk wine.

The Lady glided to a small bamboo bureau in the corner. She returned bearing a round tray with two wine cups and a jug. She filled both cups. "I wish I had more to offer for your act of bravery."

She kneeled, handing a cup first to Chen Yong, then to Ai Ling, her back curved. Embarrassed, Ai Ling quickly took the cup and sipped without thinking. The liquid cut a hot path down her throat, easing the coldness within her belly and the bitter ache of her chest.

"Who held you captive, Lady?" Ai Ling tried to keep the tone of her voice respectful, rather than accusing.

Chen Yong raised his head from his wine cup and met her eyes with an inscrutable look. Ai Ling pursed her lips—she never knew how he felt or what he thought—and turned her full attention to the Lady.

"My twin brother," she said in a quiet melodic voice that brought to mind lute strings plucked beneath a full moon.

Ai Ling gasped. She took another sip of the wine, welcoming the searing heat that filled her, slowly numbing her anger, her pain.

The Lady turned to gaze out the window, her face filled with sorrow. "I was well loved by my father, educated, encouraged to learn and travel, treated as if I were a son. My twin brother was intelligent and talented in his own right. I know not why the jealousy burned so deep within him; it ate away at him, tainted his spirit. . . ."

Her porcelain face flushed with color. "We were never close while growing up, so I had no inkling of his resentment toward me. There were just the two of us. Mother died when we were but six years.

"It was only when Father died ten years later that I understood how deeply my brother despised me. He locked me within my quarters, refusing me the right to visitors, turning away friends as well as suitors."

The Lady remained on her knees, her back straight,

turning her face from Chen Yong to Ai Ling as she told the story.

"After two years of imprisonment in my own home, I escaped. I traveled as far away as I could, until I reached the summit of this mountain. And it was here I made my home. For years I stayed here alone, the mist and stars as my companions, the birds and pine rodents as my friends."

"But your brother found you?" Ai Ling asked.

"He appeared on this summit five years later, unrecognizable. I looked into his face and saw nothing of my twin. He ranted and raved about how I was favored by my father— but the truth was, I was treated as an equal to him, never more.

"And as he spoke and paced, my beautiful mountain darkened, the leaves blackened and shriveled, the life bled away. He raised his arms, and a crystal tower thrust upward from the peak. He stripped me of flesh and body and imprisoned my spirit within those walls."

The Lady finally bowed her head, her hair ornaments clinking like chimes. "That was more than a thousand years ago," she said.

"A thousand?" Ai Ling breathed.

"He had given himself to the dark arts. He conjured the monster you slew to hold me captive in the tower and prevent rescue or escape. My home, this mountain, has been under an enchantment." She surveyed the room. "It's as if time stood still."

"That is an incredible tale, Lady. I'm glad we were able to help free you."

Ai Ling's jaws tightened. "What about Li Rong?" She spoke too loudly.

His eyes were wet when they met hers. She regretted her callousness, felt her lower lip tremble at having caused him more pain.

Rash, stupid girl.

"Li Rong died performing a good deed," Chen Yong finally managed in a husky voice.

Ai Ling felt even more wretched. Surely Chen Yong blamed her for Li Rong's death, as much as she blamed herself.

Later, Chen Yong and the Lady retreated into the night to fetch water from the well. It was cool and refreshing; Ai Ling drank two cups. Without bothering to change her clothing or wash, she climbed beneath the thick blankets on one of the pallets the Lady had laid down and immediately fell into an exhausted sleep.

CHAPTER FOURTEEN

Ai Ling woke from a dreamless sleep. Bright sunlight shone through gossamer silks draped across the paper panels of two large windows, forcing her to squint for a few moments.

"Finally," Chen Yong said, smiling. He sat at the low table, a calligraphy brush poised over a bound journal. He put down the brush on the ink stone and crossed the room in two strides to her pallet, an expression like relief on his face.

His closeness made her self-conscious. She rubbed her eyes with limbs still heavy from sleep. "Good morning," she said.

"A peaceful afternoon to you," he replied with a wry smile. "You slept for two days. We couldn't wake you. I was beginning to worry."

Two days? She shifted back on her pallet and glanced around the room. "Where's Li Rong?" Her mind skewed the moment the words left her mouth, instantly followed by a spasm of grief. Chen Yong winced as if kicked in the chest. She covered her face with her hands, wishing she had not woken. Could one sleep anger and grief away?

Chen Yong touched her shoulder, and she dropped her hands; he rose and walked away from her, his movements stiff. "The Lady went out to gather fruit," he said. "She brewed tea."

Ai Ling crawled out of her warm nest, and Chen Yong passed her a cup. "Thank you," she said, drawing the steam into her face, unable to meet his gaze.

"I can't believe he's gone," he said, staring into his own empty teacup.

"I can't either. I'm so sorry."

She hid her face until the intensity of his gaze forced her to look up. Chen Yong carried his grief in his eyes. The sunlight hit his face at angles that made him look foreign, exotic.

"It's not your fault," he said after a few moments.

She blinked several times, caught off guard.

"We knew it was a risk, and we chose to come with you," he continued in a quiet voice.

"He shouldn't have died," she said.

"Who knows what the fates have planned?" He filled his cup from the delicate porcelain tea jug.

"You sound like one of those esoteric monks . . . or the goddesses." Anger swelled within her, and she swallowed the sour taste in her mouth. The gods didn't care. Her eyes found her knapsack leaning against the pallet. She fought the urge to go to it, rifle through the contents—make sure it was still there. One month. It was enough time.

"Perhaps the monks know of what they speak. And who are we to question the Immortals?" He leaned toward her, both palms open, accepting.

She turned from him. Chen Yong could never know, not until she succeeded. The Lady entered. Her white gossamer gown shimmered, offering glimpses of the colors of dawn— vermilion, pink, and gold. She smiled as she placed a tray of berries and apples before them.

"I hope they're as sweet as the last batch." She sat in one fluid motion, tucking her long legs beneath her. The scent of honeysuckle drifted through the air.

Ai Ling became aware of the gnawing hunger in her stomach. But she had no desire to eat. "I'm not hungry," she said, realizing only after that she sounded ungrateful, spoiled.

"You both need sustenance." The Lady proffered the tray.

Ai Ling plucked a few dark berries from it with reluctance, and Chen Yong did the same. They ate the ripe berries at the same time. The sweet tang of juice exploded in her mouth, making her stomach growl in anticipation. She was starved.

The Lady offered slices of crisp green apples next, and they both ate in silence. Ai Ling kept her head down, painfully aware of Li Rong's absence, missing his easy banter.

The Lady grasped prayer beads in one hand, her fingers gliding over the iridescent stones. Ai Ling could not read her serene face. "You will have to continue on your journey soon. You need to return to the mortal realm below."

The clear jewels of her hairpin reflected light across the room. "It's not a straight path from these peaks to your world. It is ever changing. There may be foe or friend on your journey. I am hoping you will find the latter to guide you."

She put a small bundle wrapped in blue satin on the low table. "Some fruit to take with you. It is not as filling as rice or broth, but it will sustain you."

"Thank you, Lady. Yours rival those from the Gardens of the Golden Palace," Chen Yong said.

"They were grown with cuttings from that garden."

Chen Yong and Ai Ling took time to wash their faces and rub their teeth with coarse salt. They put on fresh clothing before stepping outside.

Ai Ling's breath caught. What had been a black peak had turned verdant green, alive with lush plant life. A clear brook bubbled outside the doorstep. The house perched high; clouds mingled with thick mist drifted below, jade crests jutting through them for as far as she could see.

The scent of wet earth filled her senses; she could almost see the spring buds unfurl, feel the velvet moss on stones. The hard knot of grief expanded in her chest. Li Rong was not here to witness this. He would not be there to finish their journey.

Ai Ling turned slowly to admire the landscape, more stunning than any painting. She would bring Li Rong back and make it right. It would be worth the risk.

"Follow the path," the Lady said. She bowed before them, her palms raised at the chest and pressed together. "My gratitude for freeing me from my curse."

It did not take long for the opaque mist to envelop them, so thick she could not see her hand in front of her face. Chen Yong used a long branch as a walking stick, feeling for the dirt path.

"We could plunge to our deaths," she said. "Or walk completely off the path."

"Hold on to me. It can't be like this for much longer," he said, his voice a disembodied phantom. She reached out and touched his knapsack, moved her fingers to grip his shoulder. She shuffled forward with slow hesitant steps, trusting him to guide her.

The mist pressed against them like a living entity, making her chest feel constricted. It was difficult to breathe. She took comfort in the warmth of Chen Yong's shoulder beneath her hand.

After what seemed like an endless time, the haze began to dissipate, revealing the side of a rocky cliff on their left and thick foliage to their right. Relieved to be able to see again, she looked back. There was no mist behind them, simply a wide, rutted path that rose slowly, instead of the steep one they had just descended.

"Chen Yong." She squeezed his shoulder, then dropped her hand, realizing that she no longer needed his guidance.

He stopped and half turned to follow her gaze. "I know. We can't return from where we came."

They continued to descend the gentle slope until Chen Yong paused and flung one arm out to stop her. She drew up to his side, and he pressed a finger to his lips. He tilted his head as if he were listening for something.

The sound of faint laughter drifted up to her, and she tensed. Women laughing. Chen Yong cocked his head toward the noise, and they continued around the bend.

He stopped abruptly again and stepped behind a large pine tree. She followed his lead. Two women were bathing in a small pond. Water cascaded from jutting rocks above, filling the pool.

They splashed each other and laughed. They chattered in a language that Ai Ling almost knew, the words tugging at her from some distant memory that did not seem her own.

One woman was tall and sleek, her hair a dark auburn. Her features were not entirely Xian, with wide-set round eyes and a high nose. Her lips were dainty, the color of pink lotus; dappled sunshine glanced off the milky skin of her small breasts. Her companion's skin tone was like wet sand, darker than any person Ai Ling had ever seen. Her eyes were wide, tilting upward; the mouth sensuous, full. Her breasts were ample and rested on her swollen, pregnant belly like ripe fruit.

Ai Ling's ears grew hot. She could not believe she was spying on these women with Chen Yong by her side.

The darker-skinned woman swept back raven hair with one hand, the waves falling well past her shoulders. Ai Ling could not fathom how the two could reveal themselves with their hair unbound. Were they sisters? The tall woman brushed her tresses with an ivory comb; they giggled and chattered. Something about stone and sleep . . . or dreams?

Ai Ling pulled Chen Yong back with a hard tug. "What should we do?" she whispered. "We can't spy on them like this. They're naked!" The moment she said it, she regretted being so obvious. She almost stomped her foot in embarrassment.

Chen Yong grinned, his face boyish again, the tautness in his features softening. "It's now that I miss my little brother the most. Li Rong would love this."

Ai Ling's mouth tilted upward, a soft chuckle escaping her lips. Then her nose stung with the onrush of tears. She reached out to grasp Chen Yong's arm, reacting to the gleam of sorrow in his eyes, even as the smile lingered on the corners of his mouth.

He nodded, whether in acknowledgment of her comfort or to say he was fine, she didn't know, and she dropped her hand.

The two women in the pond began singing.

"Perhaps they can help guide us back to our world," she whispered.

"I can't understand a word they're saying. And I have the feeling they'll be frightened by the sight of me," Chen Yong said.

"Maybe if I approached them first."

"We won't be able to follow that path past them without being seen, besides," he said.

She stepped from their hiding place. The women did not notice her, so she proceeded with deliberate steps toward the small pond, taking care along its muddy banks. The pregnant woman saw her first, and gasped. Her friend stopped singing at the same time.

Neither woman attempted to cover her nakedness, but instead they stared at Ai Ling with their mouths agape.

"I didn't mean to interrupt. My friend and I are lost. We need help." Ai Ling spoke too loudly and wrung her hands.

The two women looked at each other, then back toward Ai Ling. They murmured between themselves, but Ai Ling caught at least one word: outsider. The pale woman pointed a slender hand toward the path. Go. Follow. Ai Ling could gather that much.

She felt a little doubtful. "Is that the way back to the King-dom of Xia?" Both women furrowed their brows. Finally the pregnant one pointed again with emphasis to the path. Ai Ling pursed her lips, unsure if they knew the way or just wanted to be rid of her.

"My friend is behind that pine tree." Ai Ling pointed to the large tree with the wide, gnarled trunk. "He's a man, so—" She did not get a chance to finish the sentence. Both women let out loud shrieks.

They scrambled up the far bank of the pond, speaking rapidly to each other. She caught the words man, hide, and far. They vanished into a thicket of trees before she could utter a reply.

She understood modesty, but had not expected them to run screaming into the trees.

"I guess you can come out now," she called.

She turned and found Chen Yong standing on the path.

"They must have understood the word 'man.'" He chuck-led, surprising her. "You understood their speech?"

Ai Ling lifted her shoulders. "Some words—but I seemed to get the gist of their conversation anyway."

"They spoke in women's tongue," Chen Yong said.

She joined him on the path. "What do you mean, women's tongue?"

"When I saw them in the pond, it brought to mind a place I had read about in *The Book of Lands Beyond*."

Ai Ling nodded.

"There's a passage about the Land of Women in the book."

"You think we are in the Land of Women? But the darker-skinned one was with child," she said.

"Yes, but—"

Chen Yong did not get a chance to continue before Ai Ling slapped her hands together. "But they become pregnant by bathing in the golden pond."

He laughed. "Now you know why they ran off in such terror at the mention of a man."

"If I had known . . . I don't know what I would've done if I had realized." She paused. "Other than not get into that pond."

There was a breath before Chen Yong roared with laughter.

She laughed with him, her cheeks feeling hot, but she didn't mind.

"And any male child never survived past three years. I remember that passage," Chen Yong said.

"I cannot imagine a world without men. I envy the men in our society for their freedom at times. I often think that the rules favor your gender, yet it wouldn't be the same without . . ." She trailed off, feeling foolish.

"The book also mentioned a Land of Men. Like you, I can't imagine such a place."

"No one would serve you tea or prepare your clothes each morning," she teased.

"I know I'm very traditional in thought. But you have to

believe that I value women for more than their roles within the inner quarters." He struck the dirt path below them with his walking stick, then stopped and turned to her. "You've helped to open my eyes in many ways."

She lifted her chin and smiled at him, somehow willing her face not to flush scarlet.

They stopped at a stream to refill their flasks. They washed their hands and faces and sliced up the fruits the Lady in White had given them. Ai Ling nearly choked on the last bite of apple when she heard the trot of an animal approach. Chen Yong jumped to his feet, his sword drawn.

A man emerged, riding a white horse with red stripes like licks of flame on its flanks. Its mane was red as well, the color of the skies at dusk. Its wide eyes glinted gold in the sunlight.

The man had only one arm. As he drew closer, what she thought was a mark in his wide brow emerged as a third vertical eye.

A two-headed bird, vermilion and gold, perched on his shoulder. The heads sang to each other in crisp, sweet tones. The man pulled in the reins and stopped a short distance from them. She saw there was a bow strung across his back, and a scabbard rested against his hip. But he did not look anxious, and his hand did not move toward the sword hilt. She wondered how he used a bow with just one arm.

"You are lost," the man said. It was a statement, not a

question. His accent was strong, but the words came through clearly.

Chen Yong stepped forward, not lowering his weapon. "We're from the Kingdom of Xia, trying to make our way back there," he said.

"Xia." The man pronounced their kingdom's name differently, but it seemed he had heard of it. "You are Xian?" The voice was higher than what she was used to, his skin smooth like a young boy's, the eyebrows thin and delicate.

"Can you guide us back?" she asked.

Chen Yong turned to her with a hard stare, a barely audible hiss escaping from his lips.

The man tilted his head. "To go back by foot is impossible," he replied. "I have never encountered people of Xia. I have only heard tales from elders. We may find answers in my city. If you follow?"

Ai Ling nodded even as Chen Yong drew her aside, his gaze never leaving the strange man. "How do we know he speaks the truth?" he asked in a low voice.

"He appears willing to help . . . is civil. It's a risk we have to take," she said. "We could wander for years and never reach home."

Chen Yong's jaws were set in a rigid line, his reluctance to follow this stranger obvious. "Can you read his thoughts?"

Her eyes widened. "You jest."

His silence was answer enough. She sighed, turned a fraction so her back was to the strange man on the horse, and flung her spirit toward him. She connected, sensed the anticipation from him. *The chief will be much pleased.*

"It's fine. Just as I said." Ai Ling strode over to the man. Stubbornness prevented her from glancing back to see if Chen Yong followed. Then he was by her side, his stare so intense she thought she felt the heat on her face. She dared not look at him.

The man doubled back onto the path they had already traveled. He kept his horse at a slow canter, so she and Chen Yong could keep the pace. No one spoke. The dense foliage they had passed earlier had changed to tall birch trees, their trunks glowing silver, the limbs and leaves towering above them.

Confused, Ai Ling glanced back. The pebbled path they had walked less than an hour earlier had turned to a narrow one covered in moss.

"I noticed it, too," Chen Yong said. "The landscape is changing around us, in a way that shouldn't be possible. I don't think we could find the pond where the women bathed if we tried."

How would they ever return from this strange world?

The quiet was soon broken by the triumphant trills of the two-headed bird as it took flight, leaving the perch that was its master's shoulder.

"Where does your bird fly to?" Chen Yong asked, one hand shading his face as he gazed upward.

The one-armed man did not respond but pulled the bow

from his back and rested it against his thigh. Ebony in color, the bow curved in a smooth elegant arc. He drew an arrow from his leather quiver—also black, with bright crimson feathers on the end. He notched the arrow with his one hand, drawing the bowstring taut with his mouth.

Ai Ling gaped. The arrow flew among the trees. Chen Yong stepped forward with his sword raised. The one-armed man jumped from his horse and into the woods, returning with something that resembled a hare, only its short fur was a pale lavender. His arrow jutted from the creature's midsection.

"My bird hunts, as do I," he said. He removed the arrow and slung the carcass into his saddlebag.

Ai Ling shivered.

Chen Yong rolled his shoulders before sheathing the sword. The stranger remounted his horse, and they continued on their journey.

The moss-covered path started to slope downward. Ai Ling's legs ached. They had been walking for hours. She wondered what the one-armed man's city was like. Did they take baths? What did they eat? The sun cast its heat on their backs. Ai Ling drank from her flask, grateful she had filled it at the stream earlier. The path continued steeply downward until it rounded a bend to a plateau and a lush valley opened up below them.

She drew in a breath of disbelief. A wide river wound its way through the center of the valley like a silk ribbon. Seven arched bridges spanned the river. Both pedestrians and riders on horses with flame red manes crossed the bridges, intent on the tasks of the day. All had but one arm, some protruding from the left, others from the right. Her arms prickled at the sight of so many of them.

The valley was surrounded by mountains, their round, blunted peaks forming shapes to incite the imagination. Ai Ling saw a tortoise, the side view of a hare, and a farmer's woven hat. The pinnacles stretched endlessly into the horizon, making it seem there was no other city beyond the one nestled in the valley below—no other kingdom.

"Are there other cities near yours?" she asked.

Their guide glanced over his shoulder and stared at her with three unblinking eyes. "We fly our chariots, and the journey is long. This is the reason I believe you are far from Xia."

Ai Ling's stomach fluttered with unease. No matter how gentle his manner, she was not comfortable beneath his scrutiny.

They reached the edge of the plateau. Water from tiered rock pools cascaded down the valley wall, iridescent, catching hues of turquoise, gold, and green.

"I've never seen anything like it," Ai Ling said.

Their guide's smooth face betrayed just a hint of pride. "There is none like our stair lakes anywhere. The waters in these pools formed from melting snow. The limestone was smooth-shaped by eons of water flowing."

He guided his horse to wide steps carved between the stair lakes. They were also hewn from pale limestone, but the steps were wide and not steep, allowing the horse to step down with an easy gait. It appeared the horse had navigated them many times before. Ai Ling and Chen Yong followed.

The city was well laid out, with paths paved in white quartz. Ai Ling was used to dirt and, at best, cobbled streets. They walked past a tower with a domed top, bejeweled and sparkling in the afternoon sun. Another building was constructed of hexagonal tiers, in a material that appeared silver and also reflected the sunlight. She counted thirteen floors.

Another structure was built right on the river, with five rotating arms dipping into the water, spinning endlessly.

"It's a different world," Chen Yong said.

The strangeness of the place overwhelmed her, the unfamiliar shapes of the buildings, the glint of unknown materials. The city was stunning, but completely foreign. As were these people. She ached for home.

"I know not what yours is like," their guide said from atop his horse.

"We never asked your name," Ai Ling said, feeling foolish for having forgotten the simplest etiquette.

"We do not give our names so readily. But you may give yours to the Chief if this is usual to you. My people call me Archer."

They continued to follow Archer, passing others on horse

and foot. Although no one betrayed surprise, Ai Ling felt their stares. The paths were lined with trees and plants, many bearing fruit. She saw an apple tree and a diamond-shaped fruit the color of bitter melon, as well as dark orange berries that resembled cherries.

Their guide led them to the six-sided tiered building. It reminded her of the pagoda paintings she had seen in books at home. This one appeared much sleeker in its design, the sides so shiny they reflected her image. The door was hex-agonal as well, made of a dark green stone.

Archer dismounted, petted the horse's fiery mane, and whispered in its ear. The beast flicked its head as if in response to its master, who stepped up to the green door. It split open in the middle like a gaping mouth, receding into the shiny walls. Ai Ling could see her own reflection, her mouth round as a circle. She looked at Chen Yong's image and felt better—he seemed just as astounded.

"Come. The Chief expects us. Crimson Tail brought news after her hunt."

Utterly confused for a moment, Ai Ling finally realized he was referring to his bird. She ignored the hollow feeling in her stomach, blaming it on hunger, even as her throat clenched with doubt. Chen Yong followed her down a nar-row hallway, his hand tight around his sword hilt.

The chamber Archer led them to was bright, although windowless. A giant shaft at the center flooded the room with natural light.

Another one-armed man, dressed in a dark blue tunic and leggings, walked toward them. His hair flowed from a thick topknot, unlike their guide, whose hair was shaved close to the head. Ai Ling could not stop looking at the man's hair; she had no words to properly describe the red color, had nothing to compare it to. The man's eyebrows were so light she initially thought he had none.

Archer bowed his head low.

"Your pet sent news." Ai Ling stared at his lips. His voice sounded like a woman's, yet he looked like a man, nearly as tall as Chen Yong, broad shouldered and muscular. The bird was perched on his shoulder. He raised his hand in a graceful gesture, each finger bejeweled with large rings, and it flew back to Archer, both heads twittering in excitement.

The Chief took a seat and indicated for his visitors to sit before him, on the floor. The smooth white stone was cold, but Ai Ling was glad to rest. A small sigh escaped her lips. It did not seem very welcoming, to have them huddle on the floor. She had to arch her neck to see the Chief's face.

"Crimson Tail said you come from the Land of Xia?" The Chief looked down at them with three curious eyes. They were not the same color. The middle vertical one was a dark green, and the other eyes a clear, light blue.

"Yes. I'm called Chen Yong, and this is Ai Ling. We're trying to make our way back home."

The Chief nodded. "I have heard tales of your people, but did not know them to be true or false. It astounds me to see someone so different from ourselves."

He nodded to Archer in approval. "You have done well bringing this species to us. Take them to the third floor and strip them. The Anatomist will examine them."

The words had barely sunk in when Chen Yong jumped to his feet, his sword already sweeping an arc in the air. But the sharp blade Archer pressed to the back of Ai Ling's neck halted him.

"Do not be a hero, Xian male. You are outnumbered." The Chief's lips curved into a smile, revealing sharp white teeth.

Armed guards marched into the room until they lined the six walls shoulder to shoulder. Garbed in red, they carried tall staffs with hooked blades at the tip. Each one had hair shorn short, like Archer.

"We will not harm you. We want to examine and learn." The Chief rubbed the fingers of his hand in obvious pleasure; anticipation. "Take them away." He flicked his hand in dismissal.

"Relinquish your weapon, Xian male. Fight, and the Xian female dies first," Archer said. Ai Ling bit her lip at her own rashness and stupidity. They would not be in this predicament if she had listened to Chen Yong—but she had been too stubborn, sure she was right. Chen Yong handed over his sword, the cords of his neck taut. Archer cocked his

220

head to the door and escorted by guards, they started down the long hallway.

"The stairs in the back. Go."

Ai Ling followed Chen Yong, with Archer behind her. Her mind raced. They were surrounded by guards—how could they possibly escape? She wanted to beg for Chen Yong's forgiveness, stomp her feet in anger and frustration at her own gullibility.

Chen Yong walked with his back straight and stiff, his hands doubled in fists by his sides. She wondered if she could enter Archer's spirit to search for knowledge. But could she keep herself walking at the same time?

They climbed past the second floor and onto the third. Ai Ling sensed the sharp tip of the Archer's sword behind her, its threat heavy, solid, even though it did not touch her once.

"Down this hall," Archer said. The passageway looked the same as the first, only now all six walls were made of glass, allowing a view into a room that was bare except for two single beds on raised stilts, reminding her of Li Rong's funeral pyre. Her throat tightened, the grief quickly replaced by fear. Would they seize her knapsack, rifle through the contents? She clutched the sack closer to her.

Chen Yong stepped into the chamber under Archer's direction. Ai Ling wrinkled her nose at the scent of bitter medicinal herbs. Again, sunlight flooded the room from an open shaft in the middle, glancing off the six opaque walls ol silver. Ai Ling realized that the glass only allowed one-way viewing, from the outside in, and the hairs on her arms stood on end. What did the Chief have planned for them, with the Anatomist's help?

"Take off the clothes." Archer waved his weapon nonchalantly at them.

Ai Ling didn't move.

Archer extended his sword until the tip touched the hollow of her throat, his smooth face never changing expression.

Chen Yong nodded to her. She almost wanted to laugh, hysteria welling within her. But then he turned his broad back, put down his knapsack, and pulled off his tunic. Ai Ling spun around at the sight of his bare skin. Her face burned as she removed her own tunic. She glanced at Archer, and he waved his weapon to quicken her pace.

Ai Ling took off her trousers and folded both top and bottom neatly, placing them on one of the platform beds. She still had her undershirt and shorts on.

"Everything, female," Archer said.

She peeled off her underclothing and climbed onto the edge of the bed, her back to Archer and Chen Yong. She brought her knees up to her chin and wrapped her arms around herself, unable to disguise the trembling of her limbs. Her teeth clacked in terror. Her entire body felt flushed, yet chilled from sweat; her heart pounded hard against her thigh.

"The Anatomist will come. Do as he says. We see every-thing."

Archer picked up their knapsacks, and the silver doors slid shut behind him with a faint hiss. Ai Ling wanted to retch.

"Son of a rotten turtle. He took my sword," Chen Yong said.

She had tucked her dagger in the pile of folded clothes. The Chief had said they would not be harmed. Archer had said he would help to get them home. But look where they were now.

"I'm sorry. . . ." She trailed off, unable to talk past the knot in her throat. She stared at her hunched reflection. Chen Yong's bare back was visible behind her in the silver glass.

He didn't reply. She breathed into her knees, not blaming him if he never spoke to her again.

"Can you . . . ?" Chen Yong finally said. She waited for him to finish his sentence but realized after a few moments he deliberately had not.

She snapped her head back to him. He half turned also, and tilted his head toward the doors, menacing with their gray reflection. Anyone could be watching. Anyone could be listening.

At that moment, the silver doors slid open and another one-armed man entered the room. This one was dressed in robes the color of agate. He was slender and slight, with the smooth face that seemed so prevalent. She assumed he was the Anatomist. He turned to them, the vertical eye intent on her, his two others scrutinizing Chen Yong. Ai Ling shivered, and she hugged her nakedness even closer.

"This is indeed a surprise. A real find by our Archer. We will learn much from studying you," the Anatomist said in a singsong voice. He crossed the room with a strange gait, as if one leg was shorter than the other, and approached Chen Yong.

"The guards are outside. They see all."

The Anatomist directed Chen Yong to the end of the hard bed. Ai Ling glimpsed the side view of his naked form in the reflection.

She shut her eyes and focused on the Anatomist, casting her spirit toward him, hoping to learn something—anything. They needed to escape, and fighting their way out was not an option. Not if they wanted to live. She felt the familiar tautness in her navel. She snapped into the Anatomist's being. The clarity of his vision shocked her, the colors vibrant, the light filtered more pristinely than what she knew.

The Anatomist ran his fingers across Chen Yong's scalp, massaging the skull. He twisted a strand of the hair and made a mental note of the color and texture. Through his eyes, Chen Yong's hair was a mixture of bronzes, copper, and ebony. Fascinated, Ai Ling wanted him to linger there, but instead he tugged on Chen Yong's earlobes and peered inside an ear.

The Xian male is tense. Not surprising. The pair will make good slaves—as well as their offspring. The Chief is much pleased. I must

make careful illustrations of their sexual organs. Do they procreate the same as we do?

Ai Ling's spirit recoiled, and she nearly snapped back within her own body.

The Anatomist worked his nimble fingers across Chen Yong's wide shoulders and began tracing a line down the lumbars of his back. Chen Yong's muscles tightened, became even more defined under the Anatomist's touch; he rolled his shoulders, as if to shake off a fly.

The Anatomist gripped the back of his neck, with surprising strength. Ai Ling felt the cords of Chen Yong's neck tense. "Cooperate. It will be unpleasant otherwise," the Anatomist hissed in his ear.

She folded herself around the Anatomist's spirit. She felt his confusion. He resisted, his arm slackened to his side, shocked into immobility at what was happening within his mind.

She could not fail. This was their only chance. She expanded her spirit and wrapped it around his. He continued to struggle, like a slippery fish caught in the binds of her net. Ai Ling held firm . . . until she had taken control of his physical body.

Startled by her own success, she stood frozen. Chen Yong cast a wary glance her way, his expression filled with loathing, danger.

"Get dressed," she said brusquely in the Anatomist's high-pitched voice.

Chen Yong's eyes locked with hers, gold flecked with dark green, the color even more stunning when seen with the Anatomist's heightened vision. They narrowed, even as he reached for his clothing. She hastened toward the silver doors, trying to get used to walking with the shorter leg. A deformity he had had since birth—his history and experience were open to her in a jumble of noise composed of memories and thoughts. The doors slid aside to reveal six guards standing at attention. She looked down the hallway, trying to adjust to the brighter, more intense light and color. There were no other guards.

"Leave us. I need privacy," she said. It took all her strength and willpower to speak with authority, not to tremble or shake. She gulped, feeling a small bone protrusion slide within the Anatomist's throat.

A guard stepped forward. She knew it was the highest-ranking officer, Protector West. "We were told to guard the captives at all times, Anatomist."

She made herself angry, drew the words and a snarl from the Anatomist. "You waste my time, West. Leave us." Her captive's heart beat faster. His spirit twitched. She felt a sheen of sweat begin to collect at his hairline.

"Archer gave specific instructions—"

"I am here on the direct order of the Chief." She paused, to keep the tremor from the Anatomist's throat. Slow, deep breath. "You abide by my requests, not the Archer's." It was true, she knew. The Anatomist held higher rank, though he would never have dismissed the guards. His furious screams were distant but shrill.

They stared into each other's eyes, neither blinking. Ai Ling hid a trembling hand deep within the folds of the agate-colored robe, fought hard to breathe normally. Finally, after five heartbeats, West nodded. "Summon us if you need us." He turned on his heel and walked down the hallway, the other five Protectors marching in a precise line behind him.

She felt a writhing struggle for control from the Anatomist's being. "Stop this sorcery, female," he cried from somewhere deep. His mouth jerked open, and she felt him on the verge of shouting to the guards for help. Terrified, she clamped down, her spirit quivering from the effort, and stumbled back into the chamber. The door slid closed behind her, and she leaned against the wall to steady herself.

Chen Yong was dressed and standing by the bed.

"Help me dress my body. We have to find the flying chariot."

Chen Yong turned to her naked form, saw that her head had dropped to her knees. "What did you do to her?"

"It's me, Chen Yong. I've taken control of the Anatomist's body." She heard herself speak these words in the high-pitched rasp of the Anatomist. This was not going to be easy.

Chen Yong's features tightened with suspicion. "What trick is this?"

She felt her heart, the Anatomist's heart, quicken.

"We don't have time to argue. We need to survive this—
for Li Rong's sake."

Chen Yong blanched as if she had slapped him; then his
expression hardened. He nodded.

There was no time for modesty. With Chen Yong's help,
she pulled on her tunic and trousers. Her body drooped
and appeared asleep, her breathing slow and quiet. It was
unnerving, like handling her own corpse. She sensed that
Chen Yong felt even more uncomfortable than she did.

"Can you carry me?" she asked.

Chen Yong cradled her body in his arms.

The doors opened, and they walked with quiet steps to
the green stone stairs. Chen Yong's sword and their knapsacks were tucked in an alcove in the smooth wall. He slung
her body over his shoulder so she dangled facedown, and
grabbed the sword. He shrugged as if in apology.

Ai Ling took their knapsacks and knew with the Anatomist's knowledge that they had not been searched. The
Chief had no interest in their paltry possessions. She felt
for the lump in her own knapsack and, touching its coolness
through the worn material, hissed in relief.

They encountered no one on the second floor and quickly
descended the steps. The Anatomist walked more slowly
than she was used to, the joints feeling creaky, the body
worn. But his senses were agile and alert. She knew that it
was just after the second meal, when most of his tribe were
taking the afternoon silence at home.

The first floor hall was empty. They approached the door they had walked through so naively just hours before. It slid open, and they stepped into the bright afternoon sunlight. The square was deserted.

"I can't believe our fortune, that the door is not guarded," Chen Yong said.

"They are a peaceful people. Outsiders are very rare. Protectors guard the Chief, but not the Hall of Reflection unless called."

"You know all this?" The amazement in his voice was mixed with a suspicious caution.

"This way to the flying chariots," she said. "I know every-thing the Anatomist knows—though it is like piecing together a jumbled puzzle to make sense of it." Her spirit strained to keep the Anatomist suppressed, even as he writhed against its confines.

They walked down a pathway lined with trees bearing purple diamond-shaped fruit, past homes constructed of wood and stone with glass windowpanes in every shape imaginable, stained in all hues of the rainbow. With the entire tribe at rest, the valley was quiet.

Until the Sentry stepped from a side path and halted them.

The stench of rotten eggs, Ai Ling thought.

"Sentry Amber," she said. She sensed the Anatomist curs-ing as she spoke. His spirit twisted against hers like a fly caught in rice glue. She kept her face composed, imagined the placid features she had seen on everyone in this city.

"Anatomist, where are you headed with this strange lot?" Sentry Amber hefted a shiny club over one shoulder. She had never seen such a weapon. It looked like it could put down a water buffalo with one good blow.

"Our newest acquisitions, courtesy of Archer. I was examining the male when the female became sick. We are headed to the Healer." She spoke with authority, in a steady, strong voice. She felt a spasm shudder through his weak leg. Hold still, Ai Ling. Show no fear.

"But the Healer is that way." The Sentry pointed with his club at a path they had just passed.

"Yes, but I need to go to the Herbist first, friend." A pause as she scrambled. The Anatomist simply screeched now, in an attempt to deter her, hide information. "You think I have become that senile since my six hundred and eighth?" She pursed the Anatomist's lips and arched his brows. Had it been too long a pause?

The sentry pulled his thin lips into the phantom of a smile. "Greet the Herbist for me. He gave me a good concoction for my last sunsickness—even if it tasted of baoli dung."

She nodded and walked past him, feeling his stare on her back.

"Anatomist!"

She turned, trying to control her breathing. The Anatomist's pulse, her pulse, palpitated in his throat. Somewhere deep within, she could hear him hiss and struggle, his horror bordering on madness. He managed to jerk his hand upward, and Ai Ling crushed down on his being like stone. She guided the hand up to rub the smooth chin, hoping it looked natural.

"Do you need help?" The sentry cocked his head in Chen Yong's direction. Her own body rested in Chen Yong's arms, seemingly fast asleep.

"You really do take me for senile, Amber. He is under a bind of obeyance." She let the words fall naturally from the lips. There was no room for hesitation or error.

The sentry nodded, his expression unreadable, and strolled away. Suddenly a loud gong reverberated through the city. The breath caught in the Anatomist's throat after Ai Ling grasped the meaning of it.

The Eight Chants of Returning.

The entire city would now break their afternoon silence to recite eight prayers before resuming the tasks of the day. The city would soon swarm back to life.

Chen Yong turned to her as the second gong rang, the powerful sound filling her with panic. She did not speak, but instead hurried toward the flying chariots. The Anatomist's breath came in short gasps; his heart fluttered and skipped beats. She led Chen Yong upward, to a small landing notched in the side of a hill.

Three chariots, open sedans with huge silver wheels, sat on the smooth dirt. One was painted a deep eggplant and carved into the image of a bird, golden wings tucked to its sides. One bore the resemblance of a mouse, gleaming silver in the sunlight. The final chariot was hewn in the image of a dragon, rendered in azure and sea green—so like the sea dragon that had carried them to the mountain of the Immortals. This chariot was the Anatomist's personal favorite. It had the reputation for traveling the fastest.

"The dragon," she said, and felt the Anatomist shriek and rattle against her in rage. A third gong reverberated across the hillside.

"Now you have a taste of what it feels like to be enslaved," she said aloud to his struggling spirit.

"What?" Chen Yong asked.

"Climb in, hurry!" She flung their knapsacks onto the chariot floor, then grimaced, remembering what she carried in her own. The image of Li Rong's heart tumbling forth and unraveling from its cocoon flitted through her mind, seeped into the Anatomist's. He mewed in terror.

Chen Yong opened a door on the side of the dragon and carefully placed her on the bench.

"How does this thing work?" He looked around with a puzzled expression.

"We wait for a good breeze and push the chariot over the ledge," she replied.

"Are you mad?"

"It does fly. I'll push, then leave his body." She had to shout over the reverberations of the fourth gong. It had better fly.

Chen Yong's surprise turned to worry. "Are you sure you can do this?"

"I've done it so far, haven't I?" she said, more bluntly than she intended.

She limped to the rear of the chariot and started to push with all the strength of the one arm. The chariot was heavy for the Anatomist's slight frame, and he could not run fast with the bad leg, but the large wheels sped up quickly, and very soon she was struggling to keep up.

The contraption raced off the edge of the landing and hovered for one frightening heartbeat. Ai Ling whispered a prayer, seeking aid from the Goddess of Mercy. And then a small breeze caught it and the chariot began to drift. The sound of the fifth gong echoed through the valley.

Chen Yong crouched over her body, a hand on her shoulder as if to keep her steady in the slightly rocking chariot. But his eyes were locked on the Anatomist. She needed to return to her body. A breeze swept through the valley and buffeted the chariot higher, out over a grove of strange fruit trees.

A thick arm snaked around the Anatomist's neck, dragging him back. "Taking a trip? It is not authorized by the Chief."

Ai Ling choked. The Anatomist choked. She wasn't sure anymore. She released her hold on his being, cast herself out, and pulled along the invisible cord, riding a gentle zephyr toward the chariot.

There was a jarring snap, this time so violent she gasped.

She gulped in short breaths. The world was dimmer, the colors dulled. But this sight was her own, this mind and this body her own.

"Ai Ling?" Chen Yong leaned over her, the sun catching the dark auburn of his hair. "Drink some water." He cradled her head and lifted the flask to her mouth and cool spring water splashed on her lips and chin.

"I just need to catch my breath. . . ." Before she could finish, she lunged to the side of the chariot and retched over the edge. She collapsed against the chariot door, her arms draped over the side. Her head spun, and she forced her eyes shut.

The shrill screams of the Anatomist drifted to her on the wind. She opened her eyes to see him slumped against the bulk of Sentry Amber, jabbing a weak finger in their direction, his fury obvious even as the two figures dwindled to pinpricks.

"Will they follow us?" Chen Yong asked.

She shook her head, then immediately regretted it as the world tilted again. "We took the fastest chariot."

Chen Yong knelt by her, wrapping an arm around her shaking shoulders. "Lie down. You need to rest."

About twice the length of an individual sedan and oblong in shape, the uncovered chariot held a wide bench at one end lined with plump cushions.

She let herself be led there and laid her head down on a cushion. It smelled of strange and pungent herbs, but she didn't find it unpleasant. Chen Yong arranged the other cushions and draped a blanket over her. She smiled weakly, but he did not see it.

"The valley has disappeared already," he said.

"You steer with your destination in mind," Ai Ling muttered. "That's how it works." She shut her eyes and fell into an exhausted sleep.

CHAPTER FIFTEEN

Ai Ling woke to find Chen Yong steering the pivot as if he'd done it many times before. She pulled herself into a sitting position and stretched. Her stomach churned, but her head did not spin like before.

The chariot flew gently above misty peaks. The scenery rushed past them at an unnatural speed—so fast that she could not look for long, even though the chariot itself did not seem to be racing, merely gliding on a soft breeze.

"Before I met you, I would not have thought steering a chariot with my mind possible. But now I think, what do I know?" Chen Yong turned and managed a wan, tired smile. "Are you feeling better? I don't know how long you slept, but it seemed a long time."

He sat down next to her and pulled something from his knapsack. "Let's eat. We need strength."

Her stomach grumbled. What she would not give for a large bowl of broth with hand-pulled noodles or steamed dumplings or cabbage and braised pork meatballs. . . .

Chen Yong handed her two biscuits and strips of dried squid. She gnawed on the squid, savoring the flavor. She wolfed down the biscuits, despite their stale blandness.

"If only we had some tea." They spoke at the same time. Their eyes met in surprise, and they laughed.

"It's good to see you eat. I'd be worried if you ever lost your appetite," he said, dusting his hands of crumbs.

"Why do I feel like I should take offense to that?" Ai Ling laughed at the uncertain expression that flitted across his handsome features. She rummaged through her own knapsack, careful to keep her face composed, and pulled out an apple. Chen Yong sliced it with a small knife. But she was no longer hungry, and he ate the crisp fruit alone.

"I've been thinking of nothing but the Palace while you slept," Chen Yong said.

"The Palace." Would she have enough strength to defeat Zhong Ye and save her father?

"It was the destination in my mind as I steered," he said, scanning the horizon.

The light faded fast, as if the day fled from them. The night deepened and a full moon rose. They discovered the chariot had a strong light in the front, illuminating their way. Ai Ling leaned over to investigate and discovered two round orbs embedded in the woodwork, forming the dragon's eyes. She touched one eye with cautious fingertips. It was neither cool nor hot.

The interior of the chariot itself had the same orb carved into the woodwork of the floor panel. This light glowed softly and looked like a moon, rising large and full over carved hills and trees.

"Have you ever seen anything like it?" She traced her finger around it.

"The one-armed tribe was known for their mechanical and building skills. That much I remember from *The Book of Lands Beyond*," Chen Yong said. There was a short pause in which only the sound of the wind rushing by filled the space around them.

She let out a breath that turned into a small hiss. "You're right. They are both female and male—it explains their high voices and smooth faces."

After all they had encountered, this realization still stunned her. They had visited a land, been captured by a people she thought to be story and myth. It was one thing to believe the Immortals were real—but people so different from themselves?

"You saved us," Chen Yong said in a quiet voice. "What you did was beyond my comprehension. I don't know how you took control of his body, much less acted like him so convincingly. I wasn't even sure myself it was you."

"I did what I had to do. I went into his mind and saw him thinking of . . . experiments he wanted to perform." She looked down at her hands. She sounded like a monster herself. Some sort of demon. "I think my ability has grown stronger. I've seen through the eyes of the undead—the demon that carried your image . . . and the corpse monster . . . I killed it from within."

"Within?"

"I went inside it to kill it."

"Mother of the Heavens, I thought you slew it with the blessed dagger. It's amazing, Ai Ling. It's frightening. . . ." Chen Yong trailed off.

She clasped her knees to her chest. "I wish I knew more. I just go. I didn't know I could take over the Anatomist's body until I tried. I was terrified and couldn't think of another way to escape."

She shook her head. "Li Rong was right when he called it spiritual rape," she whispered, her voice catching.

Chen Yong touched her wrist. Startled by his contact, her skin tingled.

"You saved our lives, Ai Ling. Thank the Goddess for your gift."

She tried to smile, grateful for his kind words, but could not manage it.

She stood and looked out at the world far below. She could see trees and mountain peaks, lit by the moon—like ink washes she'd done for evening landscapes. The air was cold this high up, and the stars shone and glimmered. Ai Ling pulled on an extra tunic and tucked herself back on the bench, trying to find constellations she was familiar with in the night sky.

She must have drifted to sleep again. The glare of daylight beneath her closed lids roused her. She peered, squinting, and saw Chen Yong still guiding the chariot.

"How long have I been asleep?" she asked, rubbing her face. It did not feel like long enough.

"The chariot seems to hasten the passing of time. It couldn't have been more than a few hours," he said.

"You should get some rest, too."

Chen Yong sat down next to her on the cushioned bench. "I don't think I could fall asleep even if I tried," he said. He stared at the pivot before them. "I don't believe the chariot even needs steering, once the destination is set. It helped to keep my mind occupied."

Ai Ling studied him. He appeared exhausted, his grief etched in the tense line of his jaw. He put his face in his hands, allowing his shoulders to fall forward as if in defeat. She wanted to draw him into her arms, cradle him as he had cradled her. But she did not move.

"If you're to help me save my father—and perhaps find your mother, I think you should try to rest," she said.

"I'm not sure how much help I'll be, Ai Ling. Given the nature of the creatures we've been fighting. Zhong Ye will be the strongest foe of all, the most powerful in the dark arts."

"I can't do this alone."

Chen Yong lifted his head and met her gaze. "I think you can."

"I'm glad you believe so." She clutched a cushion to her chest. "I'm not so certain."

"You haven't seen yourself, Ai Ling. You're quick-witted and brave. You're strong."

She dropped her chin, her face tingling with pleasure. "And stubborn. And rash."

Chen Yong leaned back and laughed. "Even so, I'll be there at your side until the end."

Ai Ling did not fear he would abandon her. Not now. But a small part of her wondered if she was being selfish, especially after the loss of Li Rong. The thought of him brought back both intense grief and anger. What had she done in her former life to inherit this terrible task? Li Rong was dead, and Chen Yong risked his own life for her. No one else would be hurt—not her father, not Chen Yong. She would end this.

She rose and peered over the side of the flying chariot. Nothing but infinite cerulean blue with wisps of clouds below. She let the wind brush past her. It soothed her. She was glad they were nowhere, because to be somewhere would mean fighting for their lives again. She was glad to be alone with Chen Yong.

His eyes were closed. A wild, intense feeling filled her, shuddered through her. Ai Ling turned from him, fought the urge to crouch close and see the rise and fall of his chest. Did he dream? She remembered the girl of his dreams, felt again his aching loss.

She did not notice the chariot's descent until the clouds that had been beneath surrounded them. The chariot glided faster now as it flew downward, and the daylight faded once again too soon, the remains of the full moon revealing a vast sea below. Ai Ling drank from her flask and nibbled on some dried mango.

She sat down next to Chen Yong, gathering his warmth, even though their bodies did not touch. She slept with her knapsack hugged tight against her, Li Rong's heart pressed against her own.

She dreamed of home, of sweeping the main hall and eating a celebratory feast for the new year. They toasted one another with wine and laughter. Then she sat at her mother's dressing mirror as her mother brushed her hair. The face reflected before her was not recognizable. The mirror showed a beautiful woman, with her own features, but painted with expert care. Her mother slowly wound her hair up above her head in elaborate loops, before placing a wedding veil over her face.

No.

A gentle thud jolted her from her dreams. The sun had risen. They were on the ground. Chen Yong sat up beside her. They were outside the tall walls of a city—there was no one about. She looked up and saw that watch towers spanned its entire length. She caught Chen Yong's eye. Was this the Emperor's city?

Chen Yong stepped out of the chariot, his belongings slung across his back and his sword at his side.

"I hate to leave this chariot," she said.

Chen Yong smiled and nodded to a grove behind them. They pushed the dragon chariot among the trees. It was hidden from the path along the city wall, but not as well as she would have liked.

They set out to find a gate. The city was massive, vast beyond her comprehension. They walked for more than an hour, following the edge of the mud-colored wall, before they came upon a grand entrance.

Thick black stone doors were pushed back, and a golden dragon, extended to full length, claws splayed like daggers, graced each one. An imposing ebony sign hung above the grand gate, with the characters HUANG LONG carved in gold. She touched Chen Yong's elbow.

"The City of the Yellow Dragon," she whispered. This was where they would find the Palace of Fragrant Dreams, the main residence of the Emperor.

"The chariot did not fail us," Chen Yong said.

They joined a throng of people on foot, astride their horses, or hidden behind silk drapes in sedans, all waiting to filter through the massive main gate.

The line moved quickly. Many people were waved past by the sentry at the gate while other guardsmen looked on.

Just ahead of them, a peasant in a faded tunic and trousers handed over a scroll. The sentry unfurled it. He read its contents and pushed back the peasant's straw hat to scrutinize his face. The peasant's shoulders curled forward, his hands clasped tightly together. The sentry waved him away, denying entry.

Chen Yong leaned close to her. "Let me speak for us," he whispered.

Ai Ling opened her mouth to retort that she had a voice of her own, then closed it again. For her to speak would certainly draw attention to them. A young woman outside the inner quarters stayed mute, unless spoken to.

It was soon their turn. She felt the weariness in her muscles and joints, the dust on her clothes and the travel grime on her skin. The guard studied Chen Yong's face and then looked at hers just as intently. She knew they were not a pleasant sight.

"What business do you have in the Emperor's city?" he asked, his voice surprisingly deep.

"I come to prepare for the imperial examinations. This is my wife."

The guard raised his brows, and Ai Ling hoped she did not raise her own. Why hadn't he told her? She looped one arm around his and squeezed it with her other hand. Curse the rotten turtle egg for surprising her like this.

"So fortunate to marry before you even make rank? And you a foreigner besides?" Ai Ling felt Chen Yong's arm

244

tense, but refrained from casting herself into the sentry's spirit. Not yet.

"She was promised to me at birth. I'm fortunate indeed," Chen Yong said, and took her hand.

The blood rushed to her face, and she looked down at her feet.

"And so newly wed she does not wear her hair up?" The guard was close enough that she smelled the tobacco on his breath. She pressed her chin lower.

"My wife is from the country and lax in her ways. I have promised her a handmaid who will fix her hair each morning, once I pass the exams and receive an official appointment," Chen Yong said.

He spoke with such ease that she almost believed him.

"Good luck on the examinations then. Move on." The guard waved and did not bother to give either of them another glance. They walked through the gate under the curious eyes of the other sentries standing guard.

"Don't pull your hand away," Chen Yong said softly when they were out of earshot. She knew enough not to look back, but she pinched his arm as punishment. He chuckled under his breath as they walked hand in hand down the main street of the Emperor's city.

The architecture of the city was elaborate. Each building rose at least three stories tall, with pillars carved of alabaster, jasper, and jade. The roof tiles were all gilded in gold. The main street was lined with merchant stores, selling everything from embroidered silk bedding to tai-lored clothing, cookware supplies, spices, wines, and sweets. The wide, tree-flanked cobbled street was mobbed with people. Not as impressive as the quartz walkways of the One-Armed Tribe, but certainly better than any Xian town she had visited.

A few restaurants were interspersed between the specialty merchant shops. Ai Ling's mouth watered from the scent of roasted duck. Chen Yong released her hand, and her heart dropped with it as he pulled away.

"Let's eat first," he said. "The smell of that duck is torture."

They pushed their way toward the origin of the delicious aroma, and wandered down a small side street. Tucked in the middle was a cramped one-story restaurant, looking as if it fought for its space between two tall buildings. There was no name plaque outside the establishment.

Ai Ling and Chen Yong stepped into the dark interior. The restaurant was small, and surprisingly empty consider-ing the tantalizing scent that had drawn them both. Fewer than a dozen wooden tables took up the tiny space, with a dark blue curtain draped between the dining area and the kitchen behind it.

"Goddess of Mercy, I need to eat," Ai Ling said, sliding into a wooden chair near the kitchen. They'd be served faster, she reasoned.

Chen Yong grinned at her. "It's been a long time since we've had a hot meal." He sat down across from her and put his knapsack on the floor. "Order as much as you like. My treat."

Ai Ling clapped her hands with glee, and Chen Yong laughed.

"It's the least I deserve after the shock of playing your wife without so much as a kiss or warning," she said.

Two bright points of color appeared on Chen Yong's cheekbones, barely noticeable in the dim light. Ai Ling smiled, amused that she had made him blush for once.

"It worked, didn't it? We would have had too many questions otherwise," he said.

A girl brought them hot tea.

"A plate of the roast duck, steamed dumplings, spicy noodles with beef gravy, pickled cucumbers, stewed tongue and eggs if you have them, cold please, and sticky rice pearls, too," Ai Ling said, before the server girl could open her mouth. "I don't know what he wants." Ai Ling nodded toward Chen Yong.

"I'm not sure I have enough coins to order anything more," he said, laughing.

Ai Ling was about to retort but couldn't help but laugh with him.

"I'll have fresh steamed fish, if you have it, and bean curd with shrimp and snow peas," he said.

"We are close to the sea and have fresh seafood delivered daily, sir." The servant girl nodded before she hurried away to the kitchen with their order.

"We never ate much seafood. It was difficult to get, not to mention expensive. But always a treat," Ai Ling said.

"I guess I grew up spoiled. My family had at least one seafood dish with every meal," he said.

Ai Ling glanced at the other patrons in the small restaurant. There was a stocky man drinking wine and trying various small dishes near the entrance, and at another table close by two men slurped large bowls of noodles. Her hunger worsened.

Another patron was just entering. He blocked the doorway, the sunlight from behind him obscuring his features. He raised one hand and pointed at her. The hair on her arms stood on end.

"Ai Ling," he hissed.

"Chen Yong," she said, in warning.

He did not rise from the chair, but his eyes were alert and dangerous.

The figure stepped from the doorway, and the lanterns in the small restaurant revealed his form. His white tongue lolled out past his chin, the ashen lips drawn back showing jagged teeth. Instead of hair, milk white strands thicker than noodles writhed on his head. It took a second for Ai Ling to realize that each strand was alive, with tiny gaping maws. A keening came from the hundreds of open mouths. Her teeth ached from it.

Night-worm fiends! Her mind quickly flew to *The Book of the Dead*.

The man dining with his friend was the only other patron facing the front entrance. He shrieked and scooted back in his chair too quickly, tipping backward in a heap.

The stocky man eating by himself rose in confusion. "Son of a cursed bitch, what's—" He never finished his sentence as the thing lurched from behind and laid a hand on his shoulder.

The man's eyes grew wide as they turned a filmy white, his black pupils disappearing. His lips drew back as jagged teeth erupted from his gums and his tongue fell from his mouth, widening and lengthening at the same time, until it licked his own chin. Worms sprouted instantaneously from his entire head, undulating and hissing as they grew to their full length.

"Ai Ling," he hissed.

The metamorphosis was complete in mere breaths. The man who had fallen on the floor whimpered and struggled to rise. His friend tried to help him to his feet.

But both creatures covered the space between them in two jerky strides, each laying a hand on one of the men. Ai Ling didn't need to see what would happen next. She jumped from her chair and saw Chen Yong do the same, with his sword drawn.

"Through the kitchen," she yelled.

She dashed through the curtained door, only to be greeted by the hissing of her name. Their servant girl. She crouched by the cutting table, blocking their way to the back entry.

249

Ai Ling cast a quick glance around and saw two others, stumbling toward them.

"Step back!" Chen Yong pushed past her and slashed the servant girl in the neck with his sword. The pale worms on her head spat with fury. But the girl did not falter, and she extended her hand toward Chen Yong.

The other two closed in on Ai Ling, hands outstretched, hissing her name.

She felt the crackle in her hair as all three demons were enveloped in a blinding light and flung against the kitchen wall. Ai Ling clutched her jade pendant, burning in her palm.

"Go!" she shouted.

She threw the back door open and jumped into the small alleyway that ran behind the restaurant. The stench of rotten cabbage filled her nose. She looked back past Chen Yong to see the three demons from the dining room stagger after them. She splashed through a puddle of rancid water and slipped, reeling backward. Chen Yong caught her and pushed her upright again, thrusting her forward.

She ran with Chen Yong at her heels, the sound of her heart and breath thundering in her ears. The alleyway was narrow and dark. She ran blind, hoping to come to the end of the passageway and an open street. A gray stone wall, a little taller than Chen Yong, blocked their path. They were trapped. She turned to find fiends shuffling toward them, all hissing her name.

"Climb the wall, I'll help you," Chen Yong said.

He lifted her, and her hands searched for a hold among the rough stones. She pulled herself up as Chen Yong boosted her by the feet from below. She perched on the top of the wall, the width of it no more than her foot. She reached down to Chen Yong. The demons swarmed around him, tongues lolling and arms outstretched.

He looked up at her with an unreadable expression. "Run," he said.

"Take my hand." She stretched toward him, and their hands clasped just as the wretched creatures fell upon him.

Ai Ling watched with horror as his amber eyes began to fade to white. His tongue emerged from his mouth, and his face distorted. She hurtled into his being with fury and felt the onslaught of the evil that flooded his spirit. She fought against it, whirling through him in a blinding rage, destroying the seeping filth of the night worms' tainted touch.

I can't lose you, was her only tangible thought. She held on to it as she fought. She saw nothing, only felt the blazing heat of her spirit as it coursed through his. Finally, sensing a balance return, she saw through him; she squatted on the wall, their fingers twined together, her face pallid and tight.

In a rage of violence not his own, Chen Yong knocked the demons to the ground. She snapped back into her own body. Gasping, the world spun, and she gripped the narrow wall with both hands. Chen Yong stood below her, head bent, looking at the bodies around him. They were themselves again, and all lay unconscious on the ground. The servant girl bled profusely from her gaping throat.

Chen Yong stooped down and leaned his ear over her face. He placed a hand on her breast and lifted an ashen face. "She's dead," he said.

His clear eyes filled her with relief, although they were dark with sorrow. They were his eyes. Did he realize what had happened? She could do nothing but shake her head—another innocent life lost because of her. She spoke a prayer under her breath.

"Let's go this way," she said. "I can see the main street from here." Her insides felt twisted, her chest heavy as she dropped down clumsily on the other side of the wall.

Chen Yong climbed over the stone wall with ease, and they returned to the main street. Her legs were shaking; she was barely able to walk.

"They were night-worm fiends," she said.

Chen Yong stopped and regarded her. "I was trying to think if I've come across them in any of my readings." He shook his head in obvious admiration. "You win."

"It's from *The Book of the Dead*," she said.

"I was never allowed to read it."

She knew most of the text by heart.

"The initial curse was set by someone powerful. I don't recall the passing of the evil through touch in my readings. That was something new."

Chen Yong stood in the crowd, the people moving past him like water against a stone. He shielded and protected her with his body.

"But you were stronger," he said. "I felt you within me fighting. I had no willpower against it. I would have been one of them within a moment's time."

So he knew.

"How did you do it?" he asked.

She looked down at her hands, smudged with grime. Tears began to well in her eyes. They were her friends. And now Li Rong was dead, and she had put Chen Yong in danger again.

Chen Yong guided her to a stone bench. They had walked into a lush open garden within one of the massive town squares without Ai Ling noticing. The ebony stone of the bench was inlaid with gold plum blossoms around its edge. She traced the curved lines with one finger. Only in the Emperor's city. Anywhere else, and the people would have scraped off the gold with their pocketknives.

"I'm thinking of Li Rong," she finally mustered through tears.

Chen Yong nodded. "I miss my brother more than I can express. It's a pain I've never known—not even—" He stopped abruptly.

Not even compared to losing your first love, she thought.

"I can't lose you too," she said.

Chen Yong turned so she could see his face. "You won't."

They sat shoulder to shoulder, watching the sunlight filter through the trees, the air scented with earth and the subtle perfume of roses.

"We can pay tribute to Li Rong when this is over," he said in a quiet voice, breaking the silence.

Ai Ling looked away, feeling her stomach clench. Chen Yong would forgive her. Once he saw Li Rong again. "We should go to the Palace," she said, too abruptly.

"But how? They won't admit just anyone. The walls are too tall to climb. No way in but through the main gate."

"There's a back gate. The one leading to the inner chambers and living quarters of the Emperor," she said.

"How do you know?"

"Father told me," she said.

"Do you know anything else about the Palace layout? Its routines?"

Ai Ling sighed. "No." She scuffed the ground with her worn shoe. "I didn't plan on sneaking in."

Chen Yong cocked his head. The color had returned to his face. She remembered the filmy white that had glazed over his eyes, and shuddered.

"I thought we'd knock . . . and ask to be let in," she said.

He threw his head back and laughed. She smiled, even though he laughed at her expense.

"I was thinking too much like a man." He grinned, then his face grew serious. "But we'd walk straight into the hands of the enemy."

Ai Ling's fingers made star shapes now, triangle after triangle on the stone bench. "I think that's what I need to do. Walk into the hands of the enemy."

"You're the leader, Ai Ling. I just try to stay alive." He smiled, but it did not touch his eyes.

"I wouldn't be alive if it weren't for you." She swallowed the knot in her throat. "I would never have come this far."

"You've returned the favor more than once."

She rose, feeling weary and drained. What wouldn't she give to be home right now with Taro curled in her lap and her mother sipping a cup of tea across from her? But being home would not make things right again.

They walked north. The midday crowd thinned as the sun grew hotter and people in the packed taverns and restaurants escaped the heat. If she thought Qing He was big, the Emperor's city must have been ten times its size, the Palace secured within its heart, nestled in the inner city of Huang Long.

They finally saw the massive moon-shaped gate of the Palace of Fragrant Dreams after what seemed like a half-day of walking. Sentries guarded either side of the gate, but their post was so high up she could not see anything except moving shadows within the observation decks. No one was down below to indicate how a person could enter.

Ai Ling scanned the wall. It stretched on for as far as she could see in both directions. "This way," she finally said, turning right and walking along the expanse of stone.

They hugged the wall of the Palace, and rounded yet another corner after a long stretch of walking. Her legs ached, and her chafed feet felt on fire.

"Perhaps we should rest at an inn. Gather our strength," Chen Yong ventured as they stared at the endless wall.

She pressed on. Something told her it was time, that lingering would not be an advantage at this point.

"I think they're waiting for us." Her scalp prickled at her own words.

"Who?"

"I don't know. But I'm drawn there, Chen Yong."

They turned another corner. She felt no fear, only a sense of resignation mingled with determination.

They finally arrived at the back entrance. The moon-shaped gate was demure compared to the main entrance, a few hand spans taller than their heads, its edges set with a thick band of carved ivory.

Ai Ling approached the gate and touched the elaborate carving. It was wider than her hand. She saw etched peonies, magnolia, jasmine, and plum blossoms. She traced one finger across a long-legged bird perched among chrysanthemums and butterflies. She recognized it as a phoenix, but it did not look like the actual red-breasted pair she had seen wandering in the Immortals' garden.

Magnificent bronze lions stood on either side of the door, perched on ebony stones. Chen Yong examined them with a cautious air. "I almost expect them to move," he said with a wry smile, reminding her of their experience approaching the gate of the Golden Palace.

"I guess I'll knock," she said.

Chen Yong moved to stand beside her, his posture relaxed, his expression confident.

"What are you thinking?" she asked, her hand poised midair.

He looked down at her with surprise. "I think we've finally made it, Ai Ling. The enemy may lie within, but perhaps our loved ones do as well."

She brought her hand against the door with a hard rap. But it barely made a sound. "No one will hear us."

The gate swung open just as she uttered the words. A girl of no more than fourteen years stood in front of them— a servant, according to the two braids coiled in circles on either side of her head. But she was dressed more elaborately than anyone Ai Ling had ever seen. Her sage green robes were embroidered with gold and silk thread designs. Pearls nestled within her ebony locks, and a delicate gold filigree circled her brow.

The handmaid inclined her head. "Please enter."

They walked together into the Palace grounds. The afternoon light gleamed off the gold tiles of the sloping roofs. They were in an intimate courtyard filled with the fragrant scent of gardenias—reminding Ai Ling instantly of her mother. Birds flitted from branch to branch. She saw a golden-haired cat leap into the tree, then heard the panicked flutter of wings.

"I have come to see Zhong Ye," Ai Ling said. Her throat tightened at speaking his name aloud.

"Master Zhong is occupied. I'll take you to a waiting place," the girl replied.

There was no choice but to follow her. They walked along a stone-paved path past the largest building in the courtyard, only to emerge into another. This one was empty but for a pond in the middle and huge bronze urns flanking all four corners. They wove from one courtyard to the next, from one garden filled with fruit trees to another filled with gilded cages containing singing birds. Ai Ling felt lost within the labyrinth of buildings, but the sense that she was being drawn in grew stronger.

She breathed deeply, and a quiet calm stilled her mind. Chen Yong walked beside her, his long strides full of power and grace. She wanted to touch his hand, to reassure him, to reassure herself.

He turned to her, and the corner of his mouth rose in the hint of a smile.

They finally stopped before a building more opulent than the rest. The paneled doors were red and gilded with golden phoenixes. Jade pillars flanked the entryway, and red lanterns in the shape of peonies were strung above, waiting to be lit at nightfall.

The handmaid climbed the three steps and gestured for

them to enter the hall with an elegant flourish of her hand. Ai Ling stepped inside, and Chen Yong followed. The girl began closing the paneled doors behind them. Ai Ling glanced back, and all calm fled as anxiety pooled like tar in her stomach.

"She merely gives us privacy." A woman spoke from within the deeper recesses of the room. Her voice was lyrical, lilting. A woman from the North.

Ai Ling walked forward, aware of the dampness under her arms. Afternoon sun filtered in from carved panels along the ceiling, lighting the space minimally.

Suddenly lanterns flared and lit the entire hall, illuminating a raised dais at one end. A woman sat on a magnificent seat, so massive her feet did not reach the floor. Yet she sat as if she belonged there, and Ai Ling believed it.

She had slender eyes in the classic, exalted shape. Delicate eyebrows stretched over them like wings. Her dainty mouth was rouged bloodred, and her skin was as pale as alabaster.

She was attired in a golden silk sheath; purple wisterias bloomed on her dress, with the symbol for longevity embroidered among the flowers in dark silver. She wore jade bracelets on her wrists, and a large, clear stone ring on one slender finger. A black headdress decorated with pearls and rubies rested against her brow; her ebony hair was parted in the middle and swept neatly away from her face.

She must be the empress. But Ai Ling did not fall on her

knees, as etiquette would dictate—restrained by a sense of suspicion and her own pride. Chen Yong stood tall beside her, and she gathered courage from him.

"I had to see you with my own eyes." The woman spoke regally, in a soft tone, making the lilt of her regional dialect sound even more exotic. Her face remained expressionless and imperial.

Ai Ling did not know what she meant.

"I am called Ai Ling. I've come to take my father, Master Wen, home."

The Empress regarded Chen Yong with a slight tilt of her head. "And you've brought your friend, I see. Jin Lian's son. How the dead come back to haunt us."

The color drained from Chen Yong's face. He stiffened. Ai Ling could almost feel his anger and confusion.

"You're not much to look at in this life, Silver Phoenix." The coy smile on her rouged lips deepened. "Too tall and lanky. Pity. You were breathtaking. Stunning."

The hairs on the back of Ai Ling's neck stood on end. Zhong Ye's jealous consort. She tried to cast her spirit toward the woman, but she slammed against a dark energy. The cord snapped back, and she fought not to double over.

"We shall take leave if you cannot help us," Ai Ling said after a moment, clenching her trembling hands. She turned only to discover a wall of armed guards behind them.

Chen Yong saw them the same moment she did, and his face hardened, one hand dropping to the hilt of his sword.

Ai Ling shook her head. There were at least fifty of them. How did they appear without so much as a sound? They wore gold helmets obscuring their faces, with only dark slits for eyes.

She turned back to the woman on the golden throne but was met with the same coy smile.

"I've tried to kill you many times. Even sent a demon to possess a man to deflower you. I know my master would never take you used." The woman rose. The golden sheath of her dress whispered, hugged her hips.

"You surprised me each time you managed to live." She glided toward Ai Ling without seeming to touch the ground, closing the long distance within two drawn breaths.

"I always knew that only I could finish the task." With one fluid motion, she dipped an elegant hand into her sleeve, withdrew a dagger, and plunged it into Ai Ling's stomach.

Ai Ling gasped, the sharp pain causing her to lean forward. She groped at the other woman's hand, held it. Ai Ling stared into her eyes and found no pupils, just infinite black pools reflecting her own pale face. She tried to delve into her spirit again, but could not summon the strength.

"Ai Ling!" She was aware of Chen Yong leaping toward her, only to be pulled back by a faceless guard.

The blade pulsed through her. She started to fall—her attacker cradled her like a loving mother. "Not so difficult to kill, after all." The woman twisted the dagger, her face lighting with pleasure.

Heat flared in Ai Ling's pendant. The woman, encased in a blinding white blaze, was lifted and flung to the back of the room. She landed with a hard thud against the throne, the dagger skidding across the stone floor.

"You pathetic little newt!" she screamed in a shrill voice. "You can't hurt me."

Ai Ling fell to her knees, and the room grew bright and bleary around the edges. Pain seared through her gut. She began to tremble, feeling both hot and cold.

"Why was I not invited to the festivities?" A rich male voice echoed through the hall.

Ai Ling saw him through a long tunnel. A lone figure in the doorway. She could see nothing but him, the smallest detail illuminated as if he were immersed in a shaft of sunlight.

He wore a deep slate robe with gold trim around the collar and sleeves. He walked to her with command and authority, and Ai Ling blinked, willing herself to stay conscious. He stood a hand width away from her. Her eyesight wavered, the elaborate gold embroidering on the edge of his robe blurring. She smelled the faint scent of spiced cologne.

"What games do you play, Gui Xin? You thought you could dispose of my true love right beneath my nose?" He looked over his shoulder at the woman who rose to her feet, apparently unhurt.

"Silver Phoenix was weak. She was no love match for you," Gui Xin said.

"Heal her." Ai Ling heard the annoyance in his voice. Her head ached from a dull ringing in her ears. She clutched at her wound, felt the sticky warmth of blood between her fingers.

"You were nothing beyond a temporary consort," he said. "You think too highly of yourself."

"I learned from the best," the woman replied in her lilting voice. "Do you truly believe I spent the last century merely pleasing you in the bedchamber? Embroidering?"

Gui Xin laughed.

Someone crouched close to Ai Ling, gently shifted her arm to place a hand across her stomach. A searing heat erupted at the touch. She gasped and felt her entire being shudder violently against the cold floor.

"Ai Ling!" Chen Yong. A clatter of steel and plate reverberated through the hall.

"Stay back, fool. He heals her," the other man said.

Ai Ling watched through tear-filled eyes as the small head bent over her stomach. The child nodded in satisfaction. He had no eyes; the sockets were filled with dark sapphire stones. She realized then that this was no child, but a person of short stature. He smiled at her, the sapphires glittering in the lantern light.

He then stood to his full height, the size of a child of five years, and strode away with such confidence one never would have guessed he could not see. Ai Ling drew another deep breath; was drained, but not in pain. She sat up, and the world spun momentarily.

"Silver Phoenix never loved you." Gui Xin glided toward them. "I can't believe you are such a romantic fool, Zhong Ye."

Ai Ling's heart lurched. She wanted to scream, run from him. She jabbed her nails into bloodied palms. He stood too near, unmoving.

"I've subjugated legions of demons, made them do my bidding. Your precious Silver Phoenix would be dead again, cast back into the underworld, if she hadn't proven to be so . . . lucky." Gui Xin paused in front of them, so close Ai Ling could see the individual gold threads of her sheath.

Zhong Ye tilted his head. "You talk too much."

Ai Ling watched as if removed from her own self. She turned to see Chen Yong, surrounded by the faceless guards. He met her gaze.

She had led him into this. She would cry now, if she had the strength.

"Perhaps I shouldn't have targeted your true love." Her melodic voice did not diminish her sarcasm. "Perhaps I should have aimed higher."

A movement from the back of the chamber caught Ai Ling's eye. The dagger Gui Xin had used to stab her rose into the air and flew like a silver streak toward Zhong Ye. Before she could grasp what was happening, the dagger erupted in a plume of dust a few feet from him.

"You surprise me, Gui Xin," Zhong Ye said. His expression and stance had never changed. "You're smarter than I thought . . . and more naive as well."

He raised a hand. Two guards strode forward and caught Gui Xin by both arms, intent on dragging her out. The same guards who had been at her bidding just moments before. But two men were not enough. She thrashed on the floor. Two other guards grasped her by each leg, and hoisted her off the ground like a sow going to slaughter.

She writhed even then, in midair. A green sheen flared around her, and the guards let go, yelping. Ai Ling smelled burned flesh.

Gui Xin stood, smoothing her hands over her sheath. "Don't be a fool, Zhong Ye. Reconsider."

A green glow still rippled about her. The guards stood at a distance, wary.

"No." Zhong Ye spoke in a quiet voice so filled with threat that Ai Ling shuddered. "Accept your fate, Gui Xin."

"Like you accept yours?" Her smile was cutting.

The green glow suddenly evaporated with a faint buzz. Gui Xin's head snapped back, and she gasped, the cords of her neck standing taut.

"Kill her," he ordered the guards.

They picked her up and she was stiff, rigid as a plank. The room spun as her rabid screaming reverberated through the hall.

"Wait." Zhong Ye raised one hand. Gui Xin had the sense to quiet herself.

"Don't burn all of her." Zhong Ye smiled coldly. "She can dwell forever with the restless spirits of the underworld."

Gui Xin gave a harsh, mirthless laugh. "I'll meet you there, Zhong Ye. You cannot live forever."

He waved the guards away, and turned from her without another glance. He kneeled down beside Ai Ling and caressed her cheek. She flinched. "My blind one healed you," he said, pulling her to her feet.

She stared into gray eyes. His hair was black, streaked with silver and plaited in a long queue. His eyebrows were so light they were nearly indistinguishable on his pale face. She willed herself to hold his gaze. And a sense of recognition sent terror ricocheting through her. Zhong Ye released her with gentle hands.

"You finally return to me." He paced across the hard floor without sound, the flaps of his ornate robe whispering with each step.

Ai Ling felt light-headed. She tried to raise her hand to touch her wound, but she couldn't move. She was frozen in place—just as Gui Xin had been. Her heart thumped harder against her chest. She took a breath, felt hysteria welling within her. She looked toward Chen Yong, who stood rigid, his arms hanging stiffly at his sides. He was bound as well. She fought the urge to scream, to sob.

Zhong Ye slipped a hand inside his tunic, drawing out a long piece of red silk. A breast binder. He raised the fabric to his nose and breathed deep. "To think you hanged

yourself with this on our wedding night, Silver Phoenix."
He fingered the delicate material. "I've waited over two centuries for you to come back to me, love."

"My name is Ai Ling."

He smiled. His brows lifted ever so slightly as he approached her, tucking the piece of fabric back into his robe. "Yes. And to think Master Wen brought you into this world. I nearly had him executed." He chuckled.

"Fate amuses me. Who knew my worst enemy would be the one to bring my love back?" He raised his hand and stroked her cheek again. She jerked her head away, wanted to step back, but she could not move.

"You're taller in this life. Not so womanly in shape. But still beautiful, if in a different way." His hand glided down to her shoulder, the palm clasping the back of her neck. His fingers massaged the roots of her hair.

She didn't realize her one braid had been freed until her hair floated around her face, settling against her neck and cascading across her chest. But Zhong Ye had not touched the ribbon that bound her hair. He had somehow loosened her braid without his hands. Ai Ling bit her lip until she tasted blood, mortified that she stood with her hair loose in front of Chen Yong and this stranger who spoke to her like a lover.

"Still beautiful indeed. And still untouched." He smiled, pale lips drawn over perfect teeth. "Yes, I can sense it. You are pure. My fruit to pluck and taste."

She spat at him. Her aim was true, and the glob of saliva hit his cheek.

Zhong Ye did not flinch. "Still feisty, too, I see." He grinned and ran one elegant forefinger across his cheek, wiping the saliva off his face, then licked the same finger with his tongue.

"And still sweet as well."

"I've come for my father," she said through gritted teeth.

"Indeed. He was the bait that lured you to me. He is safe—the guest of honor at our wedding banquet this evening."

"No," she whispered.

"If you want to see your dear father alive, you will say yes, love," Zhong Ye said.

He suddenly cast a look toward Chen Yong. "You have feelings for that mutt?" A small smile played on his mouth.

Ai Ling stared straight ahead, felt the color drain from her face. She refused to look at Chen Yong.

"Ah, but you waste your time. He has nothing to give you. He's but a shell of a man." Zhong Ye tutted his tongue. "Why waste your affections on a half-breed?" He wandered over to Chen Yong, and stood before him, considering him coldly.

Ai Ling finally looked at Chen Yong. The cords of his neck were taut, his jaws clenched tight.

"Your mother was a whore." Zhong Ye enunciated the words, and they hung heavy in the air, like a living thing. "She rutted willingly with a foreigner, one of those pale barbarians from across the sea. Spread her legs like a bitch in heat." Zhong Ye turned, walked a few steps forward.

He flicked a hand, and a faint image began to take shape beside him. It solidified into a woman, not much older than Ai Ling. She was regal, with a swanlike neck, her arms clasped before her within long silken sleeves. Her black hair was pulled to her nape and bejeweled. Her peach dress cascaded to the ground, and she seemed to float.

Her complexion was as fine as porcelain, her large black eyes filled with a sadness beyond anything Ai Ling could grasp or describe. This young woman gazed at Chen Yong, who raised his head to meet her eyes. Ai Ling saw his face crumple for an instant, then change to stone in the next.

"I made sure your mother paid for her whorish ways. Poisoned ever so slowly; she lost her sight first, then the feeling in each limb." Zhong Ye flicked his hand again, and the figure blurred, wavered like a mirage on a scorching day. He pursed his lips and took a breath, and the image of Chen Yong's mother swirled into his mouth in a fluid stream. Zhong Ye's eyes glittered with pleasure, triumph.

"It was painful. But less than what she deserved. Now her spirit is mine."

Ai Ling felt hatred for this man consume her. She did not need to cast her spirit toward Chen Yong to feel the rage within him. Their eyes met—his face did not betray his thoughts or emotions.

A line of women glided into the room, their heads bowed,

their gossamer sleeves flowing like petals on a spring breeze. Zhong Ye took a few steps toward them and nodded with a satisfied smile.

"You arrived just in time, my pet," he said over his shoulder. "The Emperor and his court are on progress at the Palace of Cerulean Sky. We are free to celebrate as the true rulers of this kingdom."

Ai Ling felt a ghostly finger trace her throat, the scent of spiced cologne filling her nose, even as Zhong Ye stood apart from her. She struggled to suppress her panic and terror, struggled to suppress her desire to lash out with her own spirit. Could Zhong Ye sense her power? Ai Ling wound herself tight, tucked it far from this monstrosity. Surprise would be her best weapon.

"I expect a splendid banquet to celebrate this wedding. Don't harm yourself this time, love. Or your father dies. And your mother. Even this half-breed mutt." He cocked his head in Chen Yong's direction. "Do we understand each other?"

She nodded, sucking on her lower lip, steadying herself with the taste of her own blood. She could not kill him now. Her opportunity would come when they were alone. She swallowed hard.

"The handmaids will prepare you. It won't be as traditional as most Xian families would like," he said, laughing, "but what it lacks in decorum will be made up for in extravagance."

A handmaid dressed in a lavender silk sheath approached Ai Ling, placing a gentle hand on her arm. To her surprise, she could move now, and the servant guided her out of the hall and into the courtyard. She turned back. But Chen Yong and Zhong Ye had disappeared like apparitions. A line of handmaids dressed exactly alike, with their plaits coiled close to the tops of their heads, followed. The silver ornaments in their tresses made clinking sounds in the dusk air.

CHAPTER SIXTEEN

The handmaid's light touch never changed as she guided Ai Ling across the vast Palace grounds. They wound their way through arched doorways, past lush gardens and dramatic courtyards empty except for giant bronze urns as tall as she was. At last she was led into a hall and quickly ushered from the public sitting room into a private bedchamber. A bed hidden behind red brocaded drapes dominated the room. The ceiling stretched high above them with bright red lanterns strung across it, suffusing everything in a festive glow—so opposite to the dark dread that threatened to smother her.

A lacquered vanity stood against one wall of the room,

the top covered with countless jars of rouge, creams, powders, and perfumes. A round mirror set in rosewood hung above the vanity. Ai Ling caught a glimpse of a large tub in the bath chamber, and the subtle scent of jasmine drifted toward her.

The handmaid led her to the bed and drew back the heavy drapes. "May we undress you, majesty?"

For the first time since encountering Zhong Ye, Ai Ling let the shock show on her face. Majesty? She was mocking her.

"Zhong Ye is not an Emperor. And I am no Empress."

The girl simply inclined.

"What's your name?" Ai Ling asked.

"I am called Zhen Ni, mistress."

Ai Ling was relieved that the girl had called her mistress. Even if that seemed odd as well, it wasn't nearly as bad as majesty.

"Zhen Ni, why does Zhong Ye act as if he's the Emperor?"

The girl raised a pale face, then quickly lowered her head again. "Master Zhong is the Emperor's most trusted adviser."

Ai Ling touched her spirit lightly.

He's worse when the Emperor is gone. Fear surged through the girl. *One mistake and I'll never win back his favor. He could kill me and the Emperor would not care. . . .*

Blinking, Ai Ling brought herself back.

"Please, mistress. If we could undress you."

Ai Ling allowed the handmaids to remove her clothes. The bloodstain remained wet on her tunic but had begun to crust against her skin. Her wound had been right above her navel, yet the skin had healed without a mark. Fully naked, she shivered as cooling air curled from the high carved windows of the bedchamber. The handmaids surrounded her like a retinue, and she was led into the steaming bath chamber.

The tub was shaped like a half-gourd and hewn of dark wood. But as she stepped in, she saw that the inside was made of gold. The metal was warm and smooth beneath her feet.

White petals swirled on top of the steaming water. Ai Ling slipped under until her chin touched the top of it. She tried to cover her nakedness, grasped her jade pendant tight, as too many hands massaged her.

Her hair was lathered with soap that smelled of spring rain, citrus, and honey. One handmaid scrubbed the soles of her feet with a rough stone. Bumps prickled her skin. She wasn't used to this. She didn't like it. Two handmaids filed her nails. It was like a dance, and she the reluctant partner.

She was relieved when Zhen Ni stretched out her hand. Ai Ling took it. The stone floor felt cold against her pruned feet. She was patted dry with plush lavender towels. Then the four women rubbed a scented cream that smelled faintly of jasmine on her body.

"The bathwater was filled with jasmine flowers, too?" Ai Ling asked.

"It's Master Zhong's favorite scent on a woman."

Ai Ling's cheeks burned.

Zhen Ni threw a luxurious gold robe over her shoulders. She ran a carved wooden comb through her hair. Ai Ling watched the deft fingers of the handmaid as she twisted her tresses into loops, pinning jeweled flowers into them. Finally she placed a gold coronet on the top of her head, with a phoenix rising from the middle, clutching a ruby in one claw and a pearl in the other.

"We dust, then dress, her," Zhen Ni said. "The makeup comes last."

The other four handmaids nodded in unison, and Zhen Ni removed the gold robe from her shoulders, revealing her naked body again.

"Please stand, mistress, to be dusted."

Ai Ling rose to her feet and raised her brows at Zhen Ni, not knowing what she meant.

"Mother-of-pearl, silver, and gold pounded into body powder, mistress. Also scented." Zhen Ni nodded, and the four handmaids, each holding a porcelain bowl, proceeded to dust her entire body using large, soft brushes. Ai Ling shivered, sickened by the cloying scent of jasmine.

She stared at herself in the mirror. Her coloring was not the pale ivory coveted by so many women, but a warm sun-kissed pink instead. Her arms and face had darkened from the days of travel; the bath had brought a glow to her cheeks. They flushed again, red hot, as she stared at her bare breasts. How much of herself would she have to sacrifice— could sacrifice—to defeat Zhong Ye? Was she even strong enough to conquer him?

She cast herself into the nearest handmaid, hoping to gather information. But the girl only thought about the end of the day, when she could return to her own quarters, away from the dangerous politics and intrigue. Another handmaid daydreamed of her lover, praying they wouldn't be found out.

When the handmaids had finished, a scented sheen covered her entire body. She unclasped her necklace and slipped it into her knapsack on the bed. She sensed it could not help her now, and she could not risk it catching Zhong Ye's attention. Her hand grazed the cold bundle that was Li Rong's heart.

Had they rifled through her belongings? Ai Ling touched Zhen Ni's spirit. The handmaid calmed herself by sweeping the floor. *My mistress must look perfect for Master Zhong. The breast binder needs to be scented. Where are the wedding slippers?* Panic swept through Zhen Ni, and Ai Ling pulled herself back quickly.

She reached for the glass vial hidden in her tunic. Her movement caught the handmaid's attention.

"What's that, mistress?"

"A good-luck charm," she said.

Zhen Ni wrung her hands. "Master Zhong would not allow it."

Ai Ling clutched the vial. "It's nothing, Zhen Ni. A trinket. I want to please him as much as you do."

The handmaid's tense shoulders dropped a fraction.

"Please make sure everything is moved to the bridal bedchamber for me," Ai Ling said.

Zhen Ni inclined her head. "Yes, mistress."

One of the handmaids retreated and returned with a red silk binder, identical to the one Zhong Ye had drawn from his tunic—the one Silver Phoenix had hung herself with. Was it the same one? What was she thinking when she had killed herself? Had Zhong Ye forced her to marry too?

Ai Ling raised both arms without being asked. Her scalp crawled as Zhen Ni bound her breasts with the fabric. She forced herself to be still, fought the urge to scream and slap the girl away. It was the custom for every virgin on her wedding night. A married woman was required to have her breasts tightly bound at all times, except within the privacy of her own bedchamber. *The Book of Making*, presented by her mother so long ago, had explained the ritual in detail.

She tried to draw a deep breath when Zhen Ni was finished, having wrapped the silken fabric around her chest with expertise. She couldn't.

"You'll adjust to it, mistress," Zhen Ni said as if reading her thoughts. "The silk is forgiving."

Zhen Ni helped her into a red silk undergarment, fastened

it around her waist with a gold braided cord. Ai Ling gasped when she saw two handmaids approaching with the wedding gown. They carried the gold-and-red gown carefully between them.

"It may not fit perfectly. But we can make quick alterations," Zhen Ni said.

Two handmaids stepped up behind Ai Ling, slipping the crimson-and-gold gown onto her bare shoulders. The weight of it surprised her, the material cool on her skin. Two golden phoenixes as well as the symbol for eternal happiness were embroidered across her chest. The handmaids moved in front of her, one standing and one kneeling, fastening with deft fingers the hidden clasps running down the center of the gown.

Ai Ling lifted one hand and saw, edged along the wide sleeves, bands of dragons with fierce expressions staring at her. After fastening every clasp, the two handmaids retreated and Zhen Ni leaned in to button the stiff collar across her shoulder. Then she stepped back.

It was as if they all waited for her approval. Ai Ling forced herself to look in the mirror. The blush that had colored her cheeks from the bath seemed muted against the expanse of gold and red that swathed her. She felt boxed in, claustrophobic from the weight of the formal gown. She stared into her own dark, slender eyes, and thought she looked too young to be dressed like this.

Wasn't this the fate of most girls?

Ai Ling inclined her head. She couldn't breathe. Despite Zhen Ni's reassurances, the binding was not at all forgiving. Slowly she nodded to Zhen Ni's reflection.

"It fits near perfectly, mistress. True, the length of the gown doesn't reach the top of your feet"—Zhen Ni bent down to tug the bottom band edged with silver symbols—"but it is hardly noticeable."

She stood again and regarded her with a pleased flush on her face.

"Now we make up your face." She put a gentle hand on Ai Ling's arm and guided her to a chair before the black lacquered table.

Ai Ling closed her eyes as Zhen Ni and another girl fluttered about her with brushes and pencils, lining her eyes and darkening her brows, rouging her lips and cheeks, dusting her entire face with scented, powdery plumes.

She ignored the urge to sneeze and instead tried to cast her spirit toward her father. Could she find him? Somehow tell him she was all right? How far could she travel from her own body? She flung the cord beyond her quarters, but it wavered and dissipated.

Chen Yong. Ai Ling pictured his face in her mind, felt her heartbeat quicken. The cord did not latch but brushed against his spirit, far away. *How . . . Ling . . . at . . . help . . .*

She jumped when a light touch grazed her shoulder, her heart lurching from the faint scent of spiced cologne. Zhong Ye. She looked around. He wasn't there. Every handmaid was busy putting away makeup and straightening the room. Zhong Ye had reached her somehow, reminded her of his power and presence. She shivered. Had he sensed her? Did he know?

She turned to face the handmaids. "Thank you. Thank you all for this," Ai Ling finally said.

She had been transformed into a woman with a few strokes of pencil and brush. Her eyes were wider now, more potent. The pale powder on her face accentuated the rouge on her lips, making them more sensuous. Seductive.

A handmaid approached her with slippers in her hand. "Your shoes, mistress." She held up the pair to Ai Ling, as if for her inspection.

The shoes were exquisite—slightly arched with a pointed toe and made of a rich crimson silk. Deep purple lotus flowers with golden leaves wound across the sides. At the center of each lotus bloom nestled a dainty emerald. Unopened buds in a pale pink blush peeped from among the blooms. The short heels were made of ivory.

"I'm not sure if they'll fit." She nodded toward her long, narrow feet.

Zhen Ni stooped down and slipped one shoe on her foot. Ai Ling winced as her toes jammed together. The handmaid struggled briefly. It fit. She did the same with the other slipper, then leaned back and smiled, obviously relieved.

"She had smaller feet. I don't believe she was as tall," the handmaid said.

"Who?" Ai Ling whispered, the hairs on her neck rising.

"Silver Phoenix, mistress. These are her wedding gown and shoes."

Ai Ling wanted to retch.

"Bring the veil," Zhen Ni said. Pearls were sewn along the hem, which helped to weigh down the gossamer red silk. She could see through the material, but her vision was shrouded in a red haze. The edge of it brushed just past her collar.

The loud bang of firecrackers from the courtyard startled her. Drums thumped and cymbals crashed outside, followed by the sound of many women in song. "The bridal sedan is here, mistress. Let us help you to your feet," Zhen Ni said.

Ai Ling felt a gentle hand on each elbow. She rose from the stool, then tottered on pinched toes. "I'm not sure if I can walk in these," she said through clenched teeth.

"We'll help you to the sedan, mistress. You'll not have to walk far."

This was true, Ai Ling thought wryly to herself. Being a new bride required much sitting, kneeling, and lying on one's back. Firecrackers popped again. The acrid smell of the smoke infiltrated the chamber as Ai Ling took slow steps forward.

They finally emerged into the open courtyard, where a red sedan with a sloping gilded roof awaited her. Men dressed in red with golden dragons embroidered on their tunics surrounded it. The entire courtyard was lit by giant red and pearl white lanterns, strung on the end of long wooden poles held by servant boys.

The singers wore sky blue gowns with sheer embroidered sleeves flowing to the ground. The air swirled with color as their arms circled in unison.

Ai Ling bit her lip as she was helped into the sedan. The taste of the berry rouge prompted her to lick her teeth. The gold bangles on her wrists tinkled as the attendants lifted the sedan and the procession made its way, she assumed, to the banquet hall. Both sides of the sedan were heavily curtained, and sounds came to her muffled.

Ai Ling wished for more time, even if it were in this stuffy dark box, with the scent of her creams and body powder overpowering her senses. She uncorked the vial and placed it to her lips.

The tiny crystal tears hit her tongue and melted into bitterness, grief, and anger in her mouth. The same feelings she felt the day they were collected—when Li Rong was slain. Her heart thudded against the breast binder. She clutched at the magnificent wedding gown and willed the attendants to move faster. To carry her with speed toward a fate she did not choose, but one she would accept in exchange for her father's life. In exchange for Chen Yong's.

She would make Zhong Ye pay. Ai Ling welcomed the grief and rage that coursed through her; hot, fresh, potent. She would kill him—or die herself.

CHAPTER SEVENTEEN

The drummers beat a slow rhythm that filled her senses until her heart, the pulse in her throat, her breathing, seemed to mimic it—be captured by it. She gripped the empty vial in her hand. The attendants slowed and halted.

The banquet master helped her onto a carpet of gold cloth that shot a path to the wedding hall. Her feet would never touch the ground. She focused on the red dragons and phoenixes embroidered on the cloth as she took one small, painful step after another.

She heard the song girls, leading the way. Their song was now accompanied by flute and strings while the drummers thumped quietly. The hall hushed when she stepped inside.

She frantically searched the crowd for her father, for Chen Yong. She twisted this way and that until the banquet master gripped her hard by the elbow, pulling her forward so abruptly that she stumbled. The crowd was ten deep, and the curious faces of strangers blurred together.

A slight breeze shifted her veil as Zhong Ye stepped forward. She smelled his cologne. Fury swelled within her. She wound it tight around her spirit, steeled herself against him. He tied a golden sash into the double same-heart knot, then bent over her, fastening the other end to her hand. The moments of silence pounded against her ears.

"The bride and groom are one. The groom may examine his bride's features," the banquet master announced.

Zhong Ye lifted the veil, and Ai Ling saw her father and Chen Yong among the guests behind him. Their faces were pale, taut with worry. Tears rushed to her eyes. He raised her chin with two fingers, causing a stir among the crowd. Forced to look up, she tucked her spirit even deeper, using her anger as a shield. Would he kiss her? Bind her with sorcery? A trickle of sweat rolled down her back.

"Proceed to the altar and pay your respects to all those who have gone before." The banquet master's warm, strong voice resonated through the long hall.

Ai Ling felt a tug at her hand as Zhong Ye walked backward to the altar, leading her by the short sash as if she were on a leash. She followed him, stumbling once, the ornate wedding gown too heavy. He helped her kneel on the ivory step before the altar and knelt down beside her.

"Bow thrice to heaven," the banquet master said.

She bowed three times, the breath crushed from her each time she bent forward in the stiff gown.

"Bow thrice to earth," the banquet master intoned. Ai Ling bowed again.

"And bow three times to your ancestors, your father and your mother." Her throat tightened. Mother did not even know her only child was about to wed. She wished that her father didn't know either.

"Rise now, and drink from one cup as husband and wife," the banquet master said.

A song girl approached with the nuptial cup—as big and deep as a noodle bowl, made of red enamel and inlaid with jewels. Ai Ling had never seen anything so elaborate, so gaudy. The song girl offered the cup to Zhong Ye, and he took it in both hands, forcing Ai Ling to stumble closer, pulled by the sash. He raised the ceremonial cup to his lips and sipped.

He offered the cup to her, and their fingers touched. Ai Ling took a deep breath, tried to steady her hand. She made sure her lips did not drink from the same place he had. The wine tasted thick and sweet, made her thirst for fresh water. The song girl took the ornate cup away. Zhong Ye reached for her knotted hand, and she clenched her teeth. His hand was as smooth as a child's and cool against her own hot skin.

"They are wed! We celebrate now at the banquet. May no one go thirsty or hungry this night, as your happiness will only augment that of the bride and groom."

The throng shouted congratulations three times in unison, the cheers thundering around the hall. Festive music and singing erupted again as Zhong Ye walked the gold-clothed path and pulled Ai Ling, tripping, behind him. Ai Ling craned her neck, desperately searching the crowd for her father and Chen Yong. But hundreds of people swarmed around her, and she could not see them.

Zhong Ye led her to a massive banquet hall. The ceiling was higher than any Ai Ling had seen in the Palace. Red-and-gold lanterns cast bright light on a banquet table that stretched the entire length of the room. It was so long she could not make out the faces at the opposite end. Guards flanked the walls, still and silent.

Just as she approached her own carved seat, she saw that her father and Chen Yong had been seated to her immediate left. She rushed toward them, but Zhong Ye held her back. Her father looked so much older; the lines near his eyes, the creases on his brow. The tall table and elaborate chair seemed to swallow him. Their eyes met, and she nearly burst into tears. He half rose to his feet, but Chen Yong restrained him with one hand.

Chen Yong's handsome face was dark with fury—so unlike him that it shocked her. Ai Ling gave a slight shake of her head. He saw and looked down. Please don't do anything foolish, she thought. Please don't.

The moment she and Zhong Ye were seated, the drums thundered to a crescendo, then ceased as servants presented each guest with the first dish of the wedding feast. Magnificent entrees presented in lacquered trays arrived one after the other. Fish, prawns, pheasant, and boar. Succulent roots, rare fruits, nuts, and tender vegetables. Ai Ling forced herself to eat. She lost count of how many dishes were brought.

Seated to her right, Zhong Ye ate with enthusiasm, washing the food down with one cup of wine followed by another. Perhaps he'd be too drunk to make a wife of her this evening. She stared at her bound hand, swallowing the bitter taste that had risen to her mouth, and listened to her groom banter with his colleagues.

The drunken din of the guests grew louder until the noise pounded within her head. She avoided looking at her father or Chen Yong, both completely silent, neither even pretending to eat. She scanned other faces; bleary, squinted eyes, mouths open for more wine, gaping with lecherous laughter. Her breaths came too quickly, and the room began to spin.

She pinched her thigh so hard her eyes teared. This was no time to faint. She needed to be strong—had to be strong. This was not the worst of it.

Before the last courses were served, Zhong Ye pulled Ai Ling to her feet. They walked down the length of the massive banquet table, receiving toasts from the guests. He spoke to them in a commanding voice, threw his head back and drank with each toast. She was silent, only pretending to sip from her wine cup. After over an hour, they finally returned to their chairs, Ai Ling tottering on numbed feet.

Finally a gong sounded, announcing the end of the wedding banquet. The banquet master rose from his seat. "The bride now leads her groom into her bedchamber!"

Ai Ling grabbed at Zhong Ye's fingers. "Not them," she said, barely audible above the noise.

He leaned closer. "What?"

"Not my father or Chen Yong."

He cupped her face in one hand, and she didn't flinch. "You've behaved so beautifully, love. Anything for you."

Zhong Ye nodded, and four guards stepped forward. "Take Master Wen and Master Li back to their quarters. Secure them."

Her father leaped to his feet. "We will go with Ai Ling!"

Chen Yong shoved the guards from her father. Airborne, he spun, fists flashing. But he was no match for Zhong Ye's guards, who surrounded him from all sides.

"Daughter!" her father shouted.

Her chest seized. She drew a shuddering breath but did not look up as they were dragged away.

She entered the bridal bedchamber backward, leading Zhong Ye by the sash. She felt the beating of many fans before she saw anything. The song girls were arranged in a semicircle, fanning the bed with graceful movements, as if in dance.

The gold brocaded curtains were drawn, the wide bed covered with cushions in satins and silks of deep plum and red, emerald green and sky blue. Crimson sheets embroidered with the dragon and phoenix motif were draped across the bed. The edges of the coverlet were sewn with the character for eternal happiness, woven between peaches, lotus, and pearls—all symbols of happiness or fertility.

The banquet master untied the same-heart sash. "Your heart is one," he said, bowing.

The song girls parted. Zhong Ye offered a hand, which Ai Ling did not refuse, and helped her climb the carved steps into the massive bed. She knelt down, facing away from the door of the bedchamber and the crowd that had followed them in.

"The husband unbinds his wife's hair out of love and service," the banquet master chanted.

"He'll unbind more than that tonight!" someone shouted, and everyone burst into rowdy laughter.

She closed her eyes.

Zhong Ye kneeled behind her. He pulled the first pin from her hair. Then another. Her locks began to unfurl across her shoulders. She kept her head bowed. Her cheeks burned. This was just the beginning. Her mind wandered to what she could remember of wedding rituals—all she had read in *The Book of Making*.

Zhong Ye's fingers brushed against the nape of her neck, sending shivers down her spine. She steadied herself. Don't react. Don't give them the satisfaction. The song girls cast red and white flower petals on the bed; the banquet master threw grain. Her hair was entirely loose.

"Make her a woman tonight, Master Zhong!" The crowd cheered and laughed, whistled loudly and stomped their feet.

"May she be soft and pliable! She certainly looks it!"

Zhong Ye turned her around to face the crowd. She navigated across the bed on her knees. Her fury blazed, and she feared what she would say if she saw their faces . . . what she would do. She too had a role to play, for now.

The noise grew until Zhong Ye raised a hand. The hush that followed was immediate. "Thank you for joining us in this celebration, esteemed friends and family. . . ."

What family could he possibly have? He was an ancestor, ancient.

"I ask now to be alone with my bride," Zhong Ye said.

The whistles and foot stomping began again. The crowd was in a frenzy. But the last of the ritual words had been spoken by the new groom, and the inebriated well-wishers retreated quickly, knowing there was more food and drink waiting for them in the banquet hall.

Six guards stayed behind, standing at attention. Zhong Ye waved a manicured hand. "Leave us. I hardly need your protection tonight."

Zhong Ye was beside her, his long hands resting on his thighs. She did not move. He finally rose and inclined onto the thick cushions of the bed, resting casually on one elbow.

"We're alone at last, love. I've waited for this night for so long. Too long." He reached for her hand, brushed her fingers with his. His skin was smooth, flawless.

"I know how you're feeling. But you will grow to love me, Ai Ling. Just as Silver Phoenix did."

She blanched. Silver Phoenix could never have loved him.

He wanted her to meet his gaze. She refused, and he sighed.

"I became a eunuch when I was twenty years . . . centuries ago. Most were forced, sold, or bought. But I chose my path."

Ai Ling swallowed hard. He wasn't whole. A thin thread of hope wound through her.

He continued to stroke her fingers. His gaze was tangible; it touched her brow and traced her cheekbone and jaw, fluttered against her lips. He was attempting some sort of sorcery. The white rage within her crackled, expanded, grew taut again. She remained still.

"You're more strong-willed than I realized, my pet. I shouldn't be surprised." He sounded amused. Perhaps even pleased. "You're my match indeed. We'll rule together through all the dynasties. We'll always be here. Our love will last forever."

He released her hand. Repulsed, she clutched them together. He was delusional—a madman.

"Come now, don't play games. Look at me. Let me see the lovely face of my new bride." She finally met his gaze with a defiant tilt of her head.

"Fiery eyes, just as I remembered them. You may have a different face, a different body, but yes, I do remember the spirit behind those eyes."

He must have been handsome in his youth. His true youth. His strong cheekbones lent boldness to his face. But he lacked color now. His lips were wide, drawn thin. Whomever he may have been when he was born—that person no longer existed—was long gone. He climbed off the bed and moved to a low chest in the corner.

"Would you like some wine?" He poured himself a cup. She shook her head.

"Please stop kneeling at least, Ai Ling. I grow tired just looking at you." He made his way to one of two wood-carved chairs in the room and sat down, stretching his long legs before him. "I'll enjoy my wine here. You have the bed all to yourself." He laughed.

Ai Ling did not argue. She stretched out her legs as well. Both feet were asleep and tingled painfully. She sank back into the pillows, bone weary.

She lost herself in the bright lanterns strung across the ceiling as she waited for his next move. Her mind kept returning to the drawings in *The Book of Making*. Not all of them involved . . . Her neck grew hot, and she wrenched her thoughts away.

If the man chose to talk, she would listen and rest—gather her strength and energy. It was not yet the right time to touch his spirit. He was too strong. She needed to distract him.

Zhong Ye poured himself a second cup of wine and downed it. "I remember the day so clearly. Not the pain, the pain is just a distant memory. But how does a man ever forget the moment his manhood is taken from him?" Zhong Ye rose and began pacing the room, making Ai Ling think of a caged creature, lithe and restless.

"I swore in writing and by word that I gave myself to the Emperor of my own volition." He poured a third cup of wine, drank it in gulps. His pale face began to color. The more wine, the better, she thought.

"After all the paperwork, the talk, they took me into the back room to perform the ritual." He stood by the side of the bed now, looking down on her. She felt exposed, regretted lying down, but met his gaze without wavering. Ai Ling did not want to hear his story. What would he try next?

Zhong Ye sat down on the edge of the bed. "They tied me down with leather straps. My arms. My legs. And gave me another piece of leather to bite down on."

She heard a distant roar from the banquet hall. It surprised her. The crowd was celebrating still, probably more drunk than ever. Father. Chen Yong. O, Goddess of Mercy, let them be safe.

"They washed me with hot pepper water, to help numb the pain. But I think that was a ruse. The pain from that merely made the agony from the actual act seem less so."

Music now, muted singing and drumbeats from afar.

"The remover gripped me in one hand. All of it. And I watched him raise the curved knife, cut everything away in one motion." Zhong Ye stared into his wine cup.

"Why are you telling me this? Do you expect my sympathy?" Ai Ling spoke softly, controlling her voice. She did not show fear or anger—refused to show anything to him.

"I tell you, beloved wife, to demonstrate how far I will go to gain power. I risked everything to enter the Palace, worked my way up from latrine boy and kitchen sweeper to the Emperor's most trusted confidant. Every Emperor's trusted confidant. I have guided dynasties for enough centuries that the people do not even know me as a eunuch—do not realize what I sacrificed. . . ." He spoke in a quiet voice, too. Ai Ling tilted her face away, studied the carvings on the bedpost instead. Two golden cranes wound themselves among the blooming lotus flowers and buds.

"But power wasn't enough for you. You had to go further than that." She met his eyes now, and they widened in surprise.

"What do you know about any of it?" The tone of his voice changed, from honeyed warmth to hard-edged flint.

"What do I need to know? You've lived centuries. You say I'll rule with you for more to come." Her eyes burned from tiredness, from wanting to close and sleep for days. But did they betray all that she tried to contain within herself at this moment?

Rage.

Vengeance.

"Is it so strange that a man who has seized power should choose to keep it?" he asked.

"It's wrong to live beyond the life that was given you." Something within her spirit shifted. Ai Ling blinked, as if she heard the words she spoke from another's mouth. Had she said these words to him before . . . in another life?

He gripped her chin so fast her breath caught. "I won't argue about this with you again. And I won't lose you either."

Again? She twisted her face away.

"You don't believe Silver Phoenix loved me." He traced her lower lip with a finger. When he pulled his hand back, she saw a smudge of red on his fingertip. "You don't remember."

He removed her shoes, and the heat rose to her face when he touched her feet. "Would I wait over two centuries for you if she had not? When I can have anyone I choose?" He stroked her instep.

She refused to believe his lies.

"Don't worry, Ai Ling. My manhood may be sitting in a jar, but I can still satisfy you in every way." His hand slipped beneath the heavy wedding gown, stroking her calf. "I've gained considerable power in the dark arts and will be whole for you tonight."

The heat that had blazed across her cheeks spread to her neck, down her chest. Terror seized her limbs, and Ai Ling clenched every muscle so she would not tremble. Of course he would consummate the marriage. Zhong Ye kissed her brow, her closed lids. She wished he were less gentle, less loving in his manner. It would make it easier for her. And quicker.

His mouth covered hers, and even though she had expected this, her back still arched from shock, and a small gasp rose from her, smothered by his kiss. He broke away and pulled her to her knees to face him.

Slowly, with great care and patience, Zhong Ye began to undo the hidden clasps of the wedding gown. His fingers were swift, and he was pushing the gown off her shoulders within heartbeats.

He stroked her bare arms and shoulders with both hands, ran his fingers along her collarbone. Her flesh pimpled at his touch. Ai Ling willed herself to stay still. He bent over again to kiss her, longer now, more deeply. She tasted the wine he had drunk as his arms encircled her and began to unravel her breast binder.

Her heart raced, but she was pliant beneath his hands and mouth. She coiled her spirit tighter—not yet; wait, wait. The red silk fell like shuddering wings to the bed. Zhong Ye drew back to take her in with those pale gray eyes, hungry now, bright with a heat she did not want to recognize.

He began to work the clasps of his own tunic. "Help me," he said in a thick voice. She obeyed, bringing stiff fingers to the gold brocade, unclasping one hook while he undid three. He drew off the tunic, revealing a pale and toned form. Completely naked. It was not what she had expected so soon. The shock must have registered on her face as Zhong Ye smiled, amused.

"I can't be that terrible, my wife. But if it pleases you, I can take on the form of anyone I choose." His body blurred around the edges, wavered for moments—then Chen Yong kneeled before her, naked.

It was so convincing, her heart leaped. Longing and terror catapulted through her. She wanted to slap him, shove him away. Ai Ling fought not to collapse in surrender, fought for control. She looked up. His eyes stayed a pale gray. He smiled at her, and there was a glint in them, a cutting twist to the lips that she'd never seen on Chen Yong.

Ai Ling turned her head.

"I knew you'd prefer your husband to that mutt," Zhong Ye whispered into her ear, his breath warm on her neck.

He was himself again, his silver-streaked head bent and pressed to her chest. She bit her lip when she felt his tongue on her breast. She fisted her hands, forced herself not to scream.

His hands were on her bare hips now, worked their way down until they cupped her buttocks. He pulled her closer to him, kissing her midsection, licking her navel. She wanted to cry, tear the hair from his head. Instead she reached down for his face.

Zhong Ye looked up, desire suffusing his pallid features.

"Kiss me," she said.

He smiled and rose to his knees. Ai Ling wound her arms around his neck, clasped her hands at the nape of it. She opened herself up to him, opened herself up entirely. She kissed him deeply and released all the light that burned within her, letting it flow in a blinding rush into him.

He twitched slightly as their spirits met. She did not attempt to take control, but continued to fill him with her own unleashed being. She felt her lips through his, and his through her own.

All at once, it was as if hundreds of beings kissed her—all the souls Zhong Ye had stolen to keep himself alive. She heard a low moan, more within his mind than from his lips, which pressed on her mouth like hot coals. Sensing his distraction, the spirits worked as one to break free from their prison.

She folded her spirit over Zhong Ye's.

He felt their frenzy, was suddenly aware of her presence. His mind roared in fury, with abrupt understanding. He tried to pull away, both body and spirit. She pressed herself to his bare chest, wrapped her arms about him more firmly, deepened her kiss. His mouth was slack now, his lips brittle and cold. He struggled for control, struggled to harness the souls clamoring against him. But he was powerless, his spirit bound within hers.

His body began to convulse, and a deep-throated scream reverberated inside him, between them. He tried to push her off, but he was too weak, trembling in her arms. He began to slip, his bare back slick with sweat, yet she clung to him. A white heat radiated from him until a blazing light filled the room, blinding even beneath her closed lids.

For a mere breath, the world hung motionless between them. Then she heard Zhong Ye speak in his own mind. *Why?*

"Because I loved you," Ai Ling replied, in a voice not her own.

She felt herself lifted into the air from the force of hundreds of spirits passing. They slashed across her bare flesh in a thunderous roar before she fell back onto the bed.

Small lights danced across her vision, and the room came back to her in a slow blur. Zhong Ye was sprawled beneath her, emaciated, barely human, unrecognizable. She twisted away from him, her hand pressed to her mouth. His sunken eyes were open, staring up at the red-and-gold wedding lanterns. But no life flickered within them.

A soft sob fell from her bruised lips. She tottered and reeled before darkness smothered her consciousness.

CHAPTER EIGHTEEN

Ai Ling dreamed of Li Rong. They sat in the gardens of the Golden Palace, by the banks of the Scarlet River. He showed her a coin trick, and she laughed. The gold coin then turned into an emerald duck and waddled into the shallow water. She clapped her hands with enthusiasm. "Do another!"

"But I need my heart back," he replied.

A gaping hole bloomed across his chest. Ai Ling shivered in the sunlight.

"Without it, I cannot be reincarnated." There was the same mischievous glint in his dark eyes, the same smile on the corners of his mouth. She ached to see him again. Of course he was right; she had been led so far astray. By her own pride, her stubbornness—her anger against the gods.

"Besides, you always had my heart. I just never had yours." Li Rong extended his hand and she reached out her own, sobbing and laughing at the same time.

"I know, it's an awful jest, even for me," he said, his fingers brushing hers like a kiss.

Ai Ling woke with a start, her throat parched, the salt of tears on her lips. She turned her head. Zhong Ye's skeletal hand grazed her cheek, and she jerked away, choking back a cry. She felt no triumph. Her teeth clacked violently, and she hugged a cushion to her nakedness. Were Father and Chen Yong all right? She tore her eyes away from the corpse to glance up at the lattice panels. The sun had not yet risen.

She stepped from the bed, bent, like an old woman. She took several deep breaths, her hands pressed against her trembling thighs, before she was able to straighten. She searched the bedchamber and found her knapsack in the red wedding cabinet. Zhen Ni had not failed her.

She pulled on a pale green tunic and trousers, then retrieved the cloth bundle containing Li Rong's heart, still ice cold to the touch. She placed it with care on the bed. Ai Ling reached for a lantern and poured the lamp oil on the coverlet, lowered the burning wick to its braided edge.

"Forgive me, Li Rong. I only wanted to make things right."

She murmured a prayer to the Goddess. The material caught fire, fed on the silks and satins of the bed.

She stumbled backward, clutching her knapsack. The fire's heat burned her throat, seared her skin. She turned and ran. Her last glimpse was of the golden drapes of the bed bursting into flames.

The night air revived her. The courtyard was empty. She sat underneath a plum tree, pulled her knees to her chest, and watched as the fire grew. The blaze from within the bedchamber cast menacing shadows through the high lattice windows.

It was Zhen Ni who discovered her, teeth clattering, despite the heat from the inferno. "Mistress!" The alarm in the handmaid's voice was clear.

Ai Ling rose to her feet, only just realizing they were cold and bare. "Bring my father, Master Wen, to me. And Chen Yong." It was a command, as regal as any empress could make.

Uncertainty flickered across the girl's delicate features. Ai Ling lifted her chin. "Master Zhong is dead. You need not fear him." Zhen Ni's mouth grew as round as a goose egg. She half bowed before rushing out of the courtyard.

Several eunuchs charged in from another entrance, shouting over one another. Huge urns of water were wheeled by servants who suddenly swarmed the courtyard. Alarm bells clanged. More eunuchs emerged, pushing water-filled vats, the wooden wheels thudding against the cobblestones.

As if in response to their pleas to heaven, a light rain began to fall. At first, it only misted her cheeks, until it pattered, plastering Ai Ling's hair onto her neck. The handmaids who had scurried into the courtyard when the alarm sounded fell to their knees in supplication. Heavy rain doused the raging flames, aided by the eunuchs throwing pails of water.

Ai Ling crouched beneath the plum tree, rocking back and forth, the acrid smell of smoke and rain filling her senses. She felt a light touch on her back—Father. Chen Yong stood a short distance behind him. She rose and collapsed into her father's arms, sobbing onto his shoulder as he smoothed her damp hair, unbound for her wedding night.

"Come. Let's take refuge from the rain," her father said.

Zhen Ni had stayed close, and Ai Ling asked, "Can you show us to empty quarters?"

"I can take you to where we prepared you for the wedding . . . only"—Zhen Ni bowed her head lower—"men are not allowed there, mistress."

Ai Ling could not suppress a wry smile. "I hardly think decorum matters now. Please lead the way."

The handmaid turned, and they followed her. Her father walked with his hand clasped protectively around her shoulder, and Ai Ling leaned into his thin frame. Chen Yong strode on her other side. She couldn't look at him. How could she ever speak to him again?

They followed Zhen Ni's bright lantern in silence. When they reached the steps of the bridal dressing quarters, Chen

Yong touched her arm with a light hand. Ai Ling glanced up in surprise.

"I'm so glad you're all right," he said.

More tears gathered in her eyes, and she was grateful for the rain.

"Me too." It wasn't what she meant to say, but it didn't matter.

The handmaid led them into the darkness of the dressing chamber. She began lighting the lanterns on the tables and in the corners of the room.

"Can you bring food and tea?" Chen Yong asked.

The handmaid retreated. Ai Ling shivered in her wet tunic, which clung to her skin like rice paste. Her entire being felt numb, from each fingertip to her fogged mind, which turned with random thoughts and images.

"You should change." Her father crouched beside her, concern etched in every line of his face.

"I have no more clean travel clothes."

Chen Yong handed her the luxurious robe she had worn after her bath so long ago. "This will keep you warm." He carried a small peony-etched lantern into the bath chamber. "You can change in here."

Ai Ling smiled, even though her face felt too numb to do so. Chen Yong, ever chivalrous. "What about dry clothes for you? And Father?"

"Do not worry for us, Ai Ling." Father stroked her damp hair. "I must take leave now to find Master Cao. He was an old friend and remains adviser to the Emperor. He may be able to help us." He turned to Chen Yong and clasped his shoulder. "Can you keep my daughter safe?"

"I'll stay with her," Chen Yong said.

Ai Ling emerged from the bath chamber after combing her wet hair and braiding it. The plush robe warmed her, and she pulled it tighter. Chen Yong sat at the enameled table, a tray laden with small dishes of food and a large pot of tea before him. A grin spread across her face.

"That's what I hoped to see," Chen Yong said. He poured tea into two celadon cups.

She slid onto the stool across from him and examined the tray's offerings: a small bowl of thick beef stew with white radish and carrots, sticky rice and chicken wrapped in lotus leaves, young bamboo shoots with mushroom and tender greens cooked with sliced garlic. Ai Ling breathed in the delicious aroma wafting from the dishes. She took a sip of hot tea, delighting in the warmth that wound from her throat to her core.

"Thank you, but I'm not sure I have the appetite. . . ."

Chen Yong raised a hand to stop her. "Eat a little, you need the strength. I'll worry if you refuse good food laid in front of you!"

Ai Ling smiled and picked up her eating sticks. "Only if you eat with me."

"Agreed."

They ate in silence. She sneaked glances at Chen Yong from under lowered lashes. He appeared puzzled, his dark brows drawn together.

"Were you treated well?" she finally asked.

He poured more tea for her. "I was housed in very opulent quarters and locked in." He clenched his fist. "Zhong Ye threatened to kill you if I tried to escape, tried to aid you. I'm so sorry, Ai Ling."

"It's not your fault. It didn't happen like I thought it would." She prodded at her food with the eating sticks. "I don't know what I expected."

He too had stopped eating and straightened his back. "I know what happened to my mother now."

She saw again in her mind the beautiful woman with the haunting eyes.

"What was it like?" he asked, after a moment of silence.

Ai Ling averted her face, feigned interest in selecting more morsels for her plate.

"I thought I heard her speak through me," she said in a quiet voice.

"Who?"

"Silver Phoenix." She rubbed her brow. "I wish I knew her story—her whole story."

"It's enough for me to know yours." Chen Yong smiled.

She was suddenly limp with exhaustion.

"It's a few hours before morning. You should sleep," he said.

"And what will you do?"

"I'll stay by your side."

Ai Ling rose and climbed into the sumptuous bed. She burrowed under the thick blanket. Chen Yong would keep watch over her. She gave herself to slumber before another thought could form.

Ai Ling awoke to find sunshine filtering through the lattice windows. Chen Yong sat on a chair beside the bed, his head bent over a well-worn book bound in dark leather.

"What're you reading?" she asked, her voice rasping.

Chen Yong glanced up. "You're awake." He grinned, despite looking weary. "It's a philosophical text by Long Kuei."

"Oh." Ai Ling stretched. "Did you sleep?"

"No. Your father came a short while ago to say Master Cao has arranged carriages for our journey home." He nodded toward the foot of the bed. "And Zhen Ni brought you fresh clothes to change into."

Ai Ling climbed with reluctance from the bed and examined the clothes. A simple tunic and trousers, made of lavender silk with pearl buttons. Her hand reached for her jade pendant from habit, but grasped nothing.

"My necklace," she said.

"Did you lose it?"

She searched through her knapsack and found her necklace. Ai Ling cradled the pendant in her palm—the jade had clouded over, an opaque white.

"Can you help me put it on?" she asked.

She bowed her head and Chen Yong stood behind her, fumbling a little with the delicate gold clasp. The heat rose to her face when his fingers brushed against her nape.

"Thank you," she murmured, without turning to him. Ai Ling picked up the new tunic and trousers but paused before entering the bath chamber.

"Chen Yong, I'm grateful you stayed with me."

"I promised I would until the end, didn't I?" He winked at her and smiled. She knew he was one to keep his promises.

They took their morning meal in the reception hall outside the dressing chamber. Then her father led them to the outer courtyard, near the gate through which they had entered the Palace. A tall man dressed in a deep blue scholar robe greeted them—Master Cao.

"I've arranged royal carriages for your passage home," Master Cao said. "A courier has been sent to the Emperor, giving news of Master Zhong's passing. Of natural causes on his wedding night." He laced his long fingers together and turned to Ai Ling. "Quite sad, indeed. The grieving bride has been sent home to her family."

Her father clasped his old colleague's hand in both of his. "We can't thank you enough."

Master Cao shook his head. "The entire kingdom is in great debt to your daughter, old friend. Zhong Ye outlasted dynasties, he could not be destroyed. Those who have tried were executed . . . or murdered." The adviser dropped to his knees and bowed before Ai Ling.

Astounded, she reached down to the older man and touched his shoulder. "Please, sir, rise. I only did what I had to."

Master Cao rose. "Know you did more than that. We'll always be here to serve you, Mistress Wen."

Not knowing what more to say, Ai Ling bowed and walked to the carriage that had drawn up outside, just beyond the moon gate. She climbed in and sat down. As she waited for her father, another carriage pulled up, and she suddenly understood. Chen Yong would be taking his own journey home.

He approached her carriage as if summoned by her thoughts. "It's strange to say farewell."

"You return home now?" She looked down at her clasped hands, tried to speak in a steady voice. "Why not stay at ours for one night? It's on the way."

Chen Yong shook his head, the morning sun bright behind him. Dark shadows marked the curves beneath his eyes, making his cheekbones more prominent. He was leaner than when she had first met him. Their journey together seemed to have chiseled his features, sharpened the last remnants of youth. "I need to tell my family about Li Rong." He spoke softly, his voice raw.

Li Rong.

"I'm so sorry," she said.

These words finally brought the tears she had tried so hard to hold back, and she raised her face. "Will I see you again?" She gripped the open window of the carriage, fought the urge to reach for his hand.

He drew a step closer. "Yes, you will."

She wanted to believe him. Chen Yong moved away from the carriage as her father climbed inside, and Ai Ling leaned back. He always kept his promises, she reminded herself, as their carriage rumbled away.

CHAPTER NINETEEN

After days of constant travel, Ai Ling and her father finally pulled through the gates of their small town of Ahn Nan. There were tears in her father's eyes as he hugged her mother fiercely.

Her mother swept Ai Ling into her arms. "I'm so thankful you are both home."

Ai Ling let herself sink into her embrace. Mother, who had always appeared so strong to Ai Ling, felt frail.

Her mother waved them into the main hall. "I was worried to the bone about you. You're as pigheaded as your father in so many ways."

Her father laughed loudly—which brought youth back

to his lined face. Her mother smiled, her body leaning toward his.

"I couldn't marry Master Huang, Mother. And I couldn't put you in the position to choose, either. I knew you wouldn't let me go alone."

Her father's laughter ended abruptly. "Ai Ling told me he came and threatened you."

"Yes. He wanted Ai Ling as a fourth wife to pay for the debt you owed," her mother said.

Father slammed a closed fist into an open palm, anger coloring his face. "It was a lie."

Her mother nodded, still as elegant as ever. "We knew. But there was no way for us to contest him. He brought the contract with your seal on it." Her mother caressed Ai Ling's face, her fingers felt rough against her cheek. "I was worried senseless, but I know you. I don't fault you."

Ai Ling grabbed her hand and kissed it. "I'm so sorry, Mother."

"Don't be. You brought your father back. And Master Huang didn't bother me again. He died soon after you left." Her mother's voice lowered. "They think he was murdered."

The Life Seeker. Ai Ling recalled the entrancing song of the woman in Lao Song's restaurant, that first day away from home, so long ago. She knew she should feel pity or remorse for Master Huang's passing. But she did not.

They sat down, and Ah Jiao brought in a tray of teacups for everyone. Ai Ling gasped in surprise and jumped to her feet to hug the servant. Her mother laughed with pleasure. "She returned without pay when she found out you had left."

"You'll be paid triple that for your devotion and loyalty, Ah Jiao," Ai Ling's father said.

Ah Jiao's broad face colored, and she wrung her hands. "It's so good to have you and Mistress Wen back, master."

Ai Ling yelped as a gray blur streaked into the room, winding itself around her ankle.

"Taro!" She swept the purring cat into her lap, her heart filling with a bittersweet joy, unable to believe she was home at last.

Five long weeks passed before Ai Ling received a letter from Chen Yong. She had refrained from writing herself, unsure of what she would say, afraid of all she wanted to say. The Li family was in mourning for the loss of Li Rong, but he would visit soon. Her father had promised to tell Chen Yong the story of his birth. Surprised, Ai Ling asked her father. But he refused to divulge anything, saying she would learn the story at the same time Chen Yong did.

Ai Ling read Chen Yong's letter each day until she knew it by heart, the curves and lines of his calligraphy, the parchment folded and unfolded so many times it wore and softened beneath her fingers.

On the promised day, Chen Yong arrived at the Wen manor in the early afternoon. Ai Ling ran to the door before the house servants could respond, stopping abruptly to slow her breath. She ran her hands over her green tunic, the color of new grass, embroidered with cherry blossoms, before pulling the heavy door open.

Chen Yong stood with his hands clasped behind his back. He was dressed in elegant clothing, a formal robe in dark blue with silver embroidering and matching trousers. His face was clean shaven, his amber eyes clear. He seemed taller, his frame filling their doorway.

He smiled, the lines of his cheeks turned boyish, and Ai Ling resisted the urge to throw her arms around him. Instead she reached out her hand and he clasped it, his skin feeling warm and rough all at once against her damp palm.

"How was your journey?" she asked, her voice squeaking before she cleared her throat.

"Much easier than the last." He released her hand too soon. "I had the luxury of a carriage this time. My father insisted."

They stared at each other until Chen Yong grinned. "May I come in?"

She pulled the door open, blushing. "Mother and Father are waiting for you in the main hall." They walked through the courtyard side by side, the autumn flowers in full bloom against the walls and within the stone urns, offering bursts of orange, gold, and red.

"Who cultivates the flowers?" Chen Yong asked, studying them with admiration.

"I do." She could not refrain from smiling with pride. "It's a task Mother passed on to me. Our courtyard is small, but I find peace here. I paint here often."

"I can see why."

She entered the main hall to find her mother and father standing beside the round tea table. Chen Yong made an informal bow. "Thank you for inviting me to your home, Master Wen, Lady Wen."

Her mother stepped around the table to draw Chen Yong into an embrace. "I had hoped my husband would find you one day, to tell you your story."

Two bright spots colored his cheekbones. Ai Ling sat down on one of the lacquered stools in an attempt to hide her astonishment. Her mother already knew Chen Yong's history; that much was obvious. Why did no one ever tell her anything?

Their late midday meal consisted of fresh steamed fish—a luxury that was only served during New Year's, usually— along with deep-fried squash from the garden coated in a rice-paste batter. Ah Jiao served small savory dishes of pickles and salted meats, along with a large crock of rice porridge simmered with sweet yams.

The conversation between them was lighthearted and easy, much to Ai Ling's relief. After the meal, her father retired to his study, asking them to join him as soon as Chen Yong felt ready.

Ai Ling led Chen Yong to his bedchamber, a room they

used for sewing. Overnight guests were a rarity in their household. He placed his knapsack on the low bed while she eased the lattice panels open to bring in the crisp autumn air.

"Would you like to rest awhile?" she asked.

He did not appear at all travel worn and seemed even more alert after the meal. Ai Ling felt the heaviness of her limbs and could have done with a nap herself.

"No, thank you. I'd like to see your father, if it's not too soon?"

"He's anticipated this meeting for weeks," she said. They walked through the courtyard again, weaving between the potted chrysanthemums, gold leaves crunching beneath their footsteps. She veered onto a narrow pathway by the side of the house, and Chen Yong followed a step behind.

"I see why you found it hard to leave your family. It's obvious you are close to your parents."

"We aren't traditional by any means. I'm an only child; my father did not take on any other wives." One of the gnarled branches of the wisteria plant climbing up the manor wall caught her hair, and she jumped, startled.

"But your parents are content with each other. They love each other," Chen Yong said, freeing the twig from her braid.

Flustered, Ai Ling's hand flew to her hair. She half turned to find his gaze on her. "Yes, they do. They married for love."

"I believe my parents love each other too—they grew to

love each other. Their marriage was arranged before they turned three years."

Joy filled her, to have him here, in her home. Safe. "That's fortunate. I would not want a marriage without love," she replied.

Chen Yong nodded, looked away.

They arrived at her father's study, which had its own private garden and entrance. It was Ai Ling's favorite part of the house, and she went there often, even when her father was not there.

They passed through the round moon gate and entered an intimate courtyard. Silver fish darted in a deep, clear pool. Two pine trees provided shade, and large rocks were arranged for casual seating and contemplation.

"How unexpected," Chen Yong said, glancing around the small garden.

Ai Ling breathed in the pungent tang of pine. "Come, Father is waiting for us."

It was not a big study; the room was bright and cozy. A long rectangular desk was set beneath the paneled windows, allowing whoever sat there a view of the tranquil garden. Two walls were lined with books from floor to ceiling. The last wall had a low ancestor altar set against it. Her father had just lit new incense, and the subtle scent of sandalwood curled through the air.

Her father turned his wooden chair and smiled at his visitors. "Bring the stools. I'm afraid I don't have anything more comfortable here." Chen Yong pulled two wooden stools from under the large desk.

"Chen Yong, it's so hard for me to believe you're the same infant I smuggled out of Palace grounds." Her father poured tea and offered a cup to each of them.

Ai Ling stared wide-eyed from Chen Yong to her father.

"How strange the fates of human lives," her father said. "I feel you were destined to journey with my daughter to the Palace, so we could find each other again."

"Master Wen, what do you remember about my mother . . . about that night?" Chen Yong's eyes gleamed with emotion. Now it was her father who held the key to his past. Father took a sip from his wine cup and leaned back against his chair before beginning his story.

THE sharp rap at the door startled me. I was unsure I even heard it, but there was no mistaking the three taps that followed after the pause. It was the signal. I never slept in a dark room in those days. I never truly slept during my last two years at the Palace. To be one of the Emperor's most trusted advisers came at a price. Zhong Ye and I did not look square in the eyes. He despised me.

I pulled on a robe, hurried to the secret panel, and pressed the concealed button, a pearl clutched in the claws of a lion. The door opened. I hardly knew what to expect. Surely, Jin Lian would not come in person. Jin Lian was your mother's name.

The pale face of her handmaid peered up at me. She held the lantern at shoulder level, in front of her, like a weapon. "My mistress said to come quickly." Her voice trembled when she spoke.

My heart leaped in my throat. Had something gone wrong? I could only nod and follow her. I made sure to close the hidden panel behind me.

I knew my way to Jin Lian's room but was impressed by the young handmaid's assured steps back to the bedchamber. The passageway had many turns and could be confusing at the best of times. Of course, it was never used during the best of times.

Those corridors were constructed by the order of an Empress long gone. She was convinced everyone plotted against her, and she used the passageways to spy and scheme with her cohorts.

When we arrived outside your mother's bedchamber, the girl drew aside so I could stand close to the door and listen with one ear. There was no noise, and then I heard the small cry of a baby. I can't tell you how my pulse raced. I rapped on the door thrice, paused, and knocked once more.

The panel opened.

Jin Lian greeted me. Her face was swollen from crying, her nose rubbed raw. She held an infant in her arms. I knew right then you were Master Wai's child.

I did not ask, and your mother didn't need to explain. I had suspected the romance took place even as Zhong Ye plotted to ingratiate your mother with the Emperor—hoping to use her as another puppet to augment his influence and control.

The punishment would be death for everyone involved. I surveyed the room and saw the old midwife standing in the corner, looking calm and resolute. Impressive.

Your mother spoke in a quiet voice, her gaze never leaving your face. No one expected the babe so soon, not for four weeks yet, she said. She looked at me then. The tears coursed down her cheeks. She was even more beautiful than when she was dressed in her regal concubine clothing.

Her tears seemed to agitate you, as if a cord still connected your thoughts and feelings as one. She rocked you, could not stop brushing her lips against your brow and cheeks.

I asked for rice wine.

The handmaid returned within moments, bearing a cup and decanter on a lacquered tray. I gestured to the small round table, and she placed the tray on it. "It's to help the baby sleep," I explained. "It's a boy," she told me, and hugged you closer to her.

The old midwife approached me with a tiny gold spoon. I poured the wine and dipped the spoon into the cup.

Jin Lian coaxed you into drinking the wine. You scrunched up your face at the taste of it but took a couple spoonfuls at last. "I think he was tired already," your mother whispered, gazing down at you.

I could only pray so. A wail at the wrong time, and we

would all be dead. The midwife swaddled you in a thick silk blanket of imperial yellow. The irony was not lost on any of us.

I promised your mother I would do my best to smuggle you out of the Palace.

She turned to thank me, the pain and sorrow so bright in her eyes. Your mother was a stunning woman, Chen Yong, but her eyes were her most unforgettable feature.

"Do you have a plan?" I asked.

She did. The baby had come early. A stillbirth and deformed. Cremated and buried before defiling the presence of the Emperor, as according to custom.

I reached for you. There was no time. The only thing I could do was to take you and disappear as quickly as possible. The main gates were all guarded, and leaving the Palace at this early hour would surely garner suspicion. The guards would not allow me to leave with a baby in my arms, that much was certain.

For all the hidden passageways within the Palace, there was no secret way out of the Palace walls that I was aware of. I would have to leave from one of the gates—preferably guarded by someone I knew. There were advantages to having the Emperor's ear. I wouldn't be questioned if I acted with authority.

"May the Goddess of Mercy be with you," I said to your mother.

She reached out an elegant hand to stay me when I turned

toward the hidden panel. "His name is Chen Yong," she said, and she removed a jade beaded bracelet from her wrist. She asked me to give it to you.

She swayed away from me then, and the midwife rushed toward her, her gnarled hands outstretched, as I stepped through the secret panel.

You were asleep now in my arms, making small suckling noises. I'd never cradled a newborn before, and I clutched you close to me. Hong Yu led the way again with her bright lantern. The girl was smart. I hoped that she was truly loyal too.

Back within my bedchamber, I quickly changed and packed a bag. I wrote a brief note saying I had to hurry home to my mother's sickbed, would return within two weeks. I stamped the letter with my seal and enclosed it in a leather tube.

I asked the handmaid to deliver it to my page to give to the Emperor the next morning. She took the sealed tube from me and disappeared into the secret passageway.

I gently placed you in a saddle pack I kept for traveling purposes. It served as a makeshift sling. I threw the travel bag over my back and slung the pack across my shoulder with care.

I managed to avoid the guards who patrolled the Palace through the night, being familiar with their routine. You were born under a full autumn moon, and its light shone as bright as midday. I was as easy to glimpse as a snow goose mired in mud. As I walked across the immense main quad of the Palace, I saw another dark figure. No one wandered the grounds alone at night.

I placed a hand on your back. I continued walking toward the royal stables, even as the figure darted, straight at me.

I paused beneath the shadow of the Palace wall. I could deal with anyone, even Zhong Ye. I had to. I murmured a prayer and kept a hand close to the hilt of my dagger.

The figure approached, but the face was hidden; I heard his voice before I saw his face. I could not have been more astonished.

It was Wai Sen. The Emperor had given your father his Xian name.

Your mother had sent Hei Po to tell him the news. He drew close, and there was no mistaking the pale yellow hair beneath the black cowl drawn over his head. He was a sharp man and had guessed I would be headed for the stables.

I told him your name.

"Chen Yong," he repeated, his voice rough like an ink stick ground against stone.

He said he could leave the Palace the same night, take you with him to Jiang Dao. His whispers were urgent, earnest. He folded his tall frame over your sleeping form, and I saw the glint of tears in his eyes.

A newborn could never survive the long journey by ship, I told him.

He peered into the saddle pack one last time at your face.

He clasped my shoulder and thanked me. He promised that he'd send word, that he'd return for you.

He turned abruptly and walked away in silence, his head bowed low.

* * *

"I later learned that your father left the Palace the next day. Both your mother and father were heartbroken to lose you, but there was no other way." Ai Ling's father looked at Chen Yong, sympathy softening his sharp features. He sat back in his chair. The soft trickling of water into the pond outside filled a long moment of silence.

Chen Yong reached inside his robe and pulled out a woman's jade bracelet, made for a slender wrist. "I keep this near me, always. It was the only item I was delivered with, my father said."

"Your father, Master Li." Father nodded. "I was able to bring you to his estate with little trouble. The Goddess of Mercy heard my prayers, and you made not a sound as I rode out on my horse."

Ai Ling imagined her father, unmarried, with a newborn jostling at his side, riding for his life and safety. She shook her head imperceptibly, unable to believe this tale, unable to believe how their lives wound so inextricably together. Is this why she felt she had always known Chen Yong? Why she had trusted him so easily from the start?

"What happened after you returned to the Palace, Master Wen?" Chen Yong asked.

Her father stared into his wine cup. "The Emperor took Jin Lian's story of the deformed stillbirth at face value. He saw it as an ill omen. His attentions were diverted with the birth of a son by another concubine. Zhong Ye, however, was suspicious. He was enraged that his careful manipulations were for nothing."

Her father's kind face hardened as he spoke. "He had his spies root for information and pieced together the story as best he could. He was no fool, and probably surmised the truth. Zhong Ye convinced the Emperor to have me tried for treason—supposedly I had been plotting to poison him until he was so incapacitated, I could rule in his stead.

"There was no evidence, and the Emperor did not believe it truly. But Zhong Ye had his ear. He manipulated and cajoled, whereas I always gave my honest opinion and advice. It was he who was the puppeteer, but the Emperor could not acknowledge it. Zhong Ye had been the adviser even to the Emperor's own father; how could he disregard him?"

Ai Ling remembered his gray eyes, and almost smelled his spiced cologne. Her heart raced, and she reached for her jade pendant.

"I was cast from court in disgrace, barely escaping execution. My own family refused me." His expression was pained now, and Ai Ling's throat tightened with fierce love for him.

"After this, I sent a letter to your father, Master Li. Only he knew the truth behind your birth. We decided it wouldn't be safe to tell you your history, Chen Yong. Not as long as Zhong Ye lived. We were too fearful of how far he would go for vengeance." Her father took another sip of wine. "I never corresponded with Master Li again, though I wondered about you all these years."

Chen Yong glanced down at his hands. "I asked my father once, when I was thirteen years. He said he knew nothing, not even the person who delivered me to his doorstep. He died last year."

Her father's eyes widened. "Ah, I didn't know. I am so sorry. He was a great colleague, and so kind. I knew you would be safe with him, that he would protect you."

"A few months later a messenger arrived from Jiu Gong, carrying a letter from Master Tan. He didn't know my father, but they shared a mutual acquaintance, who had spoken of me. He wondered if I was the same Chen Yong he knew of. I had to find out what he knew." Chen Young rolled the jade beaded bracelet between his fingers, finally looked up to meet her father's eyes.

"My life is indebted to you, Master Wen," Chen Yong said, his voice steady as always. "But why—why did you risk your own life, your position at court, to save me?"

"How could I not help? You were an innocent newborn."

"And did my birth father ever write?" Chen Yong asked after a pause.

Her father shook his head. "I suspect any letters addressed to me and sent to the Palace were confiscated and read."

The disappointment showed so clearly on Chen Yong's face. He tucked his mother's jade bracelet back in his robe.

"Master Wen"—the uncertainty in his voice made him sound younger—"what else can you tell me about my mother and father?"

Ai Ling rose quietly and slipped out of the cozy study. She wanted to be alone—needed to prepare herself. Chen Yong was leaving the next day. When would she ever see him again?

CHAPTER TWENTY

Ai Ling tapped on Chen Yong's bedchamber door at dawn. He was already dressed. She wasn't surprised; he always rose early. His silk tunic was the color of wet sand.

They walked into the kitchen and pilfered red bean and lotus paste buns from the giant bamboo steamers. Ai Ling plucked out four buns with wooden eating sticks and wrapped them in a deep purple cloth for later. She also filled two flasks with hot tea and wrapped some salted pork with scallion flatbread in another muslin cloth. The persimmons in a cobalt bowl on the windowsill caught her eye. She grabbed two.

"Are we going far?" Chen Yong asked, laughing. Ai Ling

328

responded by handing him the bundles and flasks to carry.

They passed her mother and father, taking tea in the main hall.

"You're up early, Ai Ling." Her mother smiled, her face beaming with pleasure.

Father sat beside her, with Taro nestled in his lap. "I'm sure Chen Yong and Ai Ling have much to catch up on." He winked at his daughter as if they shared a secret. Ai Ling's eyes widened in consternation.

"A peaceful morning to you." Chen Yong bowed to her parents, saving Ai Ling from speaking.

"Enjoy your day together," her mother said.

Her parents exchanged a glance. The twinkle in Father's eyes and the small curve on Mother's mouth were not lost on their daughter. Ai Ling spun on her heel and stepped from the main hall, before her parents did anything more to embarrass her.

The gravel in the courtyard crunched beneath their feet. Chen Yong pulled open the main door, and they slipped into the narrow alleyway, still damp and cold from the previous evening.

They strolled side by side toward the small gate of the town.

Ai Ling weighed her words before she broke their comfortable silence. "I've dreamed about her . . . Silver Phoenix."

Chen Yong slowed his stride, turned to see her face. "What were the dreams about?"

329

"They're hazy, unclear. I always wake with a sense of urgency." With her hair damp from sweat, her heart galloping.

"You cannot draw meaning from them?"

She shook her head.

They walked past the rickety guardhouse, but a comment from the man on watch slowed her stride.

"Out early this morning, eh?" A dark, gaunt face peered from the hut. Ai Ling saw the familiar awe in his expression as his head bobbed in sudden recognition. "Mistress Wen! Out for another one of your strolls?" He cocked his head toward Chen Yong, then noticed her glare. "Enjoy yourself, miss."

Chen Yong lifted one dark brow as they walked through the gates. "What was that about?"

"It's been like this since I've returned. The town people consider me both martyr and oddity—someone they can gossip about at the markets."

"What do they know of our journey?"

"Only that I wed a corrupt adviser to the Emperor, and that he died on our wedding night."

"You've not spoken of what happened to anyone?" Chen Yong tilted his face to her, and she looked him square in the eyes.

"I've spoken to Father and Mother about it some. But who else can I tell? No one would understand, or believe me."

"It hasn't been easy," Chen Yong said.

Ai Ling led him down a less traveled path, barely the width

of a palm, winding between tall golden wild grass which reached beyond their knees. "It is fine," she said and realized how terse she sounded. She drew a breath and turned, causing Chen Yong to nearly collide into her.

"They treat me with reverence, smile from a distance. The older women who knew me before my journey are kind. Their daughters, the few who are unmarried, try to befriend me, but"—Ai Ling gave her head a slight shake, feeling her single braid sweep against her back—"but I'm not interested."

A small breeze rustled the grass. It undulated like waves, carrying the scent of burned rice fields. Chen Yong studied her in his quiet way, something that had always made the heat rise in her cheeks. This time, she simply met his gaze.

"Why not?" he asked.

Ai Ling's eyes swept across the fields, to the dusty road that had led her away from home so long ago. How could she explain her need to be alone? To contemplate their incredible journey—to try and make sense of it. "How do I tell them that the feel of dragon scales beneath my hands is more real to me than the embroidery I'm working on?"

She saw a flicker of understanding in Chen Yong's face. "They speak of betrothals, discuss bridal outfits and fertility recipes. Their life is nothing like my own."

"You don't wish to remarry?" Chen Yong asked.

This time, the heat did rise to her face. "Who wants a bride of such ill fortune?" Ai Ling turned and continued down the narrow path. "And you? Have your parents not arranged a betrothal yet?"

The silence lingered forever before his reply. "It's too soon after Li Rong's death."

She released a breath, not realizing she had held it.

The grass gave way to slender birch trees, silver in the morning light. She stopped to arch her neck and look skyward; Chen Yong stood beside her and did the same. The sky was a deep indigo, reminding her of their chariot ride. A wild exhilaration radiated from her belly, expanded through her lungs and quickened the beating of her heart.

Ai Ling turned to Chen Yong, and realized only after he smiled at her that she grinned so widely her cheeks ached. They strolled through the trees, until they reached a small meadow with a moss-covered knoll. A stone figure no more than waist high perched on top of the mound, like a strange ancient ruler from another realm.

"What's that?" Chen Yong nodded toward the statue.

"I don't know, really. I found him during my wanderings." She approached the rough-hewn figure, its lines smoothed by time, the crevices tinged green and brown. She ran her fingertips over the round head, bare except for deep grooves perhaps signifying hair. Her hands glided around the large, curved earlobes and generous nose.

"He's my friend. I come here often, it's a favorite place of mine."

"You travel outside the town gates often?" he asked.

Ai Ling pursed her lips, amused. "I can take care of myself."

"And your . . . ?" He traced a fingertip over the moss on the statue.

Ai Ling dropped to her knees and began to pull items from her knapsack—a bowl, gold- and silver-foiled spirit money. "My ability grew stronger after what happened. . . ." She did not want to speak Zhong Ye's name. "I keep my spirit to myself; it's too easy for me to hear others' thoughts now, without some vigilance."

Chen Yong kneeled beside her, and they filled the deep bronze bowl with spirit money—for Li Rong in his travels through the underworld. He brought his oval striker down against the flint, and after two strikes, a gold-foiled coin caught fire, curling around the edges. Soon the coins had turned into a small blaze. They remained kneeling, continued to feed the dancing flames with the foiled coins.

"I dream about him," Chen Yong said in a low voice.

Ai Ling's eyes snapped open. He was concentrating on the task of feeding the spirit money into the fire.

"I did as well. Once."

"Was he well?"

She nodded. "He was himself—laughing, jesting."

"I know my mother blames me for his death. I blame myself, too."

She reached over to touch his shoulder. "He ventured to that dark mountain because of me—my duty. If anyone is at fault, I am."

"It should have been me."

Ai Ling leaned closer, not believing what she heard.

"Don't you understand? I was in front of that wretched monster when his claws came down. If it had not made us switch positions . . ." Chen Yong punched the earth with a tight fist.

"Please don't think that. Li Rong wouldn't want you to carry this guilt." She withdrew her hand and stared into the flames.

"He is at peace," Ai Ling said after a heavy silence.

Chen Yong attempted a smile. He placed the last of the spirit money in the bowl and sat back on his heels, straightening, pulling his broad shoulders back.

"I'll be leaving in a few months, on a ship for Jiang Dao," he said.

Ai Ling could only stare. "Why?" she whispered.

"My father. I have to find him. I need to know if he's alive." He held himself still as a statue, in a pose of worship—or sacrifice.

"You can't even speak the language. They won't accept you there. You are Xian." She spoke more vehemently than she intended. But Jiang Dao, across the wide expanse of turbulent seas? No. Please no.

"And you believe I'm accepted here?"

His measured tone stopped her short. "I accept you. You are more Xian than anyone I know."

His smile reached his eyes this time. "But you know me. You simply see me as Chen Yong."

The sun climbed above the tree line, casting warm rays into their small meadow. Chen Yong's dark brows drew together as he spoke. "My features betray me. Each day I'm reminded I am half foreign by how others react to me—that I am something different from them."

"You'll let others tell you who you are?" Ai Ling spoke boldly, refusing to understand.

"You don't know how it is. I'll never find acceptance from strangers—no matter where I go." Chen Yong shifted, drawing his knees up, resting his arms on them. "Those letters my father wrote to Master Tan, he spoke of me in each one, wondered how I was, what I liked, if I was diligent in my studies, if I grew tall . . ." His voice caught.

"I wish you wouldn't," she said.

"I'll return. My home is here. I'll bring a gift for you."

Was he so thickheaded that he refused to see? Surely he knew, could guess, her feelings for him? If she loosened her hold on her own spirit just a fraction, she could hear his thoughts, feel his emotions. But it would be wrong—an intrusion. She had already betrayed his trust. And Ai Ling knew the inevitable truth; his heart belonged elsewhere.

They watched in silence as the flames slowly burned the spirit money into cinders. She said a small prayer for Li Rong, who would never have blamed them, even if they were unable to forgive themselves. And a prayer for the innocent servant girl at the restaurant, whose spirit had been overtaken by the night-worm fiends. Ai Ling watched as the last red ember flickered to darkness and saved her final prayer for Zhong Ye, the man who had held her father prisoner, coerced her to wed, and refused to die; the man who, she had discovered, loved her in his own twisted fashion, even as she was ending his life.

They ate a quiet meal on the knoll, sitting side by side, their backs pressed against the ancient carving. The meadow was a lush green, dotted along the edges with fallen leaves of crimson and gold. The scent of wet earth permeated the air.

Their food was cold, but fresh, the lotus paste buns sweet, the scallion flatbread thick and savory. The tea was lukewarm within the flasks.

"Eating like this reminds me of our journey," Chen Yong said.

"I come here often with a snack. I think about it a lot."

"And by snack, do you mean two sweet buns, a thick slab of bread, and lots of dried pork?" He laughed before she could retort. But the sound of it lifted her own spirit, and she chuckled despite herself.

"I usually just have a fruit myself," he said.

Ai Ling tossed a persimmon into his lap. "I'm sorry if you don't know how to eat properly."

He threw his head back and laughed again. She tried to capture the moment like a sketch within her mind, the feeling of his shoulder pressed against hers, the warmth of the autumn sun on their faces.

* * *

Later, Ai Ling accompanied Chen Yong to the front gate. Her parents had said their farewells in the main hall, inviting him to visit again.

"What will you do now?" Chen Yong looked down at her as the birds trilled above them.

"Wed and have six children," she said with a wry smile.

Chen Yong laughed. "I don't think so. You were not meant to remain cloistered within the inner quarters."

"No, probably not. Perhaps I'll travel."

His eyes widened, then he grinned. "I don't doubt your capability to travel the world—and beyond."

He extended his hand and she took it, did not pull back as he drew her to him in an embrace. She wound her arms tight around his back and pressed her cheek against his shoulder. He smelled of soap; the faint scent of sandalwood lingered in his clothing. She stepped back before he did. Ai Ling realized then she would be willing to leave her home, her family, everything, to be by his side—and the revelation stunned her.

"I'll expect my gift," she managed.

Chen Yong smiled and stepped through the door. He half turned to wave once, his golden eyes shadowed in the dying light—those eyes which were so strange to her at first, now as familiar as her own. Ai Ling struggled to keep her spirit anchored.

Look back again, she thought, and I will follow you.

Instead Ai Ling watched him walk away, with easy grace,

until he turned the corner. She shut the heavy wooden door behind her and leaned against it, her chest tight with all the words she had not said, the tears hot upon her cheeks.

It was not until Taro came to wrap himself around her calf, purring a husky song, that she allowed herself to be led back to the house, lit brightly now against the twilight.

ACKNOWLEDGMENTS

So many people along the way have helped to make the book you hold in your hands a dream realized. I'd like to thank my agent, Bill Contardi, who took a chance on a debut author with no previous credits. I couldn't ask for a better advocate, with such sharp business acumen and wit. And to my editor, Virginia Duncan, who worked with me tirelessly to improve the story and prose. I've learned so much from our revisions together. Your insight amazes me. Thank you to Chris Borgman, who created a stunning cover, and Paul Zakris, for the incredible jacket and book design. And to all the wonderful people at Greenwillow Books— thank you, thank you, thank you!

I know I would not have made it this far without the encouragement and camaraderie of my talented critique group friends: Janice Coy, Rachel Gobar, Rich Walsh, Amber Lough, Eveie Wilpon, Kirsten Kinney, Mark McDonough, and Tudy Woolfe. There is a part of you in this novel. I look forward to our future journeys together as writers!

My gratitude to my Chinese brush painting teacher, Jean Shen, for sharing the dance of the brush with me. And my fellow brush painting classmates—I look forward to our time together each week.

Two books were essential in my research for this novel, as both guidance and inspiration: *The Inner Quarters: Marriage and the Lives of Chinese Women in the Sung Period*, by Patricia Buckley Ebrey, and *A Chinese Bestiary: Strange Creatures from the Guideways Through Mountains and Seas*, edited and translated by Richard E. Strassberg.

I'm grateful for the friends I've made online through my blog and various forums. You've made me laugh, cheered and motivated me. I invite readers to visit my website, cindypon.com, to learn more about this novel, my writing, and my art. Click on my blog and leave a comment! I would love to hear from you.

And finally, chocolate kisses to my love, Mark, who watched after Sweet Pea and Munchkin for countless Saturdays, so I could write and chase my dreams.